Carlie,
Always remember
what happens in
Vegas... ;)

Elena

Nothing Stays In Vegas

Elena Aitken

MW00681874

This is a work of fiction. The events and characters described herein are imaginary and are not intended to refer to specific places or living persons. The opinions expressed in this manuscript are solely the opinions of the author and do not represent the opinions or thoughts of the publisher. The author has represented and warranted full ownership and/or legal right to publish all the materials in this book.

Nothing Stays In Vegas

All Rights Reserved

Copyright © 2011 Elena Aitken

This book may not be reproduced, transmitted, or stored in whole or in part by any means, including graphic, electronic, or mechanical without the express written consent of the publisher except in the case of brief quotations embodied in critical articles and reviews. Your support of author rights is appreciated.

Ink Blot Communications

Http://www.inkblotcommunications.ca

ISBN: 978-0-9877457-3-6

Also by Elena Aitken

Unexpected Gifts
Drawing Free

Short Story
Betty and Veronica

To Rob

~My biggest supporter

CHAPTER ONE

April 2004

The music was too loud. Maybe it was me. Was twenty-seven too old to sip an overpriced cocktail, wearing a too-short skirt and a too-tight top? Judging by what some of the other ladies were wearing, no.

I tugged at my skirt in a vain attempt to pull it closer to my knees. Preferably over them. Nicole was late, as usual; it would take at least twenty minutes to go back to the room and change. There was no time. One thing was for sure, I'd never again buy anything an eighteen-year-old sales girl declared, "Totally perfect for Vegas."

The fluorescent blue liquid swirled around my glass as I fiddled with my straw. A "Knock Out," the bartender had called it. It was going to knock me out. Every time I took a sip, the sweetness sent bites of pain through my teeth. Yet I couldn't seem to stop drinking it.

"Excuse me," a voice from behind said.

I swiveled in my seat to see a very blond, very clean cut, very preppy guy. Good looking if you liked the college boy look.

I didn't.

He was standing over me, not even trying to conceal the fact that he was staring at my cleavage, which there was way too much of.

"Yes?"

"Can I get you another?" College Boy gestured to my drink which I was surprised to see almost empty.

That would explain the dizzy feeling every time I moved my head. Knock Out, indeed.

"I'm married," I said and turned back to face the bar. Where was Nicole?

"I'm Clark," College Boy said as he took the seat next to me, "and nobody in Vegas is married."

I twisted to look at him again. His smile dazzled. Clearly the result of thousands of dollars of orthodontic work. "Seriously," I tried again. "I'm not interested."

He leaned in and the smell of stale beer assaulted me. Over his shoulder I could see the table of his frat buddies, poking each other in the ribs and pointing in our direction.

Perfect. I was a bet.

"Listen, Kid." I couldn't have been much older then him, but maybe an insult would help. "I'm not interested in being part of your game tonight."

"Come on, Baby." His breath was hot and moist in my ear. I leaned back as far as I could without falling out of my seat but his arm snaked around me and yanked me toward him. "I just wanna have a little fun."

"Maybe I can suggest a playground nearby."

"Ouch," College Boy said and pulled back in mock injury. "That hurt."

"You think that hurt?"

"Come on," he leaned in again. "Don't be a bitch."

Really?

Changing my approach, I slid my hand up the side of his face, being sure to give his cheek a little caress as I went.

"Yeah," he murmured and closed his eyes. "That's what I'm talking about."

Without wasting anymore time I grabbed his soft, fleshy earlobe and twisted, hard.

"Ow!" His eyes snapped open and he jumped back but I still had a grip on his lobe. "Shit! Let go."

"Have I made my point?"

When he didn't answer immediately, I applied a little more pressure.

"Shit! Yes, you've made your point."

I let him go and his hand flew to his ear. He shot me a look which made it clear that whatever he was feeling towards me, it was no longer romantic. I gave him an innocent smile and a little wave as he retreated to his buddies who were howling with laughter.

Yes, I was definitely too old for this.

I turned around intending to return to my drink but my eyes landed on a man standing at the other end of the bar. He was tall, but it was his black hair and matching dark eyes that caught my attention. From the grin on his face I could tell he'd witnessed what happened. I offered a little shrug but didn't look away.

He was handsome. No, more than handsome. He was gorgeous in a way that only guys who don't know how gorgeous they really are can pull off. And he was coming over.

"I'm not trying to interrupt you," he said. I looked him in the eyes. No, not black but perhaps the richest shade of brown I'd ever seen. Gold flecks caught the light making his eyes shine like onyx. I couldn't look away. "I saw what happened to the last guy," he continued.

"I didn't want to have to do that."

"No," he said with a grin. "It was great. I was going to offer my assistance, but it's clear you didn't need my help. I'm Leo." He extended his hand, which I took.

"I'm Lexi."

His skin was warm but a shiver went through me when he squeezed my hand before releasing it.

Leo turned and we both watched as College Boy threw money on the table and started toward us on his way to the door. When he got close enough he glared and said. "Good luck, man. She's married. And mean." He pushed past us and out of the lounge, his buddies tailing him.

Leo shook his head and turned back to me. "I only have a few minutes. Do you mind if I sit here?" He pointed to the stool at the bar next to me. "Or would you rather be alone?" He held up his hands in mock defense.

I laughed. "Go right ahead. I'm just waiting for someone."

"Since you're waiting anyway, can I get you a drink? I promise I won't try any bad pick up lines."

My defenses fell a little and I said, "Sure, since you promised not to try anything."

"Never," he said and smiled. His dark eyes lightened when he smiled which made them look even richer. I tried not to stare. "What are you having?"

I looked at the blue liquid at the bottom of my glass and shoved it away. "Anything but that."

Leo called the bartender over. "Mike, can I get a coke and a vodka tonic for the lady."

"Make that a vodka and soda," I interrupted.

Leo turned to me and gave me a sly smile. I shrugged. He turned back to the bartender and said, "Make that a vodka and soda. Thanks, Mike."

I watched while he made small talk with the bartender, who seemed to know him. There was something about his confidence that hypnotized me. But it might have been the effects of the Knock Out.

"So," he said turning back to me, sliding my drink over. "Is what that guy said true?"

"That I'm mean?" I took a long sip of my vodka, enjoying the sharp contrast of the soda from the tooth rotting sweetness of my first drink. I rolled the liquid around in my mouth before swallowing and added, "Absolutely."

"Well, I'll withhold judgment on that one," he said. "But what I really wanted to know is, are you married? Is that who you're waiting for?"

Was he flirting with me? "Actually, no. I'm meeting my best friend. It's her birthday. Well, not tonight, but this weekend. She's always wanted to come to Vegas, so I caved."

I could've smacked myself. Instead I grabbed my drink to prevent anymore random ramblings. If he was flirting with me, he wouldn't be for long. But what was wrong with a little flirting? It might be fun if I had any idea at all how to do it.

"And the husband?"

"I'm here with Nicole," I said hoping that I could avoid that particular line of questioning. Thankfully, he didn't push it.

"So, what are you going to do to celebrate Nicole's birthday?" he asked.

I smiled, relieved to talk about something else. "Her actual birthday is tomorrow and I told her she could choose what she wanted to do. So, I guess we'll go out dancing somewhere." I winced at the thought of braving a Las Vegas night club. "But tonight we're keeping it pretty tame. We're going to see a Cirque show. I can't remember which one. They're all the same, aren't they?"

He laughed, smooth and natural. The image of warm caramel on an ice cream sundae popped into my head.

"No, they're not *all* the same," he said. "Similar, I'll give you. But each one has a different focus."

"You've seen them all?"

"I have. Some more than once."

"You must spend a lot of time in Vegas."

"You could say that," he said, taking long sip of coke. "I live here."

Before I could ask him about that, Nicole's voice, preceding her by seconds, cut in. "Well, hello," she said as she sashayed over with a little more enthusiasm than normal. She looked much taller than her 5'2" in spiky heels. I wasn't sure how she could breathe let alone walk in her emerald green dress that hugged her like a second skin. She looked good; she'd been working out twice a day for months and practically starving herself in preparation for this trip. I hated to admit that it paid off. I tried not to encourage that behavior in her, but she did look amazing.

"Who's your friend, Lex?" Nicole flipped her red hair over one shoulder and held out her hand in invitation.

Leo stood and took her hand. "I'm Leo. You must be Nicole."

"The one and only." Nicole took the stool he offered and slid in next to me.

"I was just keeping Lexi company until you arrived. But I should let the two of you get on with your evening." He spoke to Nicole, but his eyes didn't leave mine.

"You don't have to leave," I said.

"Unfortunately, I do. But maybe I'll run into you again," he said with a smile that made my stomach flip.

I struggled to keep my composure. "Maybe."

"Nicole," he said turning to her. "What are you drinking tonight?"

Her face flickered and the flash of a frown transformed into a smile so fast that if I hadn't known better, I'd doubt it had even been there. She ran a hand through her hair and said, "I'm kinda in the mood for something sweet. You know what I mean?" she purred. She couldn't help it. Whenever there was a man around, Nicole transformed. She would bat her eyelashes, throw on her sexiest smile and send out vibes of pure lust. She'd been that way ever since we were teenagers and she'd figured out that boys would do pretty much anything for her with a little flirting.

I felt a small burn of jealousy, which was ridiculous, when Leo returned her smile and ordered her a Knock Out.

"So, Lexi said you're going to a club tomorrow night for some dancing," Leo said.

"Well, when in Vegas..." she said and leaned forward exposing a little more cleavage.

I rolled my eyes and looked out onto the casino floor where the lights from the slots flashed and waitresses traipsed back and forth on their stilettos carrying drinks to gamblers who were pumping money into machines at a surprising rate. Over at the blackjack tables, there was a crowd of people forming around a man in a Hawaiian print shirt. By the excitement surrounding him, he must have had a run of luck.

"Well, what do you think, Lexi?"

I shook my head and turned back to the conversation. "About what?"

"Leo has offered us VIP passes to Studio 54 for tomorrow. He tells me it's the place to be on a Saturday night."

"It's your birthday. If that's what you want to do, it sounds good to me." I did my best to sound excited. Night clubs were akin to torture. "Thanks, Leo."

"It's my pleasure." He held my gaze again.

I cleared my throat and forced myself to look away. I swiped a piece of hair behind my ear before asking, "So, how did you happen to have these tickets?"

"I have my connections." He grinned and because he looked so cute, I found myself grinning back. "Seriously," he added. "I work at the hotel. Speaking of which, I should get back." He pushed himself away from the bar.

"It was very nice meeting you, Leo," Nicole said.

"Likewise, ladies. Have a great night." He started to move to the door.

"Wait," I called and the second he turned around my face burned with embarrassment. That sounded ridiculous. "How will we get the passes?" I asked, trying to sound natural.

"Don't worry, Lexi," he said and I could tell he was trying not to laugh. My face got even hotter if that was possible. "I'll make sure you get them." And then he turned and disappeared onto the casino floor.

I watched him go, wishing with a great deal of absurdity, that he would turn around and come back.

"That's it. No more alcohol for me," I mumbled. I hadn't reacted to a man like that since, well, since ever.

Nicole didn't hear me. "He's yummy," she said licking her lips. "Now come on, we're going to be late for the show. And what are you wearing?"

I looked down and said, "What's wrong with this? The sales girl said this was totally Vegas appropriate."

"Seriously, Lexi? For such a hottie, you choose the strangest clothes." Nicole stood and pulled me from the stool. "Don't worry, we'll go shopping tomorrow and get you sexed up."

I turned to grab my purse and caught sight of my left hand. It still made my breath catch when I saw my naked finger where a ring had been for the last three years.

"Lex, come on. What are you looking at?"

I blinked hard. "Nothing," I said and grabbed my purse. "Let's go."

CHAPTER TWO

I had the pool to myself. Dropping my towel and wrap on a chaise, I dove head first into the glassy water. I must be the only person who liked to swim laps at seven in the morning in Vegas. When I broke the surface, I transitioned easily into smooth, effortless strokes and headed for the opposite end. When Nicole brought up the idea of coming to Vegas to celebrate her birthday, she was smart enough to suggest we stay at the MGM Grand, where there are five pools. She knew if she eliminated most of my objections, including my need for a morning swim, I wouldn't have much of a reason to say no.

I reached the other end, tucked into a smooth flip turn pushing off the slick blue tiles and started back to the other side.

A sigh escaped me as a bubble after my second lap. It always took me a few minutes to warm up, for my muscles to relax and loosen as memory took over and my body fell in line with the exercise. I'd been swimming so long that if I missed a day, my body seemed to crave the fluidity of the water, the lengthening of each muscle as I strove for an ever-changing goal.

As I reached the wall on my fourth lap, a shadow fell over the water startling me into stopping. I popped my head out of the pool, grabbed the slippery tiles and peered up into the already intense desert sun.

"I found you," the shadowy figure said.

I shivered involuntarily at the voice and shaded my eyes trying to bring him into focus.

"Sorry," he said as he squatted, blocking the sun so I could see him. "Is that better?"

"Yes. Thanks, Leo." I smiled at him.

"You remember me, then?"

"Why wouldn't I?" I tugged my goggles onto my head.

"Well, this is Vegas, and I'm sure a beautiful woman like you meets lots of guys in one night. I wasn't sure if I made the cut of being important enough to remember."

I blushed at his compliment, before laughing at the absurdity of his statement. It was Nicole that met men; I was just along for the ride.

"What's so funny?"

"Nothing," I said and swallowed hard. "So, why did you say you were looking for me?"

"I didn't." He grinned.

I shot him a look and started to pull my goggles back into place.

"No, wait." The smile fell from his face, and he looked genuine enough that I paused. "I was looking for you," he said. "I wanted to give you these." He pulled two tickets from his back pocket and held them out to me.

"What're those?"

"I told you I'd get you and...your friend..."

"Nicole," I supplied for him and couldn't help being just a little bit pleased that he remembered only my name.

"Right, Nicole. I told you I'd get some club tickets for tonight."

"Oh, those. Thanks."

"Why do I get the feeling that you don't really mean that?" He smiled and tilted his head.

He was flirting with me again. At least I thought he was.

"I do mean it," I said trying my best to sound genuine. Nicole once told me that I was too standoffish, and came off like a bitch sometimes. Normally I didn't care. But with Leo crouching on the deck in front of me, I found that I did care. A lot.

"You may not sound very excited," Leo said, "but Studio 54 is a great club. One of the best in Vegas. It's over 22,000 square feet, it has four dance floors, and...you don't look impressed."

I shrugged. "I'm sorry. I really am. I don't mean to sound unappreciative, but I'm not the nightclub type."

"So why is it that you want to go?"

"Well, I'm not the nightclub type, but Nicole is and it's her birthday so I'll put on my best friend hat and go dancing with her."

Leo smiled again and the simple action had the effect of making his already handsome face absolutely deadly. I was happy to be submerged, because I could feel my entire body heat up.

"You're going to have an awesome time," he said. "Honestly, it's a great club."

"I'm sure it is," I said. "I know we'll have fun." What I wanted to say was that it would be great if he were there, but even I knew that would sound pathetic.

"Do you want me to put these somewhere for you?" Leo waved the tickets. "Unless you're ready to get out?"

I wavered. I'd enjoyed talking to him, a lot. Definitely more than I had enjoyed talking to any other man in recent memory, but I wasn't quite ready to abandon my swim. Besides, he looked like he was dressed for work. It crossed my mind to ask him what he did at the hotel but before could, he spoke.

"Should I just put them with your stuff?"

I shook my head trying to remember what he was talking about. "Oh, yes. That would be great." I pointed to the chaise where I'd left my things. "Thanks again, Leo. I mean it. Nicole will be so excited."

He pushed up from his crouching position so his face was in the shadows again. I put a hand up to shade my eyes, but I still couldn't make out his features.

"It was my pleasure, Lexi. Oh, and don't forget to give them your name at the door tonight. You'll be on the list."

He didn't make a move to leave right away, and I searched my brain for something else to say, anything.

"Have a good day," was all I could come up with.

I had to force myself not to dunk my head under the water. I could not believe those words came out of my mouth.

"Thanks," Leo said and I was glad I couldn't see his face. "I should get going. Enjoy your swim. It looks like it's paid off already."

I watched him tuck the tickets under my towel before he turned and waved. Then he was gone, up the stairs back to the casino floor. I pulled my goggles back down and dove under the water, extinguishing the blush that burned on my cheeks at his last comment. It was only after I reached the other end that I realized I'd never asked how he'd known to find me at the pool.

***

"Oh, the sun is burning my retinas," Nicole moaned as we stepped outside and into the waiting taxi.

"It's the desert, Nic. It's sunny and hot, remember?" I nudged her as I slid into the seat beside her. "Premium Outlet Mall please," I told the driver before turning my attention back to my friend. "Besides, shopping was your idea."

"Not so early though," she whined and pushed her oversized sunglasses further up her nose.

"It's two in the afternoon, Nicole. It's not my fault that you were up drinking all night."

"Of course it's your fault. You should've dragged me back to the room with you when you went back."

I gave her a look. "Right, cause you were ready to go to bed?"

After the show Nicole and I walked down the Las Vegas strip laughing and joking. We stopped in front of the Bellagio to take in the fountain show, and it was amazing, but it was more fun people watching. One of our habits since college, we would make up elaborate life stories for people, creating dialogue and situations that sent us into hysterics. I could have stood there all night, but Nicole had other plans. She dragged me into the casino where I lost at least a hundred dollars at the craps table, but she was on a roll and clearly wasn't going anywhere.

"I'm done, Nic. I'm going to bed," I said stifling a yawn.

"No, Lexi. Stay. Please? I'm winning here."

"I know, I know. But I'm done."

"Woo hoo!" Nicole yelled as the ball landed on her number, again. She whipped around and grabbed me in a hug. "You're my good luck charm!"

"I'm sorry, Nic. I am. But I'm going to fall asleep on my feet here." She let go of her grip on me and pulled away.

"Let me rest, and tomorrow I'll be ready for an all nighter."

She eyed me and asked, "Promise?"

"I promise. All night, as long as you want." I knew I would regret that promise later, but I really needed to get some sleep. I'd worry about that later.

Nicole broke into a huge grin. "Okay, Lex. Get some rest. I won't be too late."

Hours later, I woke for a moment when she came back to the room. It was 3:30.

"I hit the blackjack tables after you left," she said now. "And I may have had too many drinks."

I raised my eyebrow at her.

"Okay, I definitely had too many drinks. But, I'm ready to shop. So grab me a coffee and I'm good to go. Oh, and get me inside and away from this sun."

"You poor thing." I laughed and put my arm around her. "I'll get you all fixed up." I pulled her towards me and let her rest her head on my shoulder until we arrived at the mall.

***

"Lexi. You have to try this one," Nicole said and shoved a teal green dress at me. We were in a store that Nicole assured me carried all the latest styles but if scraps of clothing hanging on by threads was the latest style, I wasn't sure I wanted anything to do with it. I couldn't see myself wearing any of the skimpy garments hanging on the racks. I gave her a look but didn't take the dress.

"Come on, Lex. With your body, you can totally pull this off. Seriously, you don't dress to flatter yourself at all. If I had your body, you wouldn't be able to keep me out of things like this."

"The color-"

"Will be fantastic on you. I'm pretty sure teal was created for you. Only blondies with green eyes can look semi-decent in teal."

"Semi-decent?"

"You'll look smokin'," she amended. "I wish I had legs like yours. I got better boobs though." She laughed and kept flipping through the racks.

"There is nothing wrong with my boobs." I snuck a peek at my chest just to be sure.

"Your boobs are amazing, Lex. They're just not mine." Nicole paused her search long enough to flash me a grin. "But they will look even more amazing in this." She pulled out a halter top. This one red with black gemstones sewn onto the plunging neckline.

"Not too bad," I said.

She flipped it around to show me the back, if you could call it that. There was only a tie securing the sides together.

My mouth fell open. "That's more like a bathing suit top than a shirt to wear out."

"I swear, Lex. You are such a prude. Come on, it's my birthday and you have to look hot."

"I don't see why I have to look hot on your birthday," I grumbled, but let her lead me to the changing room where I obligingly tried on one outfit after another, each skimpier than the last.

***

After what seemed like forever, Nicole selected her outfits and agreed to let me treat her to a bite to eat. Desperate to get her away from anymore shopping, I grabbed a cab and we headed back to the strip where I chose a restaurant at random. Thankfully, between the lunch and dinner rush, service was fast and it wasn't long before there was a mouthwatering meal in front of me.

"How can you eat that?" Nicole looked horrified at my club sandwich as I was about to take a bite.

"It's a sandwich, not a plate of fries dipped in gravy." I lifted the sandwich to my mouth again.

"All that bread."

"I like bread."

Nicole shuddered and resumed poking at her salad. "I think if I even look at a loaf of bread, I gain five pounds. You're so lucky."'

"I am what I am." I shrugged and took a bite. I had long since given up trying to convince Nicole that she looked amazing. I still told her every time I saw her, but I no longer kept up the constant campaigning for an improvement in her self esteem. The truth was that while I didn't take my athletic build for granted, I just didn't think about it much. I never was all that interested in appearances. Nicole said it was because I didn't have to worry about it. But I believed it was because you either liked me or you didn't. It was as simple as that. Which probably explained why I was awful at flirting, and hadn't had a lot of boyfriends. And those I did have, weren't serious, at least not until I met Andrew. Andrew was different.

Nicole's voice brought me back to the conversation. "Did you hear what I said, Lex?"

"Sorry, I missed it," I said. I took another bite of my sandwich, which I had to admit, did have a lot of bread in it.

"I was saying, wouldn't it be awesome if Leo stopped by tonight?"

I coughed, trying not to choke on my food. If Nicole noticed my reaction, she didn't say anything.

"It was nice of him to get us tickets, wasn't it?"

I nodded and swallowed hard reaching for my glass of water.

"Where did you say he ran into you this morning?"

I cleared my throat and said, "At the pool. I was doing laps."

"Seriously? You're on vacation," she said and raised her eyebrow. "Not that I'm all that surprised. Your dedication is something to be admired I guess." She rolled her eyes. "But anyway, he found you at the pool? How did he know you were there? Did you tell him last night that you had a crazy obsession with swimming?"

"It's not an obsession." I shook my head and took another sip of water. "But I was wondering that myself. It's kind of creepy that he knew where I was, don't you think?"

Nicole laughed and said, "There is nothing creepy about that man. I would be all over that, if he wasn't so clearly into you."

"What?"

"Oh come on, Lex. You cannot be that oblivious. He is so into you."

I shook my head but I could feel the heat creep up my face. There was something about the way he looked at me. Not even Andrew had looked at me that way. And Nicole was right; there was nothing creepy about Leo. "It doesn't matter," I said after a moment, "even if he was interested, I'm married. Remember?"

"Lex," Nicole said and took my left hand, flipping it so my bare ring finger was exposed. "You and Andrew have been separated for months, remember?" Her voice was soft, but firm. "It's okay to look at other men," she added. "Hell, its okay to do a whole lot more than that if you wanted to."

"I'm still married," I said and pulled away from her grasp. I rubbed my finger and tucked my hand away from view.

"Yes, but for how much longer?"

"Do we have to talk about this now?"

"I think we do," she said leaning back in her chair. "You never want to talk about it, and that's my job as your best friend. So spill."

"It's your birthday. We shouldn't talk about me on your birthday."

"That's exactly why we should. It's my birthday and it's what I want to do." Nicole smirked. She knew she would get her way.

There was no point avoiding it. "Fine. What do you want to know?"

"Anything. You never talk about it, and that's not healthy. So tell me how you feel about all this. It's okay to open up." Nicole put on her best therapist voice and I could see why the teenagers at the high school where she worked opened up to her. Lots of people were surprised to find out that Nicole was a guidance counselor, and I had to admit, if I was meeting her for the first time dressed in her tight party clothes, having a good time, I might have trouble making the connection too. But the truth was, she was fabulous at her job. She connected with the kids, maybe because she could relate so much to what they were going through. When we'd met in college, we were both in the education faculty and despite Nicole's love of a good time, she aced her exams and maintained an impressively high GPA. Opposites in every way, instead of repelling each other, our personalities complimented each other and after our first year, we became roommates. I'd always known I wanted to work with children, so I majored in child development, preferring to work with elementary kids. Nicole, fueled by her excellent grades, went back for her Masters in Psychology so she could work with troubled teens.

"Okay, Ms. Lennox," I said now in the highest pitch I could manage. "I'll tell you all of my woes."

She shot me a look and I dropped the act.

"Honestly," I tried again with more sincerity. "I don't know how to feel about it. I guess it's been a long time coming. A marriage can't work when you want different things, can it?"

She nodded, but didn't say anything allowing me to continue.

"I can't help the way I feel. And I guess it's my fault. I changed my mind."

I had changed my mind. When Andrew and I met, I had just graduated and accepted a position as a second grade teacher at Willow Brook Elementary School in my hometown of Calgary, right on the edge of the Canadian Rockies. It was my dream job and the last thing on my mind was having a family of my own. I was only twenty-three and having kids wasn't something I could wrap my mind around. Besides, I was young and idealistic and I knew everything. Including the fact that I didn't want to bring children of my own into a world with so many issues when there were thousands of children who could benefit from my guidance as a teacher. I didn't need or want children of my own which was perfect for Andrew. A recent grad himself, he landed a great position as a financial analyst for an oil company downtown and had ambitious plans to work his way up. He was a dedicated man, to his career and to me, and he didn't hesitate to shower me with attention and love; but he'd made it very clear that babies were not part of his future. It wasn't long before I moved out of my shared apartment with Nicole and into a condo with

Andrew. Six months later, he looked at me with his sky blue eyes, flipped his sun streaked hair off his forehead in the way he knew made me melt, and asked me to marry him. It happened quickly, maybe too quickly. But Andrew always went after what he wanted without hesitation. He was confident in our love and our future. And our life was great.

Until I changed my mind.

We'd been married just over two years when everything changed. My period was late. It's not like it was scary late, only two days, but I was never late. I could almost set a clock to my body's schedule. Being two days late was a cause for full out panic. But I didn't tell Andrew. I decided I wouldn't tell him until I was certain. There was no point distracting him with this, at least until there was something to worry about.

Instead of taking a pregnancy test, I stewed. I could have put my worries to rest by stopping at the pharmacy on the way home from school, but instead I let my imagination run wild. If I was pregnant, what would I do? What would Andrew say? Could we be parents? We never wanted this. But it didn't mean we couldn't do it. Did it? It was a Wednesday; I was going over the week's spelling words at the front of the class, twenty pairs of eyes trained on me when I felt the twinge low in my belly followed a few moments later by the familiar warmth. My period.

Instead of being relieved, I was inexplicably upset. For the last few days my mind had been consumed with the thought of a child. Of being a mom. Without even realizing it, something changed. In the months that followed, I couldn't walk past a young woman pushing a stroller without rushing to peek inside. Everywhere I looked, there were swollen, pregnant bellies. When I put my hand on my own flat stomach, it was like a gradual ache was building deep inside me. I wanted a child.

Andrew didn't take the news well. It was our first real fight.

"No kids. We agreed."

"Andrew, I can't help the way I feel. I want a child."

"You have your students."

"It's not the same. I need a baby of my own."

"You need?"

I thought for a moment. It was more than want. I nodded and said, "Yes. I need a baby."

That was the first time we went to bed angry. It wasn't the last.

We shared apologies in the morning, but something had shifted between us and we both knew it. When I went to kiss him goodbye, he turned away. I don't even think he realized it.

I couldn't turn off how I felt, and despite my efforts, I couldn't change the way he felt. We fought more until after awhile, almost every conversation led to an argument. Even the intimacy between us, something that came so easily before, was strained until that too stopped. Our marriage was falling apart. It only took six months of arguments to shatter what we'd built together. It became clear to both of us that unless one of us changed our mind, it wasn't going to work. I moved in with Uncle Ray. That was three months ago.

My marriage had failed.

"Earth to Lexi." Nicole waved a napkin in front of my face bringing me back to our conversation. "I was asking you if you regret it. Splitting with Andrew?"

I took a sip of water, and spun the straw in my fingers. I remembered the way he kissed me and held me in his arms like I was the most precious person in the world. How we'd take long walks through the park and tell each other about our days. How we laughed and teased each other in the kitchen when we made dinner together. Then I thought about holding a baby in my arms, and that child growing up to call me Mommy.

I shook my head. "No," I said. "I don't regret it."

"But you miss him," Nicole stated.

"I miss what we had together. But I can't hold on to something that isn't there anymore. I don't need a therapist to tell me that." I forced a small smile.

"I'm sorry, Lex," she said. "I really am. Andrew's a good guy and I know how important marriage is to you. But you're right. You can't force a piece that won't fit in the puzzle."

"You know what? I'm okay with things. More okay than I thought I'd be. It's not like I'm sitting around crying, right?"

"Right. Cause you're a toughie," Nicole said. "Just so you know, if you want to cry, that's okay."

I pushed my mostly uneaten sandwich away. I wasn't hungry anymore. We sat in silence while I watched Nicole pick at her salad.

"So," she said after a few moments, her counselor persona abandoned. "The way I look at it, you're a free agent and maybe a little Las Vegas fling is just what you need to get a fresh start."

I laughed at her shift. Nicole could always be counted on to lighten the mood. "Right, Nic. I'm not really the fling type."

"Oh, yes. I always forget that your sexual partners can be counted on one hand." She held up three fingers and wiggled them at me before reaching for my sandwich. "Seriously, Lex. You're way too young and gorgeous to miss out on so much fun. And maybe that's just what you need right now." She picked out the turkey and tossed the bread aside.

"Whatever. And I could turn this around. You're getting kind of old now for the single life, aren't you?"

"Twenty-eight is hardly old. When I meet the right guy, I'll know. He just hasn't come along yet. Besides, we're talking about you and that yummy Leo." She popped the rest of the turkey in her mouth.

"We were talking about Leo?"

"Oh yes. And how a dirty little fling with him is just what you need."

"Well, even if I wanted to, and I'm not saying I do, but even if I did, it's not like I'll ever see him again. Vegas is a big place."

"Not that big, Lexi," Nicole said with a grin on her face. "Not that big."

CHAPTER THREE

"Lexi, stop tugging on your dress, you're going to stretch it."

"That might be a good thing," I said. "I can barely breathe. And don't you think it's a bit short?"

"Are you kidding?" Nicole said as she leaned toward the mirror to apply yet another coat of mascara. "Seriously, if I had your legs instead of these little stumps, my skirts would be a whole lot shorter."

"Whatever, you look fantastic," I said and meant it. She'd chosen a black dress adorned with just enough rhinestones to look classy, but not enough to be tacky. It was a fine line. The dress clung to her in all the right places, showing off the hard work she'd been putting in.

She turned around and flashed me a brilliant smile. "I do look pretty good, don't I? We are seriously hot. We won't have to buy a drink all night."

I tried to look past her to the mirror. I had settled on the teal halter dress. It was the most modest choice even if it was more revealing than any of the bathing suits I owned. It was short, maybe indecently so, but when I tried it on with the strappy black heels Nicole picked out, even I had to admit the effect was pretty incredible. Nicole was so proud of herself after she pulled my hair out of my usual pony tail and styled it so it hung in waves over my shoulders that I caved and let her do my make-up. It wouldn't hurt to play dress up for one night.

"Before we go, I want you to promise me one thing," Nicole said and zipped up her make-up bag.

I groaned but said, "What's that?"

"Before I tell you, just remember it *is* my birthday."

I shot her a look.

"Just promise me you'll have a good time."

"Nic--"

"I mean it, Lex," she said. "I know the last few months have sucked for you and you need to have some fun. That's the great thing about Vegas. It's really easy to have fun and the best part is, no one knows you here. You can totally let loose because you'll never see any of these people again. Just try, okay?"

"What're you talking about?" I leaned into the mirror to examine my eyelashes.

"You know what I mean. Trust me, okay? Consider it a birthday gift."

"Okay, okay."

"Lex, I mean it."

"I said I would." I stood up and looked at her.

She air kissed me on the cheek. "Good. Then we're ready." Nicole tossed her lipstick into her purse and took my arm. "Tonight is going to be amazing."

***

The second we stepped off the elevator we were hit with the pulsing life force of the casino floor and I could feel myself starting to get into the spirit of the evening. Nicole had been trying to get me to come to Las Vegas with her for years, but this was the first time I'd given in. At first, I was overwhelmed with the sheer excess of the city, but after two days the crowds, lights, and noise were starting to feel almost normal.

There was a never-ending stream of people walking around at all hours taking in the wonders, and they definitely were wonders. Where else could you see lions playing with a human trainer in the middle of a hotel? Or a pirate show complete with a sinking ship right on the street? Vegas seemed a world away from my peaceful life in Canada and despite the quiet I was used to, the glitz and glamour had cast a spell over me. It was nice to leave reality behind and forget my real life. Even for a few days. But I was glad to have a return ticket. I would need the rest when the weekend was over.

"Are you sure the party isn't over?" I asked trying to stifle a yawn. "It's almost eleven."

Nicole laughed. "Lex, the party is barely getting started. No one goes out until after ten at least. You look like you need a drink to wake you up. We're almost there."

We hadn't even left the hotel, but we must have crossed the equivalent of three city blocks. The hotels were massive. I held Nicole's hand as she wove through the crowd and concentrated on not tripping in my heels. Before I knew it we were standing in front of Studio 54. A massive line snaked across the floor with people in various states of undress. I looked down at my own outfit which now seemed quite conservative.

"Do you have the tickets?" Nicole asked. She cast a quick look towards the people stopped in front of a muscle-bound bouncer, his arms crossed in front of his chest creating an impenetrable wall.

"Of course." I handed them to Nicole. "But Leo also said to make sure we gave our names."

"Names? Are we on some sort of guest list?"

"I don't really know. He just said to make sure I gave my name at the door. Why? Does that matter?"

"Lexi, it totally matters. Come on," Nicole said and floated towards the bouncer. I followed her, trying not to look at the group of girls shooting dangerous looks our way.

"Alexis Titan," Nicole said to the beefy man and flipped the tickets to him. He fixed her with a stare that was a cross between icy contempt and braindead before checking his clipboard.

"It might be under Lexi," Nicole added.

I watched as his face transformed and when he looked up he might even have been smiling.

"Ms. Titan," he said to Nicole. "Good evening. It'll be just one moment." He pressed a finger to his ear and began speaking into what I assumed was a radio. Nicole looked back at me, as bewildered as I felt. In a few moments another man, this one far less burly and much more handsome, appeared from behind the velvet curtain.

"Ms. Titan," the new man said to Nicole as he offered her his hand. "My name is Mitchell. I'll be looking after you this evening. It's an absolute pleasure to meet you."

"And you, Mitchell," she said shooting me another look. I shrugged. I didn't know anything either. I'd never been to a club in Vegas, but I was pretty sure this type of treatment wasn't normal. I didn't have time to think about it too much because Mitchell was ushering us through the curtain.

"Leo has requested that I take special care of you tonight," Mitchell said as we wound our way through the packed club. He had to yell to be heard over the music. Most people were pressed together in knots, standing, as there didn't appear to be many places to sit. The tables they did have were cordoned off with velvet ropes and plush chairs. Bouncers, clones to the one at the front door, stood at each opening, letting people in and out of the special sections.

"They must be important," I said to Nicole.

"Either that or they have a lot of money," she said. "That would be the life wouldn't it?"

"Ladies?" Mitchell had stopped walking and was watching us with concern. "Is everything all right?"

Nicole spun on her heel and crossed over to him. She looped her arm through his and purred, "Everything is just fine. We're just wondering where exactly you're taking us."

Mitchell smiled; he was just as skilled at flirting as she was. "Not to worry," he said, "we're almost there."

With Nicole's arm still linked through his, he led us up a few stairs to a platform that seemed to float above the main floor, one side looking over the dance floor. There was a wall of water along the back, and the entire area was furnished with luxurious looking couches and chairs. Of course, a thick red rope marked the area as special.

"Leo gave me strict instructions to treat the two of you very well," he said and stopped. "Here we are." The bouncer, who somehow looked even bigger than the last few I'd seen, released the barrier and Mitchell ushered us into the space. "Leo also told me to be sure that you have whatever you need."

"This is amazing," I said trying not to stare.

We were the very important people.

"All of this is for us?" Nicole said to no one in particular.

"There's a bar right here," Mitchell was saying. He gestured to a side table where a multitude of bottles sat. Next to them, another table with an array of glasses and what looked like mixes. On a large ottoman, flanked by two very comfy looking chairs, sat two champagne flutes. A bottle of champagne was chilling in a bucket next to the table. Nicole turned to me, she was beaming.

Leo did all this?

"What can I get you to drink, Ms. Titan?" he said to Nicole.

"Well actually," Nicole's voice faltered, "this is Ms. Titan." She waved in my direction and I was surprised that she gave up the ruse; she seemed to be enjoying the spotlight.

Mitchell smiled and without missing a beat, he said, "Then you must be the birthday girl, Nicole."

Nicole beamed, flipped her hair over her shoulder and said, "That's me. It's my very special day."

"Of course it is and that's why I think you should toast your birthday with a drink." Mitchell handed us each a champagne flute and with a practiced hand, popped the cork before filling our glasses.

"If there is anything you two ladies need, just ask. I'll be nearby," Mitchell said and disappeared, snapping the rope into place behind him.

As soon as he left, Nicole faced me and said, "What on earth did you say to Leo to get us this place?" She threw her arms around me, her champagne sloshing a little. "Thank you, Lexi. You're the best friend ever."

"I didn't do this."

"Of course you did." She released me and raised her glass. "You need to make a toast."

"Right." I raised my glass as well. "To Nicole. May this year be more spectacular than the last." We clinked and drank. The bubbles popped against the roof of my mouth and the back of my throat as I swallowed. I liked it.

"This is fantastic," Nicole said looking around our

space. She walked to the edge and peered down at the people dancing. "We have the best seat in the house."

"We do," I agreed. "This is pretty crazy."

"Okay, seriously, what did you say to Leo to get this set up? You flirted with him, didn't you?"

"Nothing. I swear. He met me at the pool and gave me the tickets. I didn't say anything special at all."

Did I? I thought back to our brief conversation. No, if anything, I'd made a fool of myself, but I was pretty sure I hadn't even flirted with him.

"Well, whatever you did, it worked."

I rolled my eyes. "Let's have another toast," I said raising my glass again. "To new beginnings."

She twisted around and met my glass. "And new adventures." Nicole wiggled her eyebrows at me, we clinked and drained our glasses.

A few more toasts later, we'd almost finished the bottle. I surprised myself when I realized that despite every misgiving I'd ever had about a nightclub, I was enjoying myself.

The music was loud but not obnoxiously so. Maybe it was the alcohol, but my feet started to move in time to the beat.

Nicole grabbed my hand. "Come on," she said. "That's enough sitting around. Let's dance."

"I don't dance," I objected. But I didn't put up a fight as I followed her and within seconds fell into the rhythm of the music.

I don't know if it was the pulsing beat, the champagne or just being in Vegas, but I forgot to feel self-conscious as I let my body go. We danced together, alone and soon with partners as we began to attract male attention. Nicole reveled in the spotlight and shimmied and shook with her partners. I did my best to move away from the intruders but despite my attempts, they continued to follow me. I was having fun; I didn't want to ruin my mood with some random guy trying to push up on me so I grabbed Nicole and dragged her back to our table.

"I'm thirsty," I said once we arrived in our safe haven. I checked over the table of alcohol. "What should we have?"

"Make me something fun," Nicole said and flopped into one of the plushy chairs.

I picked up a pink bottle that I didn't recognize and put it back again. "I have no-"

"Let me," Mitchell said appearing as if I'd conjured him. He slid through the velvet ropes, and took the pink bottle from my hand.

"Something fun please, Mitchell," Nicole called from the chair where she was now lounging seductively and waving at her earlier dance partners still down on the floor.

I watched in awe as Mitchell grabbed various bottles, poured multiple shots into a cocktail shaker, topped it with ice and gave it a few quick shakes before pouring the concoction into two glasses. He handed us each a pink beverage and said, "Here you go, ladies. Just shout when you're ready for another." He winked at Nicole before vanishing again.

I took a sip; it was fruity and far too sweet. I opted for more champagne instead and joined Nicole in the chairs.

"Ladies," a male voice called to us over the rope.

"Well, hello there." Nicole pushed herself up to a sitting position and fluffed her hair behind her.

"Would you two care to dance?" He was handsome, and looking right at Nicole.

"Go ahead," I said. "I'm good right now."

"You sure?" she said.

"Positive. I think my feet could use the break anyway."

I watched Nicole lead her tall, blond dancing partner toward the floor.

"It looks like she's having fun. What about you? Wanna dance?" another voice said from behind me.

Getting comfortable in the overstuffed chair, I swung my legs over the arm, letting my black heels dangle off the other side. I didn't bother to look up. "No thanks," I said. "I'm going to sit this one out."

"Oh, come on, sugar. Your friend's having fun. Why don't you at least let me in to have a drink with you?"

I looked up then and twisted around, irritated with the intrusion. He was good looking - everyone in Vegas was - he was also drunk.

Why did I attract these fools?

"No," I said again, this time with a little more force. "I'm good.

"Come on. You were dancing out there like you wanted me to come over here."

He did not just say that. Loser.

I shot a quick look at the bouncer who was watching the situation. I gave him a nod which was all he needed to remove my drunken intruder, leaving me alone again.

I could get used to this type of treatment. I turned around, closed my eyes and let the music flow through me. The beat was sensual, maybe I did want to dance. I slid my hands up my bare thighs to the silky satin of my dress to the rhythm.

"Why do I always feel like I'm interrupting you?"

My eyes snapped open and I dropped my hands. It was ridiculous, but like a teenager, I could feel my heart jump at the sound of the voice behind me. I didn't even try to stop myself from grinning before I turned around.

Leo had already undone the velvet rope barrier and was stepping onto the platform as if he owned the place, which for all I knew about him, he did.

"Hi," I said trying hard not to sound too excited. I pushed myself up to a sitting position. Maybe a little to fast. The room spun a little, so I closed my eyes until the feeling passed.

When I opened them again, Leo was watching me with a knowing smile.

"I see Mitchell made you his famous concoction." He pointed to the pink drink I'd left untouched.

"He did. But it's too sweet. I stuck with champagne. Which may not have been the best idea."

"Not usually, no," Leo said. His brow creased in concern and he moved to the bar, poured a glass of water. "Here, drink this."

The water was cool and a relief from the heat of the club. "I guess champagne and dancing don't mix. It must be the heat in here," I said.

"Do you feel better?"

I nodded and the concern melted from his face, replaced by a dazzling smile. It must have been the atmosphere, or the alcohol, but when I looked at his face, my thoughts went to what Nicole had said earlier. And technically, I was single.

"Thank you," I said.

"For the water?"

"No." I leaned forward and squeezed his arm.

Did I really just do that?

"For this," I said. "All of it. It's incredible."

"It's nothing."

"Nothing?" I sat up straight. "It's everything. I'm

actually enjoying myself, and I don't think I've ever said that about a nightclub before."

Leo's eyes locked onto mine and after a moment I had to force myself to look away. I shifted my gaze to the dance floor just over his shoulder.

"Where is the birthday girl, anyway?" he asked.

"Where else?" I pointed below us where she was wrapped in the arms of her partner.

Leo took a quick glance and faced me again. "And why aren't you out there? It seems to me that you would have your fair share of partners to choose from." There was a question in his eyes.

"I'm resting," I said and crossed my bare legs in a way I'd seen Nicole do before. I hoped it didn't look too stupid.

I watched his gaze travel up my legs and a shiver ran through me.

I guess it didn't look stupid.

Leo stood and extended his hand towards me. "I think you've rested long enough. Care to dance?"

At that moment, I couldn't think of anything I'd like more. I took his hand and he led me through the crowds onto the dance floor. The beat was fast, and I was eager to get out there.

I couldn't blame my uncharacteristic behavior on the champagne alone. It had to be Vegas. Just being in this city was making me act differently. Oh well, it was Nicole's birthday and I was having fun like she'd requested.

Conversation was out of the question with the bass pounding so I started dancing, trying to lose myself in the beat. I looked at Leo who was moving with surprising grace and rhythm for such a large man. Looking at him yesterday, I wouldn't have thought he was the dancing type. But now, still in his work clothes, minus the tie and with the top few buttons undone, he looked much more relaxed. Our bodies moved in rhythm together. We were so close that I could feel the heat from his body and the space between us was filled with an electric charge. I looked up at his face and saw his smile. Instead of closing his eyes to the beat, as I tended to do, they were fixed on mine. His smile broadened when he saw I was studying him.

He leaned over and said something at me, but his words got lost in the music.

"What?" I yelled back, right as the song changed making my voice seem much louder. I laughed at myself and moved to leave. But Leo put his arm around my waist and pulled me close.

"May I have this dance?"

Let yourself go a little. Nicole's words echoed in my ears.

I slipped my arms around him in response. The room seemed to spin a little but it may have been Leo moving me in time to the sensuous beat.

I let the music consume us both. I closed my eyes, relaxed into his shoulder and inhaled the scent of him. He smelled earthy with just a bit of spice. Was that cologne, or him? Now that we were touching, the heat he stirred in me was undeniable.

"What did you say earlier?" I asked.

"I just wanted to tell you that you looked beautiful." His voice was serious but I couldn't help the giggle that escaped my lips.

"Thank you," I said. "You're beautiful too." I wanted to take the words back right after I'd spoken them.

What was wrong with me?

I should have been more embarrassed than I was, but I wasn't. I looked up at Leo who had stopped dancing and was watching me with a strange look.

"Well, you are," I said and grabbed his hips to get him moving again.

He laughed and slid his hands across my bare back as we resumed our dance. My skin tightened in response to his touch. He must have noticed.

When the music changed again, Leo pulled back slightly and bent his head so we were only inches apart. For a crazy second, I thought he might kiss me. "Let's go sit down," he said. I could feel the hot moisture of his breath against my mouth.

I nodded, unable to form words and keeping his hand on my back, Leo guided me back to our seats.

I collapsed on the plush chair and slipped my shoes off.

"Why do people wear these things?"

"Because they make your legs look outstanding," Leo answered. "May I?" He gestured to my foot.

"Really? But, they're feet. I've been dancing and--"

"Trust me. I know a few pressure points."

I shrugged and let him take my foot in his hands. His touch was cool despite the heat of the club and his big hands made my foot feel tiny as he worked his fingers into my sole.

"That feels so good."

"You sound surprised," he said. "Don't tell me you've never had a foot rub before?"

"I don't usually like people touching my feet." I let my head hang over the back of the chair and I closed my eyes. "But, it feels so good."

"Am I interrupting something?"

My eyes flew open and I tried to jerk my foot away from Leo but he held tight.

Nicole laughed. "Sorry, I really did *not* mean to interrupt this."

"Stop it." I swatted at her but she dodged me.

Leo released my foot and stood up to give Nicole a kiss on the cheek. "Happy birthday," he said. "Are you having a good time?"

I think Nicole might have swooned if her dance partner from earlier hadn't been standing behind her to hold her up.

"This is awesome," Nicole said. "Thank you." Then remembering the man behind her, she pulled him forward and said, "This is Josh."

"Hi, Josh," I said.

"Would you like a drink?" Leo asked him and led Josh to the bar and took over the host duties for the moment. Nicole squeezed herself into the chair next to me and said, "And here I was worried that you were alone. I should've known better. I saw you two dancing. He's so into you."

"I'm just trying to do what you said. Let loose. Remember?"

"Oh, I definitely remember. And you're doing an excellent job," she said. "Are you having fun?"

"I am. But the better question is, are you? It's your birthday."

"I'm having a great time."

"I think I might be done with the club though. I can't handle anymore to drink," I confessed.

"Well..." Nicole tipped her head towards Leo. "You don't have to stay here if you know what I mean?"

"Come on, I can't do that."

"Can't do what?" Leo asked returning to his seat.

"I was just telling Nicole that I couldn't possible dance

38

anymore," I said with a smile.

"And I was just telling Lexi," Nicole said, "that as long as she was okay getting back to the room, she could go on without me." She winked at Leo and I had to stop myself from smacking her leg. "I think Josh and I are going to stay and enjoy my special VIP treatment a little longer though." On cue, Josh wrapped his arm around her and gave her a squeeze. He was cute, even if he didn't say much. Nicole knew how to pick them.

"Can you get back to the room, Lexi?" She asked me, but she was looking at Leo.

"I'll make sure she gets back okay," he answered.

"Oh, I'm sure you will."

CHAPTER FOUR

I guided Lexi into the casino, leaving the pounding bass of Studio 54 behind us. Her hand in mine felt good. Better than good, it felt like I never wanted her to let go.

"Are these people still trying to get in?" she asked and pointed to the would be party-goers standing in the line that hadn't thinned at all through the night.

"It's a popular spot."

"But it's the middle of the night."

"That's when the party happens in Vegas. It's like there's no sense of time here at all. People will be up all night. I know it's said that New York's the city that never sleeps, but if you ask me, it's Vegas. I've met people who come for a weekend and don't sleep in their bed once."

"Then why get a room?" Lexi asked.

"I said they don't *sleep* in their bed."

Instead of blushing or getting embarrassed like I would have guessed, she laughed.

"I should've known," she said. "I've heard plenty of stories."

"So, it's your first time here?"

She nodded, confirming what I already knew. Her

pretty mouth was formed in a circle, like she was going to say something, but couldn't remember what it was. I couldn't focus on anything else. Her lips were perfect. Full, but not too full. I could imagine how they'd yield when I pressed mine on hers. I shook my head.

I couldn't kiss her. She wasn't the type of woman that you just kissed out of the blue. I was pretty sure if I did, the result would not be what I was hoping for.

"Are you tired?" I asked trying to get my mind off her lips.

Again, she looked like she was going to say something but then someone hit a jackpot and she turned towards the loud bells and flashing lights coming from a slot machine a few feet away. She moved towards it, watching. The older lady in front of the winning machine was like many of the seniors I saw here on a daily basis. She'd just won big, but if it weren't for the lights and noise, you'd never know. She didn't even crack a smile. It could've been a huge win, enough to pay for a month of groceries, but the woman didn't register even a flicker of excitement.

I slid closer to Lexi, but didn't touch her. Standing only inches away from her was hard. It would be so easy to slip my arms around her waist and pull her into me. Not touching her was an exercise in restraint.

"She won big," I said in Lexi's ear.

She shivered. Because of me? Maybe, and I hoped it was true, that she felt the same way I did. The urge to touch her magnified.

"She doesn't look very happy about it," she said. "I assumed there would be a celebration. You know, flipping chairs, yelling...that type of thing.."

I leaned in a little closer and I could smell her perfume. When we were dancing, the scent of her filled my senses. Now, I inhaled deep. It was fresh, not sweet at all or flowery. More like a crisp breeze. "There are two types of gamblers, especially slot players," I said. "Some are in it for fun. Those are the ones that get excited. And then there's the hardcore players. I'm sure she's happy. But she'll keep playing until it's all gone."

"Really?" She turned around and for a moment our mouths were only inches apart.

It would've been easy to kiss her.

But worry lined her face, so I said, "I've seen so many people who can't afford to lose even a dollar pump everything they own into these machines."

"That's really sad."

"It is," I agreed. I forced myself to pull away from her, creating distance before I could no longer fight the urge to touch her lips. "Come on. We don't have to watch." I walked to the elevator bank, giving myself a moment to get my desire in check. Lexi followed me but glanced back to the slot machine and the woman who was no doubt well into spending her winnings already.

I could tell Lexi wanted to stop the woman, her concern was so genuine, so...unlike anyone I'd met in a very long time. I clenched my hands together, stopping myself from brushing a stray hair off her face. Behind me there was a steady flow of people coming and going out of the elevators.

It was late and when she turned back to me, I swallowed hard to prepare myself again to say goodbye to her.

I'd promised Nicole I'd get Lexi got back to her room safely. I'm no fool. There was so much implied meaning behind Nicole's words, I'd have to be brain dead not to catch on. But I was also a gentleman, and if Lexi was tired I would take her back to her room, without an agenda.

"It's late, isn't it?" she asked.

I nodded. I wouldn't tell her the time unless she

asked.

"What time is it?"

Dammit.

"One thirty."

"Seriously?"

This was it. I was going to have to say goodbye.

"I'll take you to your room," I said trying my best not to seem disappointed. I took her hand; the spark that never seemed to dull shot through me at her touch. Turning, I started to lead her towards the elevator.

"Why?" She pulled on my arm lurching me to a stop.

When I turned around I wasn't prepared for the mischief in her eyes.

"What do you mean, why?" I said. "I thought you were tired."

"Suddenly," she said with a smile, "I'm feeling much better."

She squeezed my hand and my heart jumped like a kid at a school dance.

"I know this sounds crazy," she said, "but I'm hungry. Can we get something to eat?

I laughed out loud, more from relief then humor, but she looked so serious that I put my hand to my mouth and tried to cover my laughter with a cough. How could this woman affect me so much that the thought of her going to bed and walking out of my life was making me nervous?

"Hungry?" I managed.

Lexi crossed her arms, which, as well as making her look out of control hot, had the added bonus of pushing her breasts up so I could see their swell. She wasn't wearing a bra.

I was suddenly very hungry myself.

"Am I funny?" she demanded. Her turned up mouth gave her away; she wasn't mad, but I was sure enjoying the way she was trying to convince me that she was.

"I'm sorry." I swallowed hard. "You're not funny," I said and then because I had nothing to lose, I added, "But you're very cute."

Another blush crept across Lexi's face, down her neck and into that cleavage I couldn't seem to take my eyes off.

I loved making her blush.

I gave her a moment to recover before I said, "I know an excellent place where we can grab a burger. Assuming your feet are okay."

She smiled and the ball bounced back into her court. "Honestly, I feel fine," she said. "It must be the oxygen they pump in here, but I'm not tired at all and my feet are doing much better after their massage."

"Good. I don't think I want the evening to end yet."

That was an understatement.

"Neither do I."

We looked at each other for a moment. I tried to read her expression. Never before had I experienced this type of instant sexual tension with a woman. But, God, it was so much more than that. I wanted to keep her talking, to hear her voice. But at the same time I wanted to silence her by kissing those lips.

The noise of the casino faded away. I leaned in to close the distance between us. My lips were so close to hers, I could feel the warmth of her breath.

"Excuse me." A man dressed in a tropical shirt squeezed through, pushing me back and completely, effectively ruining the moment.

"Well," I said trying to recover. "Is a burger okay? Or are you in the mood for something else? If you want

—
44

something fancy, I can arrange it. But, I'll be honest, it's usually a good juicy burger that I crave after a night out."

"That sounds perfect," she said and if it was possible, at that moment I wanted her even more.

***

I knew the perfect place to take her and I didn't waste any time in case she changed her mind. I led her outside, into a cab and in a few minutes we were seated across from each other in a red vinyl booth.

The minute the huge hamburgers and baskets of fries were put in front of us, I realized I was much hungrier than I thought. I took a few big bites, satisfying the growl in my stomach. And I wasn't the only one enjoying the meal. I took my time chewing and watched Lexi.

"What?" she asked and wiped a dribble of ketchup off her chin.

I took a sip of my soda in an attempt to conceal my smile. She was so damn cute, even when her mouth was full.

"I was just watching you eat," I said. "I can't remember the last time I've seen a beautiful woman with such a good appetite."

"That sounds like such a line." She laughed and popped another fry in her mouth. "I've never been afraid of eating. Besides, this is fantastic."

"I'm glad you're enjoying it. They're the best burgers in town."

She glanced down at her half eaten meal. "Oh, I don't think there's any doubt that I'm enjoying it." Her eyes sparkled. She might have been flirting with me but it was so unlike the women I was used to, the ones who threw themselves at me. Lexi's flirting was subtle, almost like she didn't know how. It was sweet and I wanted more. "So you must date a lot?" she continued.

"I don't."

"I find that hard to believe."

"It's true. Usually the type of women I meet are here for a good time, not really a long time, if you know what I mean?"

She swallowed another bite and asked, "What about women who live here?"

"You really want to know about my dating life?"

She smiled and nodded.

"Okay, but it's very boring. I work most of the time, have no interest in a fling with a tourist and haven't found a local woman who's interested in anything serious. So, that's about it."

Lexi took a sip of her drink and I watched her eyes change. The sparkle was replaced by something else.

"Go ahead," I urged. "Say it."

"What about me?" she asked. "Why are you sitting here with me then? And, since I'm asking questions I normally wouldn't, are you going to tell me how you knew so much about me?"

I took a moment to chew on a fry. I decided telling the truth would be the best route. "I don't actually know a lot about you," I said. "I found out your last name because I work at the hotel and I have friends at the front desk who owed me a favor."

"And the pool? How did you know I was swimming yesterday morning?"

"Friend that works security."

"Let me guess, he owed you a favor too?" She took a

sip of her drink but I could see the start of a smile.

I shrugged. "What can I say? I'm a helpful guy."

"So," she said, letting me see her grin, "what is it that you do at the hotel that has so many people indebted to you?"

I swirled my straw before answering. It's not that I was embarrassed of my job, but I could do better, I knew I could. And a spot in guest services wasn't really going to impress a woman like Lexi. She looked like she was used to a comfortable lifestyle. Not that she was pretentious in any way. In fact compared to most of the women I'd met, she was a rare and compelling combination of classy and down to earth. She wouldn't be impressed with my job.

"I work in guest services," I said and looked down at the table trying to muster the courage. After a moment I pulled myself together and looked up, trying to appear more successful than I was. "I help people with parties, events and things. It's not much now," I continued, "but I'm working hard and hopefully in a few years I'll move up to management."

"I'm sure you will," she said. Her voice was soft and she looked so genuine, that I wanted to hug her.

I felt my body relax again. Was it possible that even after just meeting me, she believed in me? It'd been too long since anyone believed in me.

We ate in silence for a few more minutes. I don't think I'd ever seen a woman devour a burger the way she did. Juices dripped down her chin which she wiped off before dropping the napkin in the basket on top of the fries she couldn't finish. I took a swallow of my coke and she looked up, catching me staring.

"Just watching me eat again?" Lexi tugged at her dress, wiggling in the seat.

"Yes, but I was wondering something too," I said. "Can

I ask you a question?"

"Sure."

"Last night, in the lounge. You told that guy you were married."

Her face turned that pretty shade of red again. I didn't want to embarrass her, but if I was going to sit here and flirt with her, I needed to know. I'd already checked out her ring finger, it was bare. But in Vegas, you could never know for sure, and I needed to know.

She nodded and said, "I am."

The smile fell from my face. Dammit, I should know better than to ask a question when I didn't want to hear the answer.

"I see," I said trying to keep the bitterness out of my voice. I could tell by the look on her face, I hadn't done a very good job.

"Leo--"

"So, why were you so willing to come with me tonight? Don't you think your husband will mind?" It wasn't a malicious question.

Her face transformed. She looked sad for a moment but then her expression changed again. She looked like she might laugh. Or...damn.. was she going to cry?

"What did I say?" I asked. "Lexi, I didn't mean to-"

"No," she said. "It's just, I don't think my husband," she emphasized the word, "would mind at all. We're separated."

Separated.

One word was all it took for my entire mood to shift. No sooner had the word left her lips than I could feel myself sitting a little straighter, the smile returned to my face and my heart resumed its frantic beat. With that one word, I realized that no matter how slim, I might have a chance with her. At least, I might have a chance at sitting with her a little longer and getting to know her. And right at that moment I couldn't think of anything I'd like more than to look into her eyes that made me feel like I was drowning, and learn everything I could about her. And there was one more very important thing I needed to know.

"How long?" I asked. "Have you been separated a while?"

"Six months," she said. "But it was a long time coming."

"So you're..."

"Yes," she said answering my unasked question. "It's over. In fact," she continued and I had to force myself to listen to what she was saying. "I'm sure he'd be shocked by my behavior tonight."

"What do you mean?" I leaned in towards her. I wanted to close the gap between us, but I caught myself and pulled back again. "How have you been acting?" I asked.

"Well, I'm sure you've figured out that I'm not the nightclub type," she said. "Nicole chose my clothes tonight..."

I liked her clothes. It was undeniably the sexiest dress I'd ever seen. But if it got any shorter, I would have to be resuscitated.

"...I almost never dance, and I absolutely never go out with strange men in the middle of the night for burgers."

"Well, it's a good thing I'm not strange then," I said.

She tucked her hair behind her ear and smiled in a way that made my blood rush, and said, "And I'm not usually so...forward." And then she winked at me. It took me a moment to digest the action.

Had she really done that? It was so sexy and awkward, all at the same time that the simple action had an undeniable impact on my body. I was glad to be sitting.

"Well," I said after a moment. "I like it and I'm glad you decided to take a chance tonight."

"Me too." Her voice was quiet, the false bravado of a moment ago had vanished.

I couldn't help it any longer. My arm shot out in front of me and I took her hand in mine.

I had to touch her.

She shivered and when she closed her eyes, I stroked the top of her hand. I knew my touch affected her. The heat from her skin ebbed to my core.

"Come on," I said. "We still have all night."

CHAPTER FIVE

Leo led me outside to the strip where the constant stream of people still hadn't let up. There never seemed to be a break in the action in Vegas. It was exhausting. People were everywhere taking in the lights and sights that even at two in the morning were going strong.

Some of the sights, were much more disturbing than others.

"Are you okay?" Leo asked. Until I heard his voice I hadn't realized I'd stopped moving. My gaze was frozen on the sight in front of me. "Lexi?" Leo asked. His voice was soft, concerned.

"I can't believe it," I said to him over my shoulder. "Why would they do that?"

"Do what?"

I pointed to the woman standing a few feet away. She had a cigarette in one hand and a bottle of beer in the other as she leaned over a stroller. Her child who looked to be about two or three, reclined with his legs hanging over the bar and his eyes, wide open. "It's the middle of the night," I whispered.

Leo covered my outstretched hand with his own, pushed it down and held it in both of his. "You see all kinds of things here."

"That doesn't make it okay. I would never take my..." I could feel tears building in my eyes and I blinked hard to keep them at bay.

"Your baby?" he asked. "Do you have a child?"

I turned my back on the woman and looked at Leo. "No," I said trying not to let my emotion show. "I don't. But if I did..."

"You wouldn't have them out in the middle of the night," he finished for me. "You're very sweet, Lexi."

"Just because I don't think the Vegas strip is the best place for a child in the middle of the night?"

"No," he squeezed my hand. "Because you obviously care a great deal of people, and I don't see that a lot here. It's a nice change."

"Well," I said with a shrug. "I am what I am."

"Yes, you most certainly are," he said with a laugh.

His laughter was so fresh and real that tingles traveled down my spine. I hoped he couldn't hear how my heart sped up. It was embarrasing how my body reacted to him. I would say that I felt like a teenager, except even when I was a teenager I'd never reacted to a guy like this. Even Andrew, who I loved, had loved, never made my body go crazy that way.

"Are you cold? You're shaking" he said.

"Cold?" Even with the sun down, it was still hotter than a summer day back home. I shook my head and let my hair sway across my shoulders.

Cold was not the problem. My body was in a continual state of heat with Leo around.

"Tired then? I keep forgetting how late it is and that most people aren't used to staying up all night." He sounded so concerned for me, and I wanted to wrap my arms around him and hold on.

I didn't. Instead, I shook my head again and looked into his dark eyes. "Please stop asking me, because I am definitely not tired," I said. I fluttering my lashes in a way I'd seen Nicole do. I hoped the look in my eyes would convey the message that my body was trying to send to him. A message I wasn't completely sure of yet.

For good measure, I tossed my head and tried to flip my hair. But instead of looking sexy, I'm sure it looked like I'd had a spasm of some sort and the ends of my hair flicked Leo in the face.

If the earth had opened up and swallowed me right then, I would've welcomed it.

He held a hand to his face where my hair had stung him. Not the message I was trying to convey.

"I'm sorry," I said.

"No, it's..." He coughed hard and covered his mouth.

Oh my, God. He was laughing at me. I knew I wasn't good at flirting but...

I'm such an idiot.

I turned away so I wouldn't have to watch him.

"Lexi." Leo put his hand on my shoulder and the thrill of his touch on my bare skin hit me again, but this time I shrugged him off. "Okay, I deserved that," he said. The humor was gone from his voice and he sounded sincere. I turned.

"I'm sorry," he said. "I didn't mean to laugh at you. It's just, you look so damn cute when you're trying to flirt with me."

"Trying?"

Oh, great.

"I should rephrase that," he said. "When you are flirting with me. It's so fresh, and so..."

I really wanted him to finish that thought. He didn't.

He reached to take my hands again and this time I didn't pull away. "I feel like I've known you for years and you don't really seem like the flirting type." His voice lowered and he added, "I suppose it's your turn to laugh at me. That sounded pretty dumb."

I didn't laugh because it was exactly the way I felt. No matter how unreasonable it was.

"It *was* pretty lame," I said. "But the thing is, I feel the same way."

"You do?"

I didn't answer him. Instead I scanned the street. All around us people were streaming by. Laughing and shoving. And we stood in the middle of it all, having a conversation that sounded like it had been pulled straight out of a cheesy romance novel. It was ridiculous for me to be thinking of a man this way, let alone a man I'd just met.

"Nicole would love this," I said.

"Love what?"

"We must sound so stupid. I don't think in my whole life, I've ever had a conversation like this one."

Leo's features smoothed out and he touched my cheek. His thumb slid across my face and I was afraid my legs might give out from the desire that flooded through me. "But you feel the same," he said, "like there's something between us?"

I couldn't speak. I stared at him like an idiot. I knew I couldn't blame the alcohol from earlier, but I wouldn't act like this all on my own.

Would I? I was responsible and level headed. Nicole was the wild card. The one that could go off with a strange man and have a great time without a second thought about safety or sensibility.

Leo's hand was still cupping my cheek and I had to fight the urge to close my eyes and sink into my fantasies about him. Instead, I stared at the planes in his face, examining him for some sign that he might be a mass murderer or a con man trying to rob me out of my savings. If he was any of those evil things, his gorgeous smile did a good job of convincing me otherwise.

"Come on," Leo said breaking my trance. "I want to show you something." He took my hand. I didn't offer any resistance as he pulled me into the crowd.

***

Leo led me down the strip, pointing things out and telling me stories as we walked. We were in front of Caesar's Palace when he suggested that we stop and sit for a bit to people watch.

"Did Nicole tell you?"

"Tell me what?" To his credit he looked surprised, but Nicole must have told him that people watching was one of my favorite past times.

"You really want to sit down and look at people?" I asked.

He bowed his head a little. "I know it's not very exciting, but-"

"I do it too."

He didn't laugh when I told him how I loved to choose people around me at random and make up situations and stories about them. In fact, he thought it sounded more fun than just watching them walk by, so we found a place to sit on the edge of a marble statue and jumped right into the game by choosing an overweight couple in their late fifties, dressed in shorts and matching

Hawaiian print shirts.

"I think," he said, "that this is their first time here. It was an unwanted present from their adult kids."

I giggled and took over. "They didn't want to come, but the tickets were paid for and now that they're here-"

"They love it," Leo continued. "In fact, they've embraced Vegas life and have decided they're never going to leave."

"They're going to open a chapel off the strip and share their love by marrying others."

"With a drive-thru window."

"And don't forget, the slushy drink bar," I said pointing to the tall cups the couple held. "They're going to have the first chapel with free slushy drinks when you say 'I do'."

Leo burst into laughter and I joined him. When the couple glanced in our direction, I did my best to stop, but I couldn't contain myself. Leo wrapped his arms around me and pulled me back against his chest in an effort to still me.

It worked.

The heat from his arms penetrated me and I melted into his embrace.

When the couple moved on, Leo whispered in my ear, "Can I ask you another question, Lexi?"

I nodded.

He released me just enough to free one hand and lift a strand of my hair letting it slide through his fingers. "How could your husband give you up? I mean, you're beautiful, smart, and the more I find out about you, the more I think you're fantastic."

I liked his flattery, but I couldn't seem to get used to it and the easy way he had of flirting with me.

"Was it an unhappy marriage?" he asked. I thought I detected a hint of hopefulness in his voice.

"No," I said. "It wasn't unhappy at all. Andrew is a great guy, he treated me like a queen. He was a good husband."

"Then-"

"It was me," I said. "I ended it."

"You didn't love him?"

"I did. I do. It's complicated," I sighed and looked down at my feet.

"Lexi, you can tell me," he said. "I want you to."

And I wanted to tell him.

For whatever reason, I felt he needed to know. I shifted around so I could look at his face. "The whole thing was my fault. When I met Andrew, all I wanted was a career. Which was perfect, because that's all he wanted too."

"And then?" Leo prodded when I didn't continue.

"And then I changed my mind."

"About him?"

"No, about what I wanted," I said. "I'm a school teacher. Second grade."

Leo smiled like he was picturing it. "That makes sense," he said. "So, you didn't want to be a teacher anymore?"

"No. Before we got married, we decided we didn't want children. I think it was one of the things that attracted Andrew to me."

"I doubt that was it," Leo said and let my hair slide through his fingers again giving me chills down my neck.

"Regardless, he made it clear he didn't want children. And when that changed for me, I hoped it had changed for him too."

"It didn't."

"No, and I'm not willing to give that up," I added.

There was a moment of silence.

"And you're okay?" he asked after a minute.

I nodded. "I am. It's not always easy, but I'll be fine."

Putting two fingers under my chin, Leo tilted my face so that our eyes locked. "I believe you will be," he whispered.

When he leaned forward all the words I'd been about to say vanished. I'd been waiting all night for this. The warm breath on my cheek, the musky scent of him. I could feel my own breathing become shallow. I closed my eyes, afraid that if I looked at him I would say something to ruin the moment. I tipped my chin; his lips brushed mine.

My cell phone rang.

I ignored it.

It rang again. When I opened my eyes, he was so close that with a fraction of a movement I would be kissing him. I could ignore the phone. With only a-

It rang again.

I swallowed my disappointment and reached for my cell phone in the depths of my purse.

I didn't bother to look at the call display. "Hi, Nicole."

"Lex? Where are you? Are you okay?"

"I'm fine," I said and looked at Leo who had sat back and was watching me with a small smile on his face. "We went out for a burger."

"We? Who are you...are you with... no way."

I turned so Leo wouldn't see me trying not to laugh. "Yup, and I'm fine. Honestly, I'm surprised you went back to the room so early. Are you done celebrating already?" I knew if I shifted the focus of this conversation, she would follow, at least for awhile.

"Are you kidding? I came back to the room to check on you and tell you not to wait up. Josh and I are going to, well..."

He must be standing right there.

I laughed. "Go, Nic. Have fun but be safe."

"I could say the same for you," she said. "And Lex?"

"Yes."

"Go for it. You need this. I won't be coming back to the room so-"

"Thanks, Nicole." I was glad I wasn't looking at Leo because I'm pretty sure my face had turned an unattractive shade of tomato red and I did not need him to see that. "I'll see you in the morning."

After I hung up I took my time putting the phone back in my purse and fiddled with some papers. I fished a lip gloss out of a side pocket and after I applied a thin layer, I couldn't procrastinate any longer. I put it away and turned back to Leo who wore an amused expression on his face.

"I'm assuming she gave you her blessing," he said with a grin.

"I don't need her blessing."

"But she did give it?"

How could I be sitting in the center of the Las Vegas strip with a complete stranger in the middle of the night contemplating, well, whatever I was contemplating. I didn't do this type of thing.

Maybe that was the point.

"Leo," I said facing him again. "What's your last name?"

"Mendez."

I cocked an eyebrow at him.

"My mother's Spanish and my father's Italian I believe."

That would explain his dark features and exotic olive skin. "You're not sure?"

His face took on an unreadable expression. "I never knew my father and my mother took off when I was very young. My grandmother raised me."

"Leo, I'm so sorry." I reached for his arm and there were the sparks again. I didn't pull away, but stroked the smooth fabric of his shirt. "I didn't mean to bring up bad feelings." And I didn't. I was enjoying our evening together; I didn't want to give him an excuse to leave.

"No," he said and his hand covered mine, stilling it. "You didn't know." He looked at me as if we were long time lovers instead of two people who had just met. "Besides, I had a great childhood. My grandmother was an amazing lady."

"Was?"

"She died about two years ago. It was a heart attack, she was seventy-six. After her funeral, I moved here."

"To Vegas?" I couldn't imagine anyone moving here, to this glitz, and over the top glamour. "From where?"

"I grew up in a small town in Arizona, about two hours from Phoenix. I wanted to go someplace where no one knew me, where there were no preconceived ideas about who my parents were. I wanted to go somewhere I could get ahead."

"And there's a lot of opportunities here?"

Leo took his hand away from mine and started tracing pictures on my back. I had to fight from releasing a sigh of pleasure. His touch felt good, natural.

"There are always opportunities for people who want to work hard. And I've always been interested in the hospitality industry, so Vegas seemed like the natural

—
60

choice."

I couldn't disagree with that. I'd never seen so many hotels or tourism operations in such a compressed area. I relaxed into his touch and soon his finger tracing turned into light rubs, as he worked some of the tension out of my shoulders. We could have been the only two people in the world; I was so lost in what he was doing. I let my thoughts drift until they touched on something he'd said a moment ago. "What do you mean, you wanted to go where no one knew you?" I asked.

He stopped moving his hands and for a moment and I regretted asking the question. I held my breath and soon his hands began their slow progression again, his fingers probing into the muscles.

It felt good. Everything about Leo felt good.

I didn't think he was going to answer me, but after a few moments he said, "My whole life I was known as 'little Leo'."

I couldn't imagine anyone thinking of this tall, dark man as 'little' but I let him continue.

"People treated me like trash because of my parents. I never knew my father, I doubt my mother even knew him. She's a drug addict. Always was. Grandma tried everything to get her clean, but she just didn't want to be helped. She spent her days turning tricks in alleys and occasionally showed up to steal money from my grandma. She was a good woman, my grandmother. She didn't deserve the way people talked about her. It wasn't her fault that my mother turned out the way she did.

"Up until the day she died, she had two jobs. During the day she worked at a restaurant. When I was little she was a waitress and that's where I'd spend my evenings. But when she got older, the arthritis in her elbows got to be too much. She stayed in the back, doing dishes mostly. Her boss, he was a good guy. He could've fired her, but he didn't."

"What was her other job?"

Leo smiled a little. "The second job she took when I was a teenager. She wanted me to go to the good high school, the one where kids actually graduated. But we didn't live in the right district so Grandma made a deal with the principal. If she cleaned the school at night, he'd let me attend classes there. I'd help her sometimes, but she wouldn't let me lift a finger until all my homework was done. And then when I graduated, she stayed on because the principal started paying her and she wanted me to go to college. The kids at school made fun of me, and her, but I'd never met anyone who worked as hard as she did and as soon as I was old enough, I got a job and tried to help out. She saved for years, putting everything she could spare into a jam jar because she didn't trust banks. So I went to school, and got a degree in management hospitality."

I thought I should congratulate him, but somehow it didn't seem right, so I kept quiet and let him continue.

"I thought it would change, the way people looked at me in the streets, the way people treated my grandma, like we weren't any good. But it didn't. I couldn't get a job in my town so I moved to Phoenix, and worked night shifts at hotels, learning everything I could. I sent every spare penny I could home to her, but she kept working. She never spent a cent of it. After she died, I found it. It was folded up with the notes I'd sent her, in the jam jar."

His hands stilled again. This time, I reached back, putting my hand over his on my shoulder and turned so we were facing each other. Around us, tourists were snapping pictures of the statues and the magnificent hotel in the background. "Leo," I said, "that's so sad."

He shrugged and leaned back against the marble statue. "It is what it is. You can't change people. After the funeral, I packed up the few things of hers I wanted to keep and never looked back. I guess my mother's still there somewhere. But I doubt she even remembers that she has a son."

He looked over my head at something I don't think was there. After a second his eyes cleared and he said, "So that's how I ended up here. That's my story." He looked down at me, the smile had returned to his face and his eyes glittered with the lights off the strip.

"That's quite the story."

"It's true," he said. "I can't believe I told you all that."

"I'm glad you did."

"It's easy to talk to you," he said and sat up so we were once again facing each other. "Now that you know my history. Tell me yours."

"It's boring. Trust me."

"I can't imagine that anything about you is boring." He laced his fingers into mine. "I know you're a teacher. Your parents must be very proud of you."

I winced. Even after such a long time, it still stung.

"What did I say?" Leo grabbed my hand and squeezed. "Don't you have a good relationship with your parents?"

"My parents are dead." Once the words were out, I felt like I could breathe again. It was always like that when I told someone. The pain didn't seem to lessen. "They died in a car accident when I was twelve."

"Lexi, I'm so sorry."

"It's okay," I said and I meant it. "My Uncle Ray, he's my dad's younger brother, he raised me and he was great. I couldn't have asked for better. I guess we have that in common, don't we? We're both sort of orphans."

"Sadly, I guess we are," he said. He released my hand and his fingers started stroking my arm. The action was so gentle that I had to glance down just to be sure he was touching me and it wasn't a breeze. "Tell me about your Uncle Ray. Do you have cousins?"

"No." I shook my head. "It was just the two of us. Uncle Ray's a bit of a mountain man. Big, burly and, well, he's definitely more comfortable outdoors than inside. But when my parents died, he dropped everything, left the mountains and moved into the city to raise me. I always wanted him to date, but he said nobody would have him. When I got older I realized he just wasn't looking. He took his role as my guardian very seriously. I don't think he knew how to date and be a dad."

"Well, he did a great job."

I smiled, more to myself than to Leo. "He did. He's great."

"So, now that you're all grown up, did Uncle Ray go back to the mountains?"

"Sort of," I said. "He kept his place, and he spends a lot of time at the lake fishing, but he still likes the city."

"Because you're there?"

I laughed. "Actually, her name is Sara Beth. He's been seeing her for a few years. It turns out someone will have him." I looked down at Leo's hand that was still moving and took it in mine. "And, that's my story."

"There's still so much I want to know. Like what's your-"

I reached for him, pulled him close and before I could stop to tell myself that I never did things like that, I kissed him.

His lips were firm, yet they yielded to mine. It took him a moment to react, but after a few seconds his arms wrapped around me and pulled me even closer so I could feel his heart beating in his chest. The kiss deepened, and I couldn't help but let out a small groan of pleasure as his tongue worked its way inside my mouth.

One of his hands released its grip on my back and moved down to my thigh. I jumped a little at the feel of his hot hand on my bare skin. I forgot I was still wearing such a short dress. As we kissed, the hand on my leg crept higher while the other one worked its way up my back until it was at the base of my neck. Leo's fingers twined through my hair and pulled my head away, breaking our kiss.

"I was wondering," he said, his voice coming in short bursts, "if we could maybe go somewhere a little less public."

I looked around, remembering we were still sitting outside Caesar's surrounded by thousands of people. I was no longer surprised by my behavior when I said, "Oh God, yes."

CHAPTER SIX

Leo took the key from my fingers and slid it into the slot on the door. I had a flash of something.

Hesitation? Uncertainty? I knew I was being very forward, brazen really. The total opposite from how I normally act. But when I looked into his dark eyes, I didn't care.

We'd barely stepped inside, and Leo grabbed me and spun me so I was pressed against the door. And this time when his lips met mine, I was ready for the way my body would react to him.

At least I thought I was. His lips melted into mine the same way they had earlier, my body responded with a thrill and I pulled him closer, securing my hands around his waist. As the kiss grew deeper, I needed more.

It wasn't enough.

Everything I thought I knew about myself went out of the window and I bit down on his lip in what I hoped was an invitation for more. I thought my body might explode from the heat.

Leo kissed me deeper and this time I didn't over think it. I let myself open up to each one of the sensations he stirred inside of me. As long as we were kissing, I didn't think.

I couldn't think.

It was as if all of my energy and focus was channeled into Leo. But when he broke the kiss, sucking on my lower lip as he pulled away, a million unwanted thoughts came crashing into my brain.

Should I be doing this? I didn't even know this man. I was still legally married. Am I making a smart decision?

If my uncertainty showed on my face, he didn't notice. His back was turned and he led me across the floor to one of the queen sized beds.

"This one's yours," he said. It wasn't a question.

I smiled, my concerns forgotten as I looked at the two beds. The one closest to the window was covered in clothing. Shoes, blouses, a dress and two purses lay on the comforter. It looked like that half of the room had been ransacked. Or, someone couldn't decide what to wear. The bed we were standing in front of was freshly made from housekeeping. The novel I was reading earlier lay open on the pillow.

"Only you would bring a book to Vegas," he said. He lifted it, marked the page with a napkin and placed it on the bedside table before turning back to me. He ran his thumb down the side of my face, until it touched the corner of my mouth. I closed my mind to everything except him. When he touched me, I no longer cared if I was making a smart decision, every nerve ending in my body sparked and reacted to him. That was all I needed.

I ran my hands down his chest, feeling his muscles through his shirt. His hands were on me as well. They moved down my bare arms and my skin tightened in response to his warm touch.

He didn't kiss me, but instead looked into my eyes. Somehow the connection between us intensified with the anticipation. Feeling bold, my fingers found the buttons on his shirt and began to work them free. I took my time as I undid the first two, but my pace quickened when the fabric parted, exposing his bare chest. Impatient I yanked the fabric, popping the bottom buttons free. He still didn't break eye contact with me, but I could see his lips turn up into a smile.

His hands came to rest on my upper arms, his thumbs worked slow circles on my skin.

With a small smile of my own, I pushed my hands beneath the open fabric of his shirt and slid them up his chest. The feel of his smooth skin, chiseled from what? Time at the gym? Physical work?

It didn't matter.

The feel of him under my fingers cranked up the level of my desire. I moved further up and over his shoulders, pushing the shirt down and then before I realized what I was doing, I took half a step forward and bent my head so my lips pressed onto his bare skin. With small kisses and nibbles, I worked my way from his neck down his torso. His grip on my arms tightened, and he let out a moan. When I got to his waist and his belt buckle I straightened up and looked straight into his eyes again.

"Jesus, Lexi," he groaned and crushed me to him. His lips were no longer soft or slow, but full of heat and need. His hands released my arms and reached behind my neck, untying the halter. The soft fabric fluttered down, revealing my bare breasts. He stripped himself of his own ruined shirt before his hands found me again.

God, he was beautiful.

There was no time to study his perfect form, the touch of his hands on my chest distracted me from all thought as he slid them down my chest and between my breasts leaving a trail of heat as he went. Leo's hands didn't stop moving. In a quick motion, he unzipped the back of my dress and pushed it over my hips. It pooled to the floor and I stepped out of it.

"You're gorgeous," Leo said and he pulled back to look at me. I was thankful for the red satin panties set Nicole had urged me to buy instead of wearing my usual cotton. With my hair falling over my shoulder, I felt sexy and not the slightest bit insecure.

"Kiss me," I whispered. I needed to feel his lips again. He obliged by pulling me towards him, but instead of kissing my mouth, his lips touched the sensitive spot on my neck, just below my jaw. I shivered and a moan escaped my lips. He used one hand to hold me to him while the other ran through my hair, gently tugging my head to the side, exposing the length of my neck. He nibbled and kissed his way down to the swell of my breasts. My body shuddered with anticipation and he stood up, meeting my gaze that I'm sure was clouded with lust.

"Your turn," I said and I moved my hands to his belt buckle and slid the leather through. My fingers fumbled with the button but I managed to push it through and moved the zipper down. Before I could think twice, I plunged my hands into the fabric.

I froze when my hands hit bare skin.

He chuckled. "Surprised?" he asked.

"I probably shouldn't be," I said and ran my hands over the smooth, bare skin of his rear and squeezed. His laughter turned into a groan. Encouraged, I pushed his pants down, exposing him and his excitement. It was my turn to moan. The sight of him wanting me sparked something low in my belly.

"Not fair," Leo said.

"What?"

"This," he said and ran his fingers along the satin of my panties. Electric shocks flew through me and the smoldering inside me burst into flames. I took a sharp breath in as he hooked his fingers under the elastic and slid my panties over my hips.

"There," he said and smiled. "Now, it's fair." He took a step back from me and let his eyes travel down. I knew how my body looked. It was tight, toned from swimming and running. I never had the sexy curves and round breasts that Nicole did, but mine was an athletic body and by the look in Leo's eyes, he was satisfied with what he saw.

More than satisfied.

I waited until he was done his appraisal, using the time to examine him as well. His olive toned skin was smooth, with just enough chest hair. He was lean and hard, but not so much so that he looked like he spent hours in the gym. I let my eyes trail down his chest to his hips and the incredible need waiting for me.

"Come here," he said. His voice was gruff. He reached for me and together we took two steps backwards until the bed was behind me. With a gentle push from Leo, I was on the bed, and he lowered himself on top of me. I closed my eyes as he covered my body in kisses, working his way down.

I heard a low groan. Did it come from me? He was driving me crazy with his tongue. His exquisite torment.

When the fire within me was too much to bear, I reached for him and guided his mouth to mine again. He broke away and asked me a question with his eyes.

"Yes," I whispered.

He didn't break eye contact as he entered me, filling me. We fit together. I felt like I knew every move he would take, but at the same time, everything was new, different.

Better.

I didn't think of all my troubles, or what was waiting for me. I didn't think about how un-Lexi like I was behaving or anything else. Instead, as my body rocked with his, the only thoughts I had were reserved for the incredible man that was staring into my eyes as our bodies moved together and how natural it felt to be with him and the last thought I had before I gave myself over to ecstasy, was how I could get used to feeling this way.

***

Not knowing what she would like for breakfast, or even if she ate breakfast, I had room service bring up a selection of pastries, fruits and cereals. Lexi didn't seem like she'd be the type of woman to eat a large meal in the morning, but then again, I didn't really know.

There was a lot I still didn't know.

I looked behind me at Lexi still sleeping curled up on her side, her bare back to me, her golden hair falling over her body like a curtain. The urge to slide her hair over and kiss her shoulders was strong but I didn't want to wake her. Yet.

Last night had been amazing which sounded ridiculously cliché but there really was no other word for it. From the moment I'd seen Lexi sitting at the bar only a few nights ago, I knew she was someone special. I knew I had to meet her.

Talking with her, learning about her, hell, just being with her last night felt like I'd been with her forever. I didn't have a lot of experience with serious relationships, but when it came to Lexi, I wanted to change all of that. The distance between us didn't matter; I'd worry about it later.

Lexi stirred and a small groan came out of her as she stretched in her sleep. My thoughts flashed right back to the night before when it had been me making her groan. She was so intense, so...well, hot.

I poured a cup of coffee from the urn on the cart and put it on the bedside table before slipping back into the bed next to her.

"Good morning, beautiful," I said. and ran my hand across her smooth skin. She shivered a little before waking further. She rolled over, pulling the sheet with her. I wanted to pull it down again.

"I didn't think you'd still be here," she said. Her voice was thick with sleep but she still sounded happy.

"Are you kidding?" I reached around and grabbed the cup of coffee. "I'm not sure how you take it," I said offering her the cup. "Or even if you drink it. But there's tea too, if you prefer. Or I can get juice. We have orange, apple and-"

"Stop," Lexi said trying to swallow her laughter. "Coffee is perfect.

While she adjusted herself in the bed, I prepared the cart and rolled it closer. I wanted to give her time to wake up and digest what had happened between us.

I'm not an idiot, and I didn't need her to tell me that she'd never slept with man she'd just met before. The last thing I wanted was for her to have any bad feelings, or worse, regret what we'd done.

"I didn't know what you'd like," I said taking a tray of food to the bed. "But I had a feeling you'd be hungry. We really..."

She blushed that sexy shade of red that I was getting used to.

"Leo, I-"

"Don't say it. Don't say you regret it," I said, "because I don't." I looked into her eyes and could see the confusion battling there. "I need you to know that I don't do things like this either." Her eyes flashed with what may have been doubt. "It's true, Lexi, I don't."

I took a deep breath. I might as well lay it out on the line. "When I'm with you, there's no other place in the world that I'd rather be. And before you start thinking how corny that sounds, I need you to believe me."

"I do believe you."

"You do?" I didn't mean to sound surprised, but I expected a bit more resistance from her. A little bit of...well...something. But when I looked at her sitting up against the headboard, with only a sheet wrapped around her and her hair lying over those gorgeous shoulders, she had a smile on her face as she bit into a strawberry.

When she was done chewing, she said, "You probably thought I would regret what happened, didn't you?"

I nodded.

"I don't," she said. "I've never done anything like that before and maybe that's the point, but I don't regret it. I loved it."

"You did?"

"You're surprised?"

"Well, no, not that you enjoyed it." I knew for a fact that she enjoyed herself last night. A lot. "It's just," I took a strawberry for myself and took a bite before changing tracks. "What are you doing today?"

"I don't really have any plans, we fly out at ten tonight but I figured Nicole would be hung-over and want to sleep and-"

"Spend it with me."

She looked surprised. Maybe she did think that all she was to me was a one night stand. I needed to change that. I had one day to change that. And I would.

If she would spend the day with me.

When she didn't answer I said, "Please. I'll show you the sights of Vegas that tourists never get to see. I want to be with you, Lexi. I want to learn everything there is about you." I took her hand in mine and looked into her eyes. I needed her to see that I was genuine, that I wasn't just a playboy.

It took her a minute but finally her radiant smile crept across her face and she said, "Okay. I'm sure Nicole will want to sleep today anyway."

I fought the urge to jump up on the bed and pulled her towards me instead. "Thank you," I said into her hair.

"For what?" She pushed me away.

"Just for giving me the chance," I said and then realized how lame it sounded. "Have some breakfast."

She gave me a strange look but took another strawberry from the plate. "You're not eating. Aren't you hungry?"

"Oh, I'm hungry all right." Just looking at her, let alone when she was wearing only a sheet, aroused me to a point that was almost painful. I'd been fighting the desire she sparked in me all morning.

She must have seen it in my eyes because she said, "Well, what are you waiting for then?" And when she crooked her finger and beckoned me, I needed no further invitation.

***

I looked at my watch. Only fifteen minutes had passed since I left Lexi in her room to shower and get ready, and already I was counting the minutes until I would meet in her the lobby.

Our 'breakfast' had left me with the sweet taste of her on my lips and I felt like I was gliding across the floor on the way to the staff locker room. It was ridiculous to feel that way about a woman I'd just met, but maybe that meant I was ridiculous and at that precise moment, I didn't care. There was no point examining it or analyzing it. I was just going to go with it.

But first, I needed to shower and change. And sweet talk Keith into covering for me today. It wouldn't be hard; I knew he was trying to get the long weekend off next month. If I worked double time, I'd be able to cover for him. It would be worth it for one more day with Lexi.

I looked at my watch. There was still twenty minutes until I was supposed to meet her.

When I pushed open the door to the locker room, it wasn't just the humidity from the showers that hit me, but Keith, who ran right into me.

"There you are," he said and pulled me inside. "I was just about to start scouring the halls for you. Why didn't you answer your cell phone?"

I reached into my pocket and pulled my hand out empty. I must have left it in Lexi's room. I had other things on my mind this morning.

"I must have left it-"

"It doesn't matter," Keith said his voice taking on a frantic edge, "you have exactly ten minutes to get ready. Let's go."

"What are you talking about?" I spun the combination on my lock and examined him out of the corner of my eye. Not waiting for an answer, I asked a new, more important question, "Hey, can you cover for me today?"

"Are you kidding me? We're both on duty today," he said and pushed me towards the shower, "which you would know if you had your phone or had been answering calls."

I peeled my shirt off, slipped out of my pants and got into the shower. "Seriously," I said through the curtain, "I need the day off. It's important."

"Leo, you're not paying attention. Today is huge. Huge as is in, career making huge. As in, skip your best friend's wedding, huge. There is no way you're missing this."

"Okay, since I clearly missed the memo, tell me what's up." I finished a quick shampoo and soap down and turned the tap off, grabbed a towel and headed back to my locker.

"We've been given the chance of a lifetime. Or at least of our careers. Management wants us to, get ready for it..." Keith paused and held out his hands for dramatic effect.

It only annoyed me.

"Just tell me already," I said as I slipped into a new shirt.

"Fine, fine. But you're ruining the suspense," Keith said. "We, that's you and me, buddy, have been selected to fill in and head up the opening night party for KA."

I stopped and looked at him. KA was the latest, biggest Cirque du Soliel show opening in Vegas, in the MGM. The opening night party was a big deal. No, it was a huge deal, which is why Keith and I had nothing to do with it. We were both customer service grunts, and were not in major events, yet.

"I thought Marcia was in charge of that?"

"She was in charge." I thought Keith's smile might split his face in two as he said, "Turns out our Marcia has quite the little coke habit. She checked into rehab last night which means that, we-"

"Get the opportunity of a lifetime," I finished for him, my grin matching his.

"I knew you'd catch on quickly. This is our big break, man. If we pull this off, we'll be moving into big events by tomorrow morning."

"What do you mean, *if*? More like *when* we pull this off. How much time do we have?" I yanked on my pants and tucked my shirt in at the same time.

"We have to go like, right now," Keith said. "Don't want the day off now do you?"

Keith's question slammed me back to reality and my stomach dropped as I realized that Lexi would be waiting for me in the lobby in less than fifteen minutes. "Shit."

"What? Don't tell me you still want the day off?"

"No. I mean, yes. I mean...shit." I slammed my hand into a locker.

"Leo, what the hell?"

"There's this girl-"

"Stop." Keith held up his hand. "Don't even think about telling me that you were going to take the day off for some chick and that you are even remotely considering the possibility of passing up the career opportunity of a lifetime for her."

"I-"

"Don't tell me."

"Keith," I said and pushed his hand away. "She's not just some chick. Lexi's different. With her, it's... I can't even explain it."

"So see her tomorrow."

"She leaves tonight."

"Oh man, she's a guest?" Keith laughed and turned to face the mirror. "That's even worse. It's not like that's going to amount to anything. Forget her, she'll be gone tomorrow and your career will be on fire. What's to think about here?"

"She's special."

"Sure she is. And I bet, the minute she gets home from her Vegas weekend she'll tell all her friends about her wild weekend fling with a local and that'll be the end of it. Don't kid yourself, Leo. It's not worth it. Let's go."

Was it just a fling? Would I ever see Lexi again? Of course I would. Making love to her this morning was just that, love.

My thoughts battled in my head as I tried to replay the last twenty four hours. It was more than just sex, it felt like more. But how could I know for sure? And what Keith was saying was true, the KA party would be a career maker. I couldn't pass it up. That would be the stupidest thing I could do.

"Come on, Leo," Keith said. "Let's go. We'll get Tamara at the front desk to get you a new phone. Now there's a girl you should busy yourself with. She's hot as hell and would jump into bed with you in a flash."

"What are you talking about?" I shook my head and tried to clear thoughts of Lexi.

Maybe I could call her from the house phone and explain?

"Tamara, she'll do anything for you. Come on."

I let Keith lead me through the hallways, listening as he filled me in on the details of the KA event, as least as much as he knew. When we got to the lobby, I found Tamara and asked her to get housekeeping to retrieve my phone for me. Keith was waiting at the end of the counter tapping his foot but I turned my back to him, picked up the house phone and dialed Lexi's room number. It rang three times before going to the voice mail service.

She must have already left.

"Keith," I called, "do we have time to-"

"No."

Damn. I scribbled a note for Lexi, trying my best to explain and left my phone number asking her to please call me. She'd understand.

She had to.

Locating Tamara again, I handed her the note. "Could you please get this to room 2634? Or watch for a blond woman, tall, with legs that- she'll be down here in a few minutes."

"Isn't that the same room you just told me to send housekeeping to fetch your phone?" Tamara asked. She smiled and before I could stop her, opened the note and scanned it. "Looks like someone had a little fun last night," she said. I thought I detected a bit of jealousy in her voice, but that might have been because what Keith had told me earlier. Maybe Tamara was interested in me.

"It was nothing," I said trying my best to flirt with her so she'd help me out. "Can you just make sure the note gets there? I would really owe you."

"Anything for you, Leo," she said and smiled in a way that needed no clarification.

"Leo," Keith yelled. "It's go time."

"Thanks, Tamara," I said. I glanced at the note to Lexi in her hands, and turned to meet Keith.

"I'm ready, Keith. Let's do this."

"Leo, buddy. Today is going to change your life."

CHAPTER SEVEN

People flowed all around me. Coming and going in every direction. I felt like I was trapped in an arcade game of Frogger. I scanned the crowd. Women teetering on impossibly high heels, rolling suit cases behind them, business men with lap top bags, tourists in a combination of tacky shirts and sweat pants, and what looked like a staggette party with a bunch of ladies wearing pink boas, streamed past me.

"Lex, over here." I heard Nicole's voice and turned. There she was dressed in black yoga pants and a tight t-shirt. Her hair was pulled back and oversized sunglasses covered most of her face despite the fact that we were inside. I picked up my duffel bag, shouldered my way through the crowd towards her and prepared myself for the barrage of questions I knew I was going to get.

"So, how was your day with yummy Leo?" she asked the moment I got close enough. "No, wait. How was your *night*?"

After Leo left the room to get changed and make arrangements for work, I'd called Nicole's cell to let her know I was going to spend the day with him. Just like I thought, she was more than okay with it, opting to spend the day sleeping off her hangover.

I shrugged. "We didn't get together after all."

"What? Well, where have you been then?"

I hadn't told her that I'd spent the day alone. After packing up my bags, I went to the lobby to meet Leo like we'd planned.

I waited for an hour before I gave up.

I'd been stood up. And worse, I had his cell phone that he'd left in my room. For a moment I thought about throwing it away as revenge for ditching me. But I didn't.

I couldn't.

I stood there making up million different stories for why he hadn't shown up. I refused to believe our night together didn't mean anything to him. I'd seen him that morning, the way he looked at me. I didn't imagine that.

Did I?

I took the phone to the front desk and gave it to the girl across the counter. "I need to turn this in," I said. "It belongs to Leo Mendez, he works here."

When I said Leo's name, the girl's face changed, like she was shocked for a moment.

"Do you know him?" I asked her.

"I've seen him around," she said. "Don't worry, I'll make sure he gets it."

"Thank you," I said and turned to leave. Then I had a thought and turned back to the desk. "While I'm here, I'd like to check to see if I have any messages."

"Sure, what room are you in?"

"2634."

The girl tapped her fingers along the keys before looking up. "Sorry," she said, "no messages."

"Nothing? You haven't seen Leo, have you?" The moment I asked the question, I wished I hadn't.

The girl grinned and said, "I think I saw him with a

girl. Petite. Dark hair."

My stomach flipped and the floor tilted under my feet.

I was so stupid.

"Oh, well thanks, Tamara," I said reading her name tag and doing my best to sound in control.

After that, I was too embarrassed to tell Nicole that I'd been stood up. Besides, she was going to sleep anyway. So I checked my bag and spent the day walking down the strip. Trying not to think about Leo.

"Well, even if you didn't do anything today," Nicole said now, "I still want to hear all about your night. And I want to tell you all about Josh and my night too. But first, I need another coffee." She started walking towards a coffee shop in the terminal. "We have time, and you can tell me all the juicy details."

***

Half a coffee later, Nicole was still drilling me about my night with Leo. I let her ask all the questions she wanted. If I didn't tell her details; she'd worm them out of me somehow. I finished my story with how Leo had ordered up a breakfast buffet to the room. I left out the part about the fantastic sex we'd had instead of eating it.

"Wow," she breathed. "You sure know how to pick 'em. Your first fling and you find a guy who treats you to VIP club access, room service and a private breakfast. It makes my evening look almost dull."

Grateful for the change of subject, I jumped on it. "How was your birthday night?"

Nicole brightened. She pushed her sunglasses up to her forehead, and said, "It was awesome. I may not have had room service. But Josh had a suite at Planet Hollywood.

What an amazing view. And the sex!" She continued to give me the play by play of her escapades and I did my best to listen but my mind kept drifting back to Leo.

"Earth to Lexi," Nicole said. She was waving her hand in front of my face.

I shook my head and took a sip of my drink. It was cold and I pushed it away.

"Were you even listening?" she asked.

"Of course." I racked my brain for clues to what she'd said. "So," I took a chance, "are you going to see him again?"

She almost spat out her coffee. "You're kidding, right? Please tell me you're kidding."

I wasn't.

"Of course I am."

Nicole stared at me for a minute then said, "Shit. You weren't kidding were you? Please tell me that you weren't thinking of seeing Leo again."

I didn't answer. I looked down at my tea and contemplated another sip.

"Shit, Lexi. You were, weren't you? It was a fling. That's what Vegas is all about. Flings and mindless sex. Safe of course. But mindless none the less."

I still didn't say anything. How was I supposed to explain to her about the connection I had with Leo?

"Have you ever heard the expression, 'What happens in Vegas stays in Vegas'?"

"Of course."

"Well, there's a reason that expression came to be," Nicole said. "You don't form relationships here. You have fun. That's it, end of story."

Leo was more than a fling.

I rolled the napkin in front of me into a tube. "I don't

know, Nic. It felt like more than that."

"Lex, you have got to be serious. You didn't even hook up today. What was that all about anyway? Did he stand you up?"

"No, he didn't stand me up," I said straightening in my chair. "He just didn't show. We were supposed to meet in the lobby, but something must have happened. He probably couldn't get out of work."

"Wow, was he that good in bed?"

I could feel my face heat up, but I didn't answer.

"Well, good or not," Nicole continued. "It doesn't matter. Even if you wanted to see him again, he lives in Vegas and you, my dear, are Canadian. Long distance, especially that long, would never work."

The thought had crossed my mind as well.

"Besides, Leo, as hot as he was, was just a fling," Nicole said. "A rebound. I mean, you just finished things with Andrew. It's only natural that you would need a little release, you're only human. And good for you for choosing someone so completely scrumptious."

Andrew and I had been split up for months. Had he slept with other women by now? He must have. I shuddered at the thought, but it didn't seem to bother me as much as it once would have.

"It felt like more than a rebound, Nic." I unrolled the napkin and start shredding it into a pile on the table.

But why didn't he meet me? And the girl at the desk said he was with another woman. It didn't make sense.

"Trust me, it was just rebound sex, Lexi. Relationships do not happen in Vegas." Nicole spun around in her chair and got the attention of two young men nursing coffees and cookies. "Excuse me," she said to them. "Sex in Vegas, it's never serious right? I mean, Vegas is just for fun, not relationships. Am I wrong?"

Both men stared at Nicole like she'd just offered herself up as a test case. The blond on the right, gave her a smile that suggested he was more than willing to prove the theory. His friend, recovered from his shock, said, "Absolutely. People come to Vegas for one thing and one thing only. Fun."

"Nothing serious, right?" Nicole asked and winked at the blond,

"Nothing serious," he agreed.

"Nothing serious," I mused and considered the pile of napkin I had created.

Nicole flipped around in her seat, leaving the guys staring open mouthed at her back. "Lex? It was just a one night thing," she said, her voice soft, almost consoling me. I looked up.

For some reason, I felt like I might cry.

"You got it out of your system. Now you can go home and get started on your new, Andrew free life." She put her hand on mine, stopping it from tearing up more napkin. "Trust me."

I blinked hard but the memory of Leo kissing me before leaving the hotel room invaded my brain. He'd looked into my eyes and said, "I don't even want to leave you for a half hour. We don't have much time together. I'll just call in sick and shower here."

"Don't be silly," I said. "Just go and change. I'll see you soon."

"Are you sure?"

"Go," I said and I laughed.

I'd laughed. I was so sure I would see him later that I laughed.

He kissed me again, and touched my cheek before he walked through the door.

I didn't even have his phone number. I could've looked at his phone when I had it, but I didn't think of it. Why would I? And now, even if I wanted to, which I did, I couldn't contact him.

"Maybe you're right," I said to Nicole.

"Of course I'm right. In two weeks, you won't ever think about him again. Trust me."

CHAPTER EIGHT

The flight home was uneventful, the way good flights should be. Nicole slept, her sunglasses in place, her mouth hanging open. It was a good thing we still had a day before we had to be back at school. Nicole would need at least that long to make herself acceptable to advise her students on their career choices and solve their latest teenage dramas.

I should've slept myself since I'd only had a few hours the night before, but every time I closed my eyes, all I could see was Leo. His mouth right before he kissed me, his back as he lay sleeping, his hands running down my body, his smile before he walked away.

I tried to push those thoughts from my mind and remember what Nicole said. It was only a fling, a Las Vegas adventure. It didn't mean anything. I didn't even have his phone number.

God, I was such an idiot.

The minute my marriage breaks up, I fall for the first random guy that shows me any attention. But, I couldn't shut off that little voice in my head that kept telling me it was more than sex.

My brain wrestled back and forth like this until finally the pilot's voice came on and announced our landing. I didn't have time to think about Leo while we gathered our bags, waited in line and eventually cleared customs.

When Nicole and I pushed our way through the double doors into the main terminal, I had my eyes on a reunion between a man and his wife and child. They were hugging and kissing and when he spun around, a child in his arms, I saw his face. He was one of the young men from the Starbucks back in Vegas. The blond one that was ready to hop into bed with Nicole. He saw me looking and had the decency to look embarrassed before he turned around again.

"Lexi, check that out." I turned and followed Nicole's gaze to see a man holding the biggest bouquet of flowers I'd ever seen. The arrangement was so large, his face was obscured.

"Wow," I said. "It looks like someone was missed. A bit much though, don't you think?" I tightened the strap of my duffel bag over my shoulder and began to squeeze through the crowd to the taxi stand.

"I wonder who she is," Nicole said. She followed close behind me so we didn't get separated in the crowd.

"Who?"

"The woman who's getting the flowers."

"Lexi," a familiar voice called over the crowd. I stopped in my tracks and Nicole slammed into me from behind.

"Geez, Lex." Nicole took a step back.

"Lexi," the voice called again and shivers rippled down my body. I turned, slowly.

There was no way.

The massive bouquet of flowers seemed to be floating over the sea of people, coming straight for us.

"It looks like you're the lucky woman," Nicole muttered as the man with the flowers broke through the crowd.

"Andrew?"

"Lex, I'm glad I caught you," my ex-husband said. I guess technically we were still married, but still.

"What are you doing here?"

Andrew glanced at Nicole who wasn't even trying to hide her shock. "These are for you," he said and thrust the flowers at me.

I juggled my purse and duffel around for a moment. "I don't really..."

"Right," Andrew said and withdrew the flowers. "I didn't think about that. I'll hold onto them."

He was nervous. Andrew was never nervous. In our entire relationship he was always so self assured. Almost always. The night he proposed to me was a notable exception when he was sweating so much I thought he might have a fever. When he finally popped the question I was so relieved that he wasn't coming down with a terrible disease that I said yes. I would've said yes anyway.

"You didn't answer her question," Nicole piped up. "What exactly are you doing here?"

"Nic, maybe you should-"

"No," Andrew interrupted. "She's right. You deserve an explanation."

Andrew dropped to one knee, right there in the middle of the crowded terminal. I could have killed him right on the spot. For a moment I considered running. But there was nowhere to go. He laid the flowers down and reached for my hand. I sort of half dropped my duffel bag; I was so stunned and let him take my hand.

"What are you doing?" I hissed.

"Oh my God," I heard Nicole say beside me.

He ignored both of us and launched into what was clearly a rehearsed speech. "Lex, I've been a fool."

"What else is new?" Nicole said.

Andrew ignored her and continued. "I miss you, Lexi. For the last few months I've done nothing but work and come home wishing you were there. I miss your voice, your beautiful face, your...I miss everything. I want to work things out. What we have is special. Love like ours doesn't come along every day. We can't just end it over a disagreement."

My mind whirled. Was this really happening?

"We're good together," Andrew was saying, "everything about us works. We work. We fit together. The last few months have been awful. I've missed you so much. Coming home every night to an empty apartment, without you there, it's wrong, Lexi. I love you."

My mind replayed his words in slow motion and then again, faster. I fixed on one word. A disagreement? Did he say that?

"Can we work it out? Please, Lexi, I'm down on my knees begging you."

"A disagreement?" I said. "Is that what it was to you?"

The long talks and debates, the heartbreak and tears over his refusal to have children were much more that a disagreement. It wasn't like we were fighting about leaving dirty socks on the bathroom floor. That was a disagreement. This. This was a deal breaker. One I agonized over for months, spent hours, days in bed, crying about. Ending my marriage because I wanted children wasn't a decision I took lightly. It was far more than a disagreement.

Andrew sensed my anger and squeezed my hand tighter. "That's the thing, "he said. "That's all I've thought about since we split. And I'm not willing to lose you over this. I'm hoping we can put it behind us and one day think back on it as a little disagreement instead of what it's become."

My sleep deprived brain was having trouble keeping up with what he was saying.

"I can't think about this now," I said and jerked my hand away. I still had Leo's touch on my skin, his kiss on my lips; I could not even begin to think about what Andrew wanted.

What did he want? To get back together? Now?

Andrew stood, but I no longer cared if he was embarrassing me. My mind was spinning and I had the strangest sensation that the floor was tilting under my feet.

"Lexi, please."

"Andrew," I said focusing on his face to keep steady, "what exactly are you saying?"

He took my hands in his again and although I wasn't sure I wanted him to hold me, it did help with my dizziness. "Lexi, I love you." He paused to let the words sink in. "And I know you still love me too."

It was true, even through my anger and hurt I hadn't stopped loving Andrew.

"I know having a child is important to you," he said.

I opened my mouth to speak, but he put his finger up to stop me.

God, I hated it when he did that. Leo wouldn't have done that.

The thought of Leo at that moment caught me off guard and again, my mind started spinning with too many things. I was so focused on trying to control my whirling thoughts that I almost missed it when Andrew said, "And if it's that important to you, then it should be that important to me too."

"What?"

Andrew dropped to his knee again. "Alexis Titan, will you do me the honor of continuing to be my wife and starting a family with me?"

I couldn't breathe. I was vaguely aware of people in the airport who'd stopped what they were doing to watch us. I heard Nicole let out a squeak from somewhere behind me. I closed my eyes and Leo's face materialized. I could almost feel the gentle way he'd touched my cheek.

It was just a fling. Relationships don't happen in Vegas. Nicole's voice repeated in my head.

Maybe it was. Maybe she was right.

Andrew was right in front of me offering me what I'd always wanted. And I loved Andrew.

Then why couldn't I stop thinking about Leo?

When I opened my eyes again, Andrew was still staring at me, a question in his eyes.

This was real. This was now. Leo wasn't real. It was just a weekend. This was my future.

I nodded slowly and Andrew let out a whoop. He jumped to his feet and pulled me into his arms.

"Lexi?" I heard Nicole ask. "You're sure? You were just saying-"

I turned to face her and the tears in my eyes must have stopped her from saying what she had planned. Instead she offered me a small smile and I turned around, buried my head in Andrew's shoulder and tried to stop the tears that had started to flow. He was offering me everything I wanted. A child. A family.

Then why was I crying?

"I'm sure," I said. Andrew's arms felt warm, comfortable. Like I everything I ever wanted.

***

It was easier than I thought to enmesh our lives again. I went with Andrew back to our apartment that night and we made love.

This time without a condom.

I kept my eyes open wide. I was terrified to see Leo's face. Terrified that I would compare Andrew to him, to his touch, his kisses. I don't think Andrew noticed my distance, my complete preoccupation with the idea that I was doing something wrong.

The next day, he helped me move my things back home and our lives seemed to pick up where they'd left off. Once in awhile, in the weeks that followed, Nicole would ask me if I was happy, which I thought was a strange question. Of course I was.

Wasn't I?

And anyway, Nicole had always loved Andrew. He was great, we were great.

Things weren't perfect though, of course they never had been. But this time it was different. I was different. I couldn't shake the feelings of doubt I had. Before our split, and before going to Vegas, I thought my relationship with Andrew was exactly how love should be but meeting Leo changed that.

Even with Andrew I'd never had the instant connection that there had been with Leo. The indescribable feeling of being whole with another person. Even though Leo had 'ditched me', as Nicole said. The knowledge that I would never see him again made me sad. Devastatingly so. I went through the motions with Andrew, but I couldn't give myself over entirely to him.

Four weeks after our reconciliation, I came home from work, dropped my purse by the door and went straight to the bathroom where I removed the box from the paper bag. I read the instructions. Twice.

When I was finished, I flushed the toilet, washed my hands, left the stick on the counter and when into the bedroom. I didn't take my eyes off the clock while I folded the laundry. I made neat piles of towels, stacking them on the bed.

Exactly five minutes passed. Five minutes where I tried and failed, to think about anything except the test I'd just taken. Not a test of skills like a driver's exam when you were sixteen. Not a test of intelligence like a course final that would determine your GPA. But a test of life changing proportion all the same.

Leaving the towels half folded, I went to the bathroom door and stopped. The little stick sat benignly on the counter. From here I couldn't see the indicator window that would tell my future.

Two lines.

I wanted, no, needed the stick to have two lines. I wanted it with a ferocity that drove me to walk to the counter despite my fear that the result wouldn't be positive. I picked up the stick.

Two lines. I blinked hard and focused.

Two lines?

Two lines.

I'm not sure how long I stood there staring at the stick. Tears blurred my vision until the lines swarmed and melded. My hand floated to my belly and the rapidly dividing cells that would be my son or daughter and I smiled. A mom. I was going to be a mom.

After a time, I left the bathroom, almost floating into the kitchen to find the phone. I had to tell Andrew. He would be so excited with the news. I dialed the number I knew by heart but paused before hitting the talk button.

Would he be excited? We'd had conversations about having children, and of course we weren't using condoms but he hadn't been enthusiastic about the idea. Every time I brought it up he found a way to change the subject. And while he didn't shut down the idea the way he used to, I couldn't help feeling that he still hadn't totally warmed to the thought of a baby.

I pushed the button that cleared the screen and dialed a different number.

"Hello?"

"Nic? Guess what?" I whispered almost afraid to say the words out loud. "I'm pregnant."

"Lex? Oh my God, that's awesome."

"I know. I just took the test. It still doesn't seem real."

"How preggo are you? I mean, you must be *just* pregnant."

"My period is four days late, so..."

"Wow, you guys don't waste any time do you?"

"It must have happened the night I got home," I said.

Nicole was quiet on the other end of the line.

"You still there?" I asked.

"Ya, I'm just...it's nothing."

"What?"

"Or, maybe it happened before," she said the words so quietly I had to strain to hear her.

"Nic!"

"I know, I know." She was quick to apologize. "It was stupid. I shouldn't have said anything. Of course you were careful, it's just...forget it. A baby! I'm going to be an

Auntie."

She babbled on about shopping, names and other things I only half heard. I flipped open the pantry and stared at the calendar that hung on the back of the door.

Of course it was the night I got home. Or...

I closed my eyes and put one hand on my stomach still hearing Nicole's voice in my ear talking about nursery colors.

I was going to be a mom. That's all that mattered.

CHAPTER NINE

June 2010

There's nothing quite as satisfying as crunching up a bag of potato chips. I took a strange pleasure in feeling them splinter beneath my hands before sprinkling them on the top of the prepared casserole. Ben liked it best that way.

Finished with the topping, I popped the dish in the oven and started on the clean up when I heard the back door open.

"Mommy!" Ben's voice rang out followed by his little body. Hurtling down the hallway, he crashed into me.

"Hey, buddy." I scooped him up and planted kisses all over his face. "How was the zoo?"

"Awesome," Ben said and wriggled in my arms already wanting to be put down. He was getting too big for the hugs and cuddles I still wanted to give him. "We got ice cream and Papa said the bears were sad."

"Oh yeah?" I said and looked to Uncle Ray who had just come into the kitchen and dumped Ben's backpack on the table. "And why are the bears sad?"

Ben looked up but it was Uncle Ray who answered, "I told him, the bears would be much happier if they were rugs on my living room floor."

I threw a dish towel at him. "You didn't."

"I was kidding," he said and bent down and ruffled Ben's hair. "You know I was just kidding right, Ben? Animals are better left in the wild, aren't they?"

Ben nodded and Uncle Ray shooed him into the living room.

"I wish you wouldn't do that," I said after he was gone. "You know Ben believes everything you say. He thinks you hung the moon, for god's sake."

"Don't worry about Ben. He's a smart kid. He'll be alright. Even after the public school system is finished with him."

Growing up, it was only Uncle Ray and me and he was the only grandparent figure Ben had unless you counted Andrew's parents, which I didn't. Jeanette and Edward had seen their only grandson twice. They lived on the East coast, and despite the fact that they had endless amounts of disposable income, they never could find the time to come for a visit. I was thankful Ben had Uncle Ray, and thought of him as his grandfather and when he'd started calling him, Papa, no one corrected him.

"You know I like spending time with Ben," Uncle Ray said. "I've been to the zoo with him more times this year alone than I think I've ever been in my whole life. That kid cannot get enough of the animals."

"He loves it there." I turned back to the sink as Uncle Ray settled into a chair. "Thanks for taking him. It was nice to have some quiet time."

"I love it," he said. "Do you know what he told me?"

"What's that?" I let the warm water run over my hands while I scrubbed the mixing bowl.

"He told me Andrew has never been to the zoo with him."

I turned the water off and busied myself with the washing. I knew what was coming next.

"How could a boy who goes to the zoo as much as your child," Uncle Ray said, "never have gone with his father? How is that even possible?"

There it was.

"Andrew's very busy," I said and put the last dish in the drying rack.

"Lexi?"

I wiped the counter down, stalling. "Uncle Ray, I don't want to talk about it. He works very hard for us. So sometimes he doesn't get a chance to go to the zoo."

"Sometimes? Or never?"

"Sometimes." I turned around. Uncle Ray had his arms crossed over his thick belly.

"Ben says he's never been."

"Why do you have to constantly criticize Andrew's parenting? It gets a bit old."

His face changed with the edge in my voice and his hands came up in defense. "What's cooking?" he asked after a moment.

I smiled, thankful for the change of subject. "Are you staying for dinner?"

"Depends," he said and pushed up from his chair to peer into the oven. "Casserole? Tuna? Is it healthy? You're a great cook, Lexi. But I can't deal with all the healthy crap."

"Don't worry, I put chips on top to up the artery clogging factor," I said and swatted him away from the oven. "You know you're staying, you love my tuna casserole. Besides, some healthier choices wouldn't be a bad idea you know. Didn't the doctor tell you to get your cholesterol down?"

"And how would you know that?"

"Sara Beth and I had tea last week. She told me about your test results."

"Women," I heard him mutter as I pulled vegetables from the fridge.

"High cholesterol is nothing to fool around with, Uncle Ray," I said ignoring him as I started chopping vegetables for a salad. "It wouldn't take much for you to make a few changes. Starting with tuna casserole."

I tossed the vegetables into the bowl with the lettuce and put them on the table.

"Whatever," Uncle Ray said. "There's nothing wrong with steak and potatoes. But as long as you're cooking, I'll eat your tuna. But I thought Andrew hated tuna casserole."

I turned away, but not before I caught the look on his face. He felt sorry for me. I knew it. He didn't have to say it. Andrew did hate tuna casserole, which is why I was making it tonight. He wouldn't be home for dinner. Again.

"How many times this week, Lex?" Uncle Ray asked, his voice was heavy with concern so I turned back and pasted the biggest smile I could muster on my face.

"Third time. But he's working on a big deal." My excuse sounded lame even to my own ears, and my eyes flicked to the bouquet of flowers on the counter.

Andrew's latest apology. They sat in my favorite vase.

"Nice flowers," Uncle Ray said following my gaze. "When I gave that vase to you, Lex, it was a symbol of love and commitment. The same thing it meant when I gave it to your mom and dad years earlier."

"I remember." Of course I remembered. The ceramic vase was a gift on my wedding day. My mother had loved it. I loved it. Andrew made a point to find me beautiful flowers to fill it. Lately those gifts seemed to be borne more out of guilt than love.

"I know you don't want to talk about it, but I'm just going to say one thing."

I leaned back against the counter and braced myself.

"A boy needs a father."

"A boy has a father."

"Not just in name," he said, "but in action too. Andrew needs to spend some time with Ben."

I opened my mouth to defend him again but closed it again. What was the point? Uncle Ray was right. Andrew wasn't a bad man. I knew he loved me, but when it came to parenting, he...well, he just wasn't around. There was always an excuse.

Even from the very beginning. Andrew wasn't excited when he found out we were pregnant. He didn't want to discuss baby names or nursery colors. I tried to ignore his lack of enthusiasm at prenatal classes, the marked differences between him and the other doting dads-to-be, but it picked away at me. When Ben was born, and I was consumed with four a.m. feedings, dirty diapers, endless loads of tiny laundry and all the other details of parenthood, I flourished with the responsibility while Andrew pulled further away. It never got better. Uncle Ray wasn't telling me anything new. I wasn't blind. Or stupid.

"You deserve better, Lex," Uncle Ray said after a moment.

"Andrew's a good man, he works hard for us."

"I used to tell you not to settle for a man who didn't treat you like a princess. Remember?"

I nodded.

"Well, I take it back."

I perked up. Uncle Ray never took back his words. Ever.

"You shouldn't settle for a man who doesn't make you

and that little boy in there," his face turned red and he jabbed a finger towards the living room, "the centre of his world. This isn't just about you anymore. If it was, I wouldn't say a word, but Ben is suffering and that's just not right."

I swallowed hard against the steel in his voice and waited for some of the color to drain from his face before I picked up the salad and walked to the table.

"Calm down," I said and patted his hand. "It's not good to get all worked up. Especially over something that isn't an issue."

"Lexi-"

I looked him in the eye and as firmly as I could, I lied to him. "It's not an issue, Uncle Ray. I promise."

"Fine." He looked away from my gaze.

"Good, I-

"One more thing," he said and I had to fight the urge to sigh in frustration. "And I won't say another word about it. If you ever decide differently, just know that you have options. You're always welcome at my place. And of course there's always the lake."

My first instinct was to snap back with a sharp retort, but I swallowed it. The thought had crossed my mind. The idea of running away to Uncle Ray's lakeside house was more than appealing some days.

"And you'll never guess what I heard from Joe," he continued. "Remember Joe? He runs the general store, at least he did. You used to play with his girl, Enid. She runs the store now."

"I remember."

"Well, Joe told me last time I was up fishing with him that they need a teacher out there. Something about the principal and a teacher and...well, never mind. It's an option anyway."

That was the moment. The moment I could have told Uncle Ray the truth. I could have told him he was right, that I was unhappy and I wanted, no, deserved, more. But I didn't. Instead I smiled and squeezed his hand before turning and calling Ben for dinner.

CHAPTER TEN

I hated to do it, but two nights later I called Uncle Ray to ask for his help with Ben again. I had plans to meet Nicole for dinner, and Andrew had an important meeting. He'd only given me three hours notice, but I couldn't help but shake the feeling that he knew he wasn't going to be able to watch Ben as soon as I told him about my dinner date. He often encouraged me to go out but almost every time I did, I needed to find someone else to babysit. It was as if Andrew couldn't handle being alone with him.

Couldn't handle it or didn't want to.

And of course Uncle Ray had to change his plans with Sara Beth which not only made me feel awful but meant he was running late coming over which in turn meant I was running late to meet Nicole at the restaurant.

I never ran late.

But on the few occasions when I couldn't help it, I hated it. I jumped into the cab waiting at the curb and glanced at my watch.

It was after six. It would take at least another twenty minutes to get downtown, which meant I would be at least ten minutes late.

"There's construction on the freeway, Miss," the cabbie said from the front seat. "Okay with you if I take side roads?"

"Sure." Now I'd be even later. "No problem."

"I'll get you there as soon as I can. Don't worry."

I nodded and sent Nicole a text to let her know. In moments my phone beeped with a message.

NP. Got news. C U soon.

If Nicole had news, she wouldn't want to hear about my concerns with Andrew. It's not like they were new anyway. She would just say the same thing she always did. She'd tell me to leave him. Life was too short and I deserved better. That Ben did too. I knew it all by heart, she'd said it so often. It was impossible to explain things to Nicole. How could I explain to someone without children that it was better for Ben to have a part-time, somewhat absent father than no father at all. And if I left Andrew, that's exactly what would happen.

I looked out the window without seeing the scenery flashing past my window. Instead I replayed for the hundredth time the conversation I had the other day with Uncle Ray. I couldn't really leave Andrew and live at the lake. Could I?

Lake Lillian was beautiful. Peaceful. Going to visit with Uncle Ray as a child I'd always felt happiest there. And Ben loved it too. But to live? Without Andrew? I loved Andrew. But Andrew didn't love Ben.

As soon as the thought popped into my head I pushed it out. No, that's not fair. Of course he loved Ben. Maybe I could try harder to foster a relationship between them. After all, even I could admit that as a parent I could be pretty overwhelming. From the moment Ben was born I threw everything I had into being his mom. I didn't leave much room for Andrew. Ben was mine. I'd created this situation.

The city lights blurred in my vision and I glanced at my watch again. The driver was right, he would get me there a lot faster than if we'd taken the freeway. We stopped at a red light and I looked out the window and into the car next to us. The man behind the wheel turned to the woman next to him who was looking at him with such open adoration and love, I could feel it from where I sat a car away. The man tucked a strand of hair behind her ear and kissed her on the lips before turning back to the wheel.

I couldn't remember the last time I'd looked at Andrew that way. Sometimes, when he looked at me I could catch some of the old spark in his eyes, but over the years it had faded.

How could it not? Every time I looked at him I felt the resentment over the way he treated Ben. And guilt. I wasn't stupid, and I wasn't blind. Every time I looked at Andrew, the guilt swamped me. I loved Ben more than life itself, but he was a living, breathing reminder of the lie I lived every day. I caught one last glimpse of the couple in love before the light changed and we sped away.

The driver pulled up to the restaurant in record time. I was only five minutes late. I handed him some bills, including a healthy tip and sprinted to the door. Opening the door I was struck by the delectable aroma of garlic and butter. My mouth watered at the thought of a big bowl of pasta. Nicole jumped up from a table across the busy floor and waved almost as soon as I walked in.

I weaved through the tables, made my way over to her and before I could even get a word out, she flung her hand in my face and said, "Look!"

I couldn't do anything but look. The diamond on her finger was huge. "No way!" I grabbed her hand and examined her ring. "Ryan proposed?"

"I know," she squealed. "It's about time right?"

I pulled her close and wrapped her in a big hug. Even with my own marriage in a constant state of disarray, I wouldn't let that shadow my happiness for Nicole. Over the years she'd tested an impressive array of men before finally finding one she deemed worthy enough to take a chance on marrying. Too bad it had taken Ryan almost two years to realize her plan. But now, it seemed, he had, and Nicole was glowing.

"I am so happy for you," I said once we'd sat down and ordered a bottle of wine. "Tell me everything."

So she did. Nicole must have been holding in every detail of the event, just to recount them to me. "He took me to that Jazz club we like, The Blue Guitar, and after the first set the lead singer announced Ryan up to the stage." Ryan was a guitar player himself. Well, really he was an accountant who'd always thought he shouldn't have given up his dream to be a rock star but every once in awhile he played a gig. "I was totally shocked and a little pissed to be honest. He didn't tell me he was going to perform and he always tells me. But when he got up on stage, he looked right at me and played for me, Lex. He wrote me a song. I'd never heard it before. I still can't believe it. It's a beautiful song and he must have rehearsed it in secret, because it was amazing."

"So the song was the proposal?" It sounded very romantic. In a rock and roll kind of way. But perfect for Nicole.

"No. After the song, he got down on one knee. Right there in front of everyone. That part was terribly cliche, but it didn't matter because..." Nicole dissolved into tears and I squeezed her hand across the table.

"What an incredible story, Nic," I said. "I'm so happy for you. I really am. You'll be perfect together."

The waiter came, poured us our wine and we toasted to their future together. Once we'd ordered our meals we settled in to discuss the details.

"So, have you even thought about a date yet? I mean I know this is still new, but I'm sure you've thought about it right?"

"You know me too well." Nicole laughed. "We've actually decided not to wait. I mean, it's been two years and I don't want to wait another day to be Ryan's wife."

"What does that mean? A winter wedding?" It was already the end of July, so a summer wedding would be totally out of the question. There wasn't enough time to plan anything, let alone book a venue.

"Well... not exactly."

"Spill it."

"We're getting married next month."

"Shut up."

"I'm serious. I told you, I don't want to wait."

"Nicole, be real. How are you going to take care of everything in four weeks? It's almost impossible." Visions of myself buried in a never-ending list of wedding tasks flashed through my head.

"That's just it, it's *almost* impossible. But not entirely. We're going to Vegas."

"Vegas?" Just saying the name of the city made me nauseous. I could feel the blood drain from my face. My fingers were wrapped around the stem of the wine glass and I only knew that because I could see them. I could no longer feel them.

Anywhere but Vegas.

Nicole was talking and I struggled to pick up what she was saying. "...a big wedding, so Vegas seemed like the logical choice. Don't you think? Lex? Are you okay?"

I shook my head in an effort to clear it. I hadn't been back there since my first and only visit and most of the time, I tried my best not to even think of Las Vegas. Or more importantly, the man that lived there.

"Earth to Lexi? Are you okay? You look strange."

"I'm good," I managed, "just hungry. I didn't eat lunch."

"Oh, good," she said. "For a minute I thought maybe you were upset about going to Vegas."

Shit.

"So you're not eloping?"

"Weren't you listening? I can't get married without my best friend. That's crazy."

"You want me to come?" I managed to regain enough feeling in my fingers to lift my glass to my mouth and take a sip of wine.

"Want you to come? Lex, I *need* you to come."

She stared at me. I knew she was thinking I'd lost my mind. I was acting ridiculous. It was dumb and childish to ban a place, especially a popular vacation destination, from your life because of one little event that happened years ago. Except it wasn't a minor event. Leo wasn't a minor event. I tried not to, but I still thought about him. How could I not when I every time I looked at Ben I saw his dark hair and tan skin? I told everyone, including myself, that it came from my mother's side of the family. It was crazy to think otherwise.

"Of course I'll be there," I heard myself say.

"Oh, thank you, Lex!" Nicole got up from her chair and gave me a hug. I felt her tiny arms squeeze me and tried my best to push away whatever irrational fears I had. It was just a city. Besides, he probably didn't even live there anymore. Even if he did, what would I do about it. He didn't need to know the truth after so long. No one did.

Moments after she released me, the waiter came with our food. I picked at my bowl of linguine, the appetite I'd had earlier vanished as memories of my first and only trip to Las Vegas flashed through my head.

The lions at the MGM.

Sitting in front of Caesar's Palace.

Kissing Leo.

Feeling Leo in-

"Hello? Are you listening to me?"

Nicole was waving a hand in front of my face.

"Yes," I said taking a chance on agreeing with whatever she'd been saying.

Nicole looked at me funny. "You'll really switch me?"

"Switch you what?" I asked.

"Your clam linguine for my Alfredo," she said as she reached across the table. "I just said I should probably start watching what I'm eating so I can fit into an amazing dress. I asked if you'd trade me."

I looked at her steaming plate of creamy pasta. Normally something so rich would make my stomach turn. I nodded. "Of course," I said and reached for her plate. "Anything for you."

Nicole gave me a strange look before plopping my bowl in front of her. I ignored my pasta and focused instead on the wine, refilling my glass and taking a healthy swallow.

"I know this is stupid," Nicole said through bites of salad, "but I thought you might be weird about going to Vegas."

"Why would you think that?"

"Oh come on, Lex. Because of...you know."

"No," I said trying for nonchalance. "I don't know what you're talking about. There's no reason on earth that I'd miss your wedding."

"I know," she said suddenly serious, "it's just, I thought maybe because of-"

"Don't, Nicole." My voice came out harder than I intended. I softened my tone and added, "Please."

We looked at each other for a moment. I know she could see it in my eyes. The uncertainty, the hesitation, the fear. She could see it because she knew me. And she knew the past. And she knew, in that way that only the very best friends know, when to back off.

She smiled and her face transformed back to the happy new bride she was. "There's so much to do," she said and the moment was over. "We need to go shopping. I need a dress."

***

When I got home the lights were off and Uncle Ray was fast asleep on the couch with an afghan pulled up to his chin and his feet hanging over the edge. The television was on one of the crime shows he loved. I fished out the remote from behind a pillow and clicked it off. There was no point waking him. He looked comfortable enough.

I tiptoed past him towards the stairs.

"Lex?"

Damn.

I took two steps back and turned around as Uncle Ray pushed himself up to a sitting position. His hair was sticking out at odd angles making him look a bit like a mad scientist.

"I'm sorry," I said, "I didn't want to wake you."

"I wasn't sleeping."

I shot him a look and he smiled.

"I never sleep while I'm babysitting," he said with a stern voice. "I take my duties very seriously, Ma'am." He saluted me and I couldn't help but laugh. "Sit, tell me about dinner. How's Nicole?"

She sends her love," I said and sat in the overstuffed chair across from him. "And, she's getting married."

"That's excellent news. To that Ryan fellow? I like him."

Uncle Ray had met Ryan exactly four times, and on each occasion he was impressed by Ryan's knowledge of music and tax loopholes. "An important combination", he'd said. "You can't go wrong with helping people save money and requesting a good band."

"She's very excited," I said. I grabbed the afghan that had been discarded on the floor and wrapped it around me. "And she's not wasting any time. The wedding's next month."

"Well, I guess there's no point in waiting is there? After all, she's not getting any younger." He wiggled his finger back and forth in a tick tock motion.

"Stop it," I said and threw a cushion at him. Uncle Ray seemed to think every woman wanted children, and if they didn't get to it by the time they were thirty-five, there was no hope.

"A month, huh? That doesn't give her much time to plan things. I don't know much about weddings but-"

"No, you really don't. Not having one of your own or anything." I grinned. "Speaking of not getting any younger..."

"Who me? I'm an impressively young looking sixty-four, thank you very much."

"You know what I meant," I said. "What about Sara Beth?"

"Lexi, you should know it's not polite to ask about a woman's age. Besides, I don't think either of us want children." He grinned.

"You can be so aggravating."

"That's my job," he said. "Now tell me about this wedding. How does she plan on getting it all planned in only a month?"

"She's got that part all figured out. The wedding's going to be in Las Vegas. They have people who do most of the work for you, so she won't really need to stress about too much."

"Seems like a good plan. So, they're eloping?"

"Sort of. Except she wants me there."

"Of course she does." Uncle Ray stood and held his back for a moment before stretching. "You really need a new couch."

"The couch is fine," I said, "as long as you don't use it for a bed."

"I told you, I never sleep on the job." He smiled and I had the sudden urge to hug him. "It sounds fun, a wedding in Vegas. It could be a little holiday for you guys."

I hadn't thought of it that way. I'd been so obsessed with memories of the past, I hadn't even thought about Andrew coming. Of course he'd have to come.

"It might be good for you," Uncle Ray was saying. "Some time away to talk about things, figure things out."

"I suppose."

"Lexi, it's not my business and I'm certainly no expert on marriage. But if you want things to work between you two, you're going to have to spend some time fixing what's broken. Maybe a weekend away will be just what you need?"

"It's not a bad idea," I said.

"Of course it's not. I thought of it." He laughed and said, "You know I'll watch Ben for you. Maybe Sara Beth and I can take him to the movies or something. It'll be fun."

"Thank you."

He waved his hand dismissing my thanks and grabbed his coat. "Okay, we'll talk about the details later. I'm off. Get some sleep." He stared at me for a moment and then said, "Are you okay? You look...well...off a little bit. Are you coming down with something?"

"I'm just tired," I said and opened the door.

"You're sure?"

"I'm sure. Goodnight, Uncle Ray," I said and gave him a gentle shove out the door.

It would be at least another hour until Andrew was home, so I clicked off the lights, making sure to leave the lamp in the foyer on so for him. Making my way upstairs I stopped to peek on Ben. He was asleep on his back, his arms crossed over his head as if he were lounging on a deck chair enjoying the afternoon sun. He'd slept like that since he was a baby.

I stood and watched as his mouth twitched with something in his dream, finally settling into a tiny smile. He didn't have a care in the world, my son. His biggest concern was what to build out of Lego, or which friend to play with at school.

And it was my job to keep it that way. He was too young to notice the cracks in our family. But for how long.?

Exhaustion settled over me so I left a kiss on Ben's forehead and backed out of the room. I'd tell Andrew about Vegas in the morning.

CHAPTER ELEVEN

As it turned out, I didn't tell Andrew about Nicole's wedding for almost a week, which meant there were only three left before we were supposed to leave. I meant to. There just never seemed to be a good time. And the more time that went by without me saying anything just made it harder to tell him. It should have been exciting. I should have been excited. And I was.

Except, I wasn't. I had gone to bed with the idea that a trip would be just what we needed, but when I'd woken, all I could think of was Leo. Being there with Andrew might destroy my memories of him. I couldn't take the risk. Memories were all I had and I wasn't ready to let it go. Not yet.

I knew that the longer I waited to tell Andrew about the trip, the harder it would be for him to get time off work. He would need time to organize and make arrangements. I knew that. Was that the point? Yet, day after day went by and I still couldn't find the words. I resolved to tell him the next chance I got.

"Hey, hon," Andrew said and gave me a kiss on the cheek then he came in the kitchen. "You have a good day?"

"It was pretty good, nothing exciting," I said instead of my rehearsed speech. I was such a coward.

"Mine was insane," Andrew said and launched into the details of whatever account he was working on. The details of what he did every day were often lost on me so I listened with half an ear and went back to stirring the tomato sauce, trying to prevent the spaghetti water from boiling over and simultaneously searching for the salad tongs.

When I'd told Ben that Daddy would be home for dinner, he insisted I make their shared favorite, spaghetti and meatballs.

"The next few weeks will be crazy," he was saying, "until this account is closed."

"Hey," I said before I chickened out. "I have some-"

The phone rang.

"Can you grab it?" I asked and gestured to the phone.

Andrew leaned back in the kitchen chair to grab the cordless receiver. "It's Nicole," he said, looking at the caller ID.

"Take a message. I'll call her back after dinner."

"Gotcha," he said and clicked on the phone. "Hi, Nicole."

I located the salad tongs in the back of a drawer and put them in the bowl right as the water I'd been so carefully watching, started to bubble over the edge of the pot.

As I turned down the flame I heard Andrew say, "Well congratulations. It must have slipped her mind."

I froze.

"Well...I have been working late a lot lately."

I turned around and offered him a sheepish smile. Well I guess that solved that problem.

"Of course I will," he said into the phone. "Bye, Nicole." He pushed the power button and set the phone on the table.

"Anything you forgot to mention?" he asked. The smile on his face was huge. I'm sure he thought it was hilarious that I could forget something so important.

"I know, "I said. "It's been crazy around here and we haven't really had a chance to talk. I was going to tell you as soon as-"

"Don't worry about it." He laughed and stood up. "It happens. At any rate, I think it's great news. I didn't think Ryan was ever going to pop the question. Oh, and she called to tell you that there's a seat sale on right now. What's that about?"

"She didn't tell you?"

"Tell me what?"

"The wedding's in Vegas," I blurted.

The smile on Andrew's face grew even larger. I knew he'd be excited. He's wanted to go to Las Vegas for years. "I'm assuming you need to be there?" he asked cautiously.

I nodded.

"Excellent! When do we leave? I'll have to take a few days off. And of course I'll need to brush up on my black jack skills, not that I have any. Hey, maybe we can-"

"Three weeks," I said and turned back to strain the pasta through the colander.

"Three weeks?"

"Yup, she didn't want to wait."

"Wow," he said and some of the enthusiasm left his voice. "That doesn't give me much time, Lex. I can't believe you didn't tell me sooner. You knew I'd need time to organize things."

I knew.

I tasted the sauce instead of answering him. Perfect. I

dished out three servings, just like the three bears, with the smallest saved for Ben.

"I'm sure it will be fine, though. I've been working so hard, I should have some extra vacation time coming," Andrew said.

Or any time at all.

I turned around, a smile pasted to my face. "I'm sure it'll be fine."

Andrew moved from the table and wrapped his arms around my waist. "I think so too. We could use a vacation."

His breath was warm against my skin as he bent down to kiss my neck. It felt good. It had been a long time since he'd kissed me. He trailed his lips up, pushing my hair over my shoulder until his mouth met mine. I wrapped my arms around him and kissed him back.

When it was over, which admittedly was too soon, Andrew pulled away but didn't let go of me. "That was nice," he murmured. "It's been too long."

"It has."

"And Vegas will be perfect, I don't know if we've ever had a holiday with just-"

"Mom," Ben called as he ran into the kitchen. "Scooby Doo's over. Is dinner ready? Hi, Dad." He spared a glance for Andrew.

I pushed away from Andrew and caught Ben in a hug before he could crash into my legs.

"Just the two of us," I heard him mumble as he grabbed the salad bowl and patted Ben's shoulder with the other hand as he walked by.

***

Wedding dresses all looked the same. At least that was my assessment after three hours of shopping. White, off white, eggshell, alabaster, oyster, pearl. They were all the same. The chiffon, satin, lace, ruffles, and tulle were all beginning to blend together in a mass of marshmallowy fluff.

With so little time before the wedding, Nicole couldn't order the perfect gown. Instead she was relegated to buying a sample dress right off the rack. Which would be fine for me but had incited a small panic with her. Fortunately for Nicole, she had the best maid of honor ever and I'd found a giant warehouse type of store that had hundreds, if not thousands of gowns. The prices seemed reasonable as well; the trade off of course was that there were no understanding and infinitely patient sales consultants to wait on Nicole hand and foot. She was stuck with me. And my patience was wearing thin.

I pushed aside a dress and lifted another garment bag from the racks.

Beading? Check.

Sweetheart neckline? Check.

Strapless? Check.

I pulled out the bag and hoisted it over my shoulder. I might as well take this one. Nicole had rejected all of my choices so far, despite the fact that they'd each met with her ever increasing list of requirements. I navigated my way to the back of the store where the changing area was.

"Here," I said and shoved the dress through the curtain where Nicole was waiting. "Try this one."

"It looks like the last one."

I sighed. "It's nothing like the last one. This one has a much deeper neck line and a little less beading." I was making it up, but she wouldn't notice.

"Okay. Here." A bundle of satin came through the

curtain. "Hang this up."

I picked up the gown and wrestled it into a garment bag. "Nic, I really didn't take you for the bridezilla type," I said.

"Lex!" Nicole's head popped out. "I am not a bridezilla. I can't believe you would say that."

"I was kidding."

"You were not," she said her lower lip coming out. "I can see it in your face. It's just that the dress has to be perfect. It's my wedding."

"I know," I said. "Seriously, I was kidding. Go. Try that one on."

She ducked back into the change room and I started back towards the other end of the store to begin my search for the next one. I only got a few steps when a flash of blue caught my eye.

It couldn't be.

Color was so rare in this sea of creamy whiteness; I must be hallucinating. I blinked and took a second look. It was color. I changed course and headed for the dress. It was gorgeous. A satin a-line, it was trimmed in the most beautiful shade of royal blue satin. The v-neck bodice was covered in gems that matched the trim perfectly and created a very elegant, very Nicole dress. It was just the thing for a Vegas wedding.

"Stop," I called. "Don't try that one on." I snatched the new dress, the perfect dress off the rack and did my best to hurry to the back of the store.

"What are you talking about?" Nicole said. "This one looks good. Besides, I've almost figured out how to get into it."

"Trust me," I said, trying very hard to control my excitement. "I am holding *thee* dress."

"What? *The* dress?"

"Yes," I said. "But before you look at it, you have to promise me you'll reserve judgment until you've tried it on. Believe me, it's perfect."

"Okay, okay. Show me already."

"Promise?"

"I said, yes."

I unzipped the garment bag and handed Nicole the dress. She didn't say anything. Nothing but silence came from behind the curtain. Soon, I heard the rustling of fabric. I held my breath until I remembered I'd have to breathe. Still, silence. And then finally, a shriek.

I threw back the curtain and let out a shriek of my own.

"It's perfect," I breathed.

I could see her face reflected in the mirror and from the tears in her eyes there was no doubt that she thought so too.

The dress was made for her. It nipped in at her waist, accentuating her feminine curves, pushed up her breasts just enough to be sexy and clung to her hips in all the right ways before falling to the floor.

She didn't say a word. She didn't have to. She had that look, the one you get when you've found the dress you know you'll wear on your wedding day. Tears came to my eyes as I watched her staring at her reflection. She must be thinking about walking down the aisle, seeing her groom for the first time, picturing their life together. I knew this because I had that moment too.

Almost ten years earlier I had tried on my wedding gown and been hit with the sudden realization that my life was changing forever. There was a magic when it came to brides. They were so full of hope for the future, envisioning how perfect their life would be. And all because their wedding day, their gown, would be perfect. No one told them there was no such thing as perfect.

"We'll have to find you some hot blue heels to go with it," I said and the moment was gone.

***

After Nicole paid for the gown and we bundled it into the car, I still had an hour before I had to be home to relieve the babysitter.

"Let's go for coffee," Nicole suggested. "The least I can do is treat you to a latte. Since you found my dress and all."

The idea of a caffeine-infused drink was appealing. I was dragging. Shopping sapped my energy on the best of days, never mind a wedding dress excursion of this magnitude. And Ben would be ready to play when I got home, no doubt amped up from all forms of sugary treats. There'd be no rest.

"That sounds better than you can imagine," I said and let her lead me to the coffee shop where we ordered fancy coffees that cost way too much and I found a table outside where we could enjoy the sun.

"So," Nicole said after we sat down, "do you think Andrew will be okay wearing a blue shirt to match my dress?"

"Andrew?" I set my drink down before sipping it. "What are you talking about?"

"I can't believe I didn't mention it," she said. "Ryan needs Andrew to stand up for him. Do you think he'll do it?"

"Why? I mean, doesn't Ryan have brothers?"

"Well, that's the thing." She took a sip of her own coffee and used a napkin to wipe the foam from her lip. "It's only going to be the four of us."

"Since when?"

"Since Ryan's family decided that a Vegas wedding wasn't classy enough. They wanted a huge, black tie, formal affair. And since that's not happening, they're not coming. It seemed strange to have one family and not the other, and my parents don't really like to travel so we decided it was easier to keep it small."

"Nicole, that's crazy. You have to have your family there."

"You think so?"

"Of course I think so. You can't get married without your mom. Is she okay with this?"

"Sure." Nicole shrugged but wouldn't look me in the eyes. "Besides, Ryan's family decided to throw us some sort of dinner in our honor when we get back and I think my parents will be happy to have a BBQ or something to celebrate. So, it's going to be an intimate affair. Nice and simple. Plus, it means that I get to wear my dress again. It's perfect."

I took a sip of my latte letting the warmth spread through me. I closed my eyes and willed the caffeine to do its work. "Of course it'll be perfect," I said when I opened my eyes. "As long as you're sure."

"I'm sure. And then I won't have to worry about my mom driving me crazy with all the details. You know how she can get. It's obsessive, really."

"You're her only daughter. It's normal." My thoughts flashed to my own mother. Would she have loved to help me plan my wedding? There were few times in my life that I'd missed her more than I had on my own wedding day. "Nic, are you really sure about not having your mom there?

It's a pretty big deal. You should be really certain."

"I totally am," Nicole said. "Ever since I made the decision, it's like a big weight has been lifted off me. I can breathe again. I was so worried about making sure mom was happy. This way, she can organize her own party and have complete control. Trust me. It's so much better this way."

"Okay. If you're sure, then I'm on board. So, Andrew's really going to stand up for Ryan? Did you ask him?"

"Actually, I think Ryan phoned him a few days ago but he hasn't gotten back to him yet. He didn't mention it?"

I shook my head. We hadn't spent much time together in the last week. Andrew was working double time to get everything taken care of at the office in time for the trip.

"I'll remind him to call Ryan back tonight," I said. And if I didn't see him, I'd leave a note but I didn't bother to tell Nicole that. "I'm sure the answer will be yes. He was pretty excited about going to Vegas. He's wanted to for years."

Nicole looked down at her drink, stuck her finger in the froth of her latte and swirled. "Thanks again, for that."

"For what?"

"For Vegas. I know the whole idea weirds you out."

My stomach clenched for a second. "I don't know what you're talking about. Vegas doesn't 'weird me out'."

Nicole looked up and sucked the foam off her finger. Her eyes challenged me and it took everything I had not to look away. "Really? Then why haven't you ever gone back? Even when Andrew surprised you with tickets for your birthday last year?"

"Ben was sick."

"Bullshit."

"What's this about? Why does it matter?"

"You can tell me," Nicole said slipping into guidance counselor mode.. "It's okay to talk about it. About-"

"Leo." As soon as the name slipped out of my mouth, I wanted to take it back. It was ridiculous how the sound of his name could make my skin tingle after so much time.

"Right," Nicole said slowly. "Leo." She was looking at me with a strange expression but I didn't say anything. "It's been a long time, Lex. Don't you think maybe-"

"Nic, stop. Please." I drank the rest of my coffee and put the cup on the table with a little more force than was necessary. "I'm not weirded out, so it's not a big deal."

"Whatever you say. But for the record, Lex? You didn't do anything wrong and besides, it's not like he's going to be there or you'll even see him again. One guy isn't a reason to avoid an entire city."

I wasn't avoiding Las Vegas because of Leo. So what if I associated the lights and glitz of the strip with him? If every time I saw a television show or movie filmed there, my mind flashed back to the night we spent together. It didn't mean anything. And last year on my birthday, Ben had been sick and deferring the tickets didn't seem right. It's not like I was avoiding Vegas. That would be dumb.

"I'm not avoiding anything," I said. "I'm going to your wedding, right?"

"Yeah, but-"

"Then drop it," I said and pushed my chair away from the table. Standing, I pulled my purse over my arm and said, "I should get going. I'm going to be late."

On the way home I half listened while Nicole rambled on about flower choices, ceremony locations and dinner options. I stared out the windshield and did my best to keep up with what she was saying while she navigated the streets. It took forever before we pulled up in front of my house.

"I'll call you tomorrow, Nic," I said and opened the door. "Thanks for driving."

"Wait." Nicole's hand shot out and grabbed my arm. "Lex, I'm sorry."

I turned around and looked at her. "What on earth for?"

"For the whole Vegas thing," she said. "I'm sorry."

"You're being silly. I told you, there's nothing to be sorry for." I squeezed her hand. "It's over. It's all in the past. Besides, you're getting married. It's going to be great."

"But-"

"It's over," I repeated and tried to ignore the tightening in my chest as I pulled away and closed the door.

It was over.

CHAPTER TWELVE

"Mom?"

I poked my head out of the closet and listened for Ben.

Nothing. I waited a second longer, shrugged and pushed my way to the back of the walk in closet again and continued searching. I knew the suitcase was there somewhere. I pushed aside a large tote, probably full of clothes that hadn't fit in years. Which is how long it had been since I needed my suitcase for anything.

"Score." I fell to my knees and started to wrestle the suitcase free. I grabbed the handle and yanked, throwing my body weight behind it.

"Mom!"

"Crap," I said as I tumbled backwards into a rack of Andrew's shoes. I looked up to see Ben standing over me. "I mean..."

"You shouldn't say crap, Mom."

"Neither should you. And don't scare me like that." I hauled myself up and readjusted the shoes.

"I called you,'" Ben said. "You didn't answer."

"What's up? I thought you were building Lego castles." I grabbed the suitcase, now freed, and yanked it out into the room. I always left packing until the last minute but with our flight leaving in six hours, this was pushing it, even for me.

Ben followed me and flopped on the king sized bed. "I was," he said, "but I wanna play with you."

I tossed two pairs of denim shorts on the bed next to him and grabbed a handful of silky tank tops that I'd bought last summer. They looked sexy and casual; at least that's what Nicole had said. "Buddy, you know I'd love to, but I have to pack."

Ben stuck his lower lip out. "Not fair. How come Auntie Nicole's getting married and I can't come? Jake, in my class got to be a ring wearer when his uncle got married."

"Ring bearer."

"What?"

"Ring bearer, not ring wearer."

Ben shrugged. "He got a present."

"He probably had to wear a tuxedo too."

"What's that?"

"A really uncomfortable suit," I told him. "Trust me. You don't want it. Besides, you'd have to worry about losing the ring, and you'd have to walk up the aisle in front of everyone. It's no fun at all."

"You're doing it."

"Yeah, but I get to wear a dress."

"Do you get a present?"

I tossed the sun dress I was holding back on the bed and looked at him. "Is that what this is all about? A present?"

Ben dove under my pillow.

"It is, isn't it?" I said and jumped on the bed causing his little body to bounce. I grabbed him around the waist and went straight for his tickle spot under the arms. He squealed and thrashed, trying, without much effort, to get away from me.

"M..M..." he was too busy giggling to get the words out.

I stopped tickling and let him catch his breath. "Admit it," I said, "you're all about the present."

"Am not," he said and crossed his arms tucking his hands into his arm pits.

"Okay, you asked for it." It didn't take much to pry his arms away and start my tickle torture again. "How about now? Ready to admit it?"

Ben managed a nod through his fit of giggles. I stopped and collapsed onto the bed next to him. "You know," I said. "I'll bring you a present even if you aren't in the wedding."

"You will?" Ben sat straight up and looked at me. His little face was returning to its normal color. "Really?"

"Of course, silly. I'm going to miss you." I reached my arms out. "Come give me a cuddle. Unless of course you're getting too old to cuddle your mom."

Ben flung himself on me and I wrapped my arms around him. He smelt good. A mixture of fresh dug earth and the laundry soap I used. It was a mystery to me how my son could smell both clean and dirty simultaneously. But it was the smell of my little boy, and there was no better scent in the world.

"I'll never be too old, Mom," he said, his voice muffled into my chest.

I stroked his silky black hair. "I certainly hope not, buddy. I'd be pretty sad if I didn't have your snuggles."

Ben wiggled out from my arms and sat up. He looked down on me, his face a serious mask. "When I'm old, I'll live next door so I can cuddle you every day."

I smiled. "I'd like that. But what will your wife say?"

Ben recoiled in horror. "Ew. I'm never getting married. Don't be gross."

I pushed myself up from the bed and grabbed the sun dress I'd abandoned. "Don't worry, Ben. You'll change your mind, I promise. One day you'll find a very nice woman to marry and you'll love her very much." I tried my best to fold the dress and laid it on top of the pile I had started.

"Do you love Daddy?"

There was something in his voice that made me stop and look at him. He was sitting on top of the duvet, clutching a pillow to his chest. His hair was ruffled and sticking up in all directions. His deep brown eyes looked sad, but he was looking right at me.

"Of course I do," I said and sat down next to him on the bed. "Why would you ask that?"

He ignored my question and asked another. "Does Daddy love you?"

"Ben, what's this all about?" I reached for the pillow and took it from his hands.

"Does Daddy love me?" Ben whispered and looked down at his toes.

"Of course he does, Sweetie." I grabbed his little hands. They were warm and a little sweaty in my own cool grasp. I gave him a gentle squeeze and asked, "What's going on?"

"Jake's daddy comes home and plays catch. He's gonna coach team next year. Daddy doesn't do that."

My heart froze. I was such an idiot. How could I think Andrew's absence wouldn't affect Ben?

I took a deep breath and said, "You know that just because Daddy works hard, it doesn't mean he doesn't love us, right?"

Ben nodded but looked down. I tipped his chin up and looked into his eyes. "Ben, you know that right? Daddy loves you very much. That's why he works so hard."

"It's okay," he said. "I don't really mind. But, Jake says you'll get a divorce if Daddy doesn't love us. Then you'll be sad."

For a moment I thought the air had been sucked out of the room. I forced myself to take a breath and swallow hard without chocking. "Ben, Mommy and Daddy aren't going to get a divorce."

"I don't want you to be sad," he said, "and if you're alone you'll be sad."

I needed to change the topic.

I mustered my bravest face and said with as much convictions as I could, "You don't need to worry about Mommy being lonely, okay?"

He nodded.

"Every family is different. Not every dad has the time to play catch and coach little league teams. But that doesn't mean he doesn't love you."

Something had to change. Five year olds weren't supposed to worry about such things.

"So, you didn't tell me what you wanted me to bring you from Las Vegas." I smiled my biggest, 'everything is alright' smile.

He looked like he wanted to say something else, but little boy greed won out and he said, "What do they have there?"

I laughed, relived that the serious mood had dissolved. "Mostly cards and dice. Can I interest you in some gambling tools?"

"Bring me candy," Ben declared.

"Candy it is." I swatted at him with a t-shirt. "Now, go

see if Papa is here yet, I have to finish packing or I'm going to be late."

Ben jumped up from the bed and raced out of the room whooping and hollering, our conversation obviously forgotten with the promise of candy. I watched him go and returned my attention to the pile of clothes on my bed. Giving up, I scooped up the pile of shirts, shorts and sun dresses and threw them into the suitcase.

It was just a weekend. A weekend in Vegas with my husband. Maybe it was what we needed, what I needed, to fix things so my son wasn't worried about our future. I stopped before zipping up the suitcase.

If I was going to try and fix things with this family it had to start with Andrew and me and I might need a little help. I returned to the cavernous closet and the bottom drawer where I kept random articles of clothing.

It was just where I'd left it two years earlier. A black, satin teddy, with lacy cups and g-string bottoms. Andrew bought it for me as a Valentine's Day gift. More of a gift for him I'd say. At the time, I had taken one look at it and shuddered. I never did wear it. I grabbed it and tossed it in my suitcase.

Might as well.

***

"We'll be fine," Uncle Ray said for the hundredth time. "Go. You're going to be late."

I looked at my watch. I had exactly fifty minutes to get to the airport to meet Andrew. He liked to be there at least two hours early.

"Okay, okay. Ben, come give me another kiss."

He flew off the couch and into my arms. I pulled him

tight to me. "Promise me you'll be good for Papa."

"Mom, I'm always good."

"It's true. He's always good," Uncle Ray said. "We're going to have a lot of fun, the two of us, aren't we, Buddy?"

Ben wiggled out of my arms and ran over to Uncle Ray. "You know it." He gave him a high five. "Guy time."

"Guy time?" I shot Uncle Ray a look.

"It's just a little something I taught him."

"Uh huh."

"You're going to be late," Uncle Ray said.

"I know, I know." I picked up my suitcase. "Come give me one more hug," I said to Ben.

"Mom," he moaned. But he came over to me and squeezed me as tightly as he could.

"I love you."

"I love you too, Mom."

Ben released his grip and I blinked hard so he wouldn't see my tears. It's not like I'd never left him before. "Okay," I said before I could change my mind. "I'm going."

"It's about time," Uncle Ray said and then winked at me.

"Thank you," I told him.

He waved me off. "Go. Have fun. We'll be fine."

I looked at them both, blew out a breath, turned and left. I was half way down the walk when I heard Uncle Ray say to Ben, "I thought she'd never leave."

I smiled and hopped in my car.

***

Andrew insisted on meeting me at the airport because he had a last minute meeting and it would be easier if we took separate cars. I parked in the extended lot and took the shuttle to the terminal where we'd planned to meet.

The concourse was teeming with people and I couldn't see Andrew right away. The thought that maybe he got held up at work and couldn't come danced through my brain. It would be easier.

"That's not the right attitude, Lexi," I muttered to myself. I needed to fix this marriage. For Ben.

Before I could dwell on it any more, Andrew's voice called to me over the din. I pushed my way through the crowd and found him in line to check in. With apologies to the couple behind us, I ducked under the rope and stood next to him.

"Hey, you made it."

"You doubted me?" And with a monumental effort, I gave him a smile I hoped was flirtatious.

"Of course not. You're very reliable," he said without looking up from his Blackberry. When he finished typing he looked up and noticed the grin that was still pasted on my face. "Oh," he said. "Is that how it is?" His lips curled into a smile of his own and he leaned down to kiss me.

His mouth was warm on mine and he tasted faintly of spearmint. I took my time kissing him and enjoyed the response I elicited in him.

"Hmm," he said. "I think I'm going to like Vegas."

I went with the moment. We needed to get the weekend off to a good start. "I think you are." I said between kisses.

We didn't notice when the line moved ahead and it wasn't until the couple behind us cleared their throat loudly that we broke apart and shuffled forward. When I adjusted the shoulder strap of my purse I couldn't help but see the look Andrew was giving me. It had been a long time since he'd looked at me that way.

Maybe it wasn't too late to fix this.

CHAPTER THIRTEEN

Encouraged by our kiss earlier, I hadn't bothered to pull my book out of my bag before checking it, thinking Andrew and I could spend the time talking and maybe flirting a little bit. But the moment passed before we even boarded and he spent the flight reading over client documents, with his iPod plugged into his ears. Before the drinks were served, I tried to distract him and slid my hand down his leg under the tray table.

"Lexi, I need to get this done," he said and took my hand off his leg and placed it back into my lap. "Wouldn't you rather I do it now?"

"I thought you were all caught up on work," I said looking down. I wouldn't let him see that his rejection had hurt me. "Wasn't that the point of working so hard for the past few weeks?"

"I'm never caught up," he said and returned to his papers shutting me out.

I tried to pass the time flipping through the in-flight magazine and surfing the complimentary channels on the seat back television.

After we claimed our baggage, Andrew turned to me and said, "Okay I'm all yours." He smiled at me in a way that used to melt me. I felt myself relax a little bit, but the mood from earlier was gone.

"Let's go check in," I said.

Andrew pulled me close and kissed my neck. "Absolutely," he said and I thought of the black negligee in my suitcase.

I can make this work.

"I can't wait," I said and together we started off in search of a cab to take us to the hotel.

We'd only gone a few steps when a voice called from behind us. "Lexi. Andrew. Over here."

I turned and saw Ryan, waving his hands over his head.

"I guess we have a welcoming committee," I said and crossed the busy terminal floor.

"So much for the hotel," I heard Andrew mutter behind me.

Nicole and Ryan had arrived in Vegas two days ago to make the final arrangements and relax by the pool before the big day. We weren't supposed to meet up with them until tomorrow morning.

"Hey, Ryan," I said as I approached. He took my bag and gave me a hug.

"How was the flight?"

"Fine. Where's Nicole?" If Ryan was here, she should be here somewhere. I glanced around but couldn't spot her.

"Hey, man," Andrew said coming to stand next to me. "What's with the welcome? I thought you were going to be busy with your bride-to-be."

"Well, that's the thing," Ryan said and ran his hand through his hair. It was then I could see how worried he looked. He did not look like a man on holiday about to get married.

"What's going on?" I asked. "Is everything okay?"

Ryan nodded and said, "Come on. Let's go. I'll tell you on the way."

We followed him outside where a limousine was waiting for us. "Nice," Andrew said as we slid inside.

I couldn't enjoy our plush transportation; worry grew for my friend. "Ryan," I said as soon as we were all inside. "What's going on?"

"Don't panic, everything's okay. Well, maybe not okay exactly." Ryan grabbed a beer from the cooler in the seat. "Want one?" he asked Andrew. "There's champagne too, but I'm more of a beer guy."

Andrew accepted the beer; I declined the champagne and tried to be patient as Ryan sucked down half the bottle before continuing with his story.

"Nic is in our suite. Everything was fine until this morning. I really don't know what happened. She woke up and totally freaked out. She's having second thoughts about everything. She won't listen to a thing I say and I'm a little worried." He polished off the beer. "Okay, I'm a lot worried." Ryan looked at me. "Lexi, you have to talk to her. You have to calm her down. I thought this is what she wanted, and now...well, I'm not so sure. She's been crying all day and is a total mess."

I grabbed Ryan's hand before he could reach for another beer, gave it a reassuring squeeze and said, "Don't worry. Things will be okay. Nicole's just got a case of cold feet. It's totally normal. It's my maid of honor duty. I'll go talk to her."

The trip from the airport to the strip didn't take long but the guys still managed to have a few beers each. The sun began to set and the city started to come to life outside our windows. Everything looked more or less the same as it had last time except for the huge new hotel complex, City Center, which had been under construction when I was here last. Now it occupied over a quarter mile of glass and steel sparkling along the strip.

It was strange to think that despite the way my life had changed, this city, where it all started, didn't change. My stomach flipped when we passed Caesar's and the statue where Leo and I sat and people watched.

Did he still live here? Was he married? Did he have a family?

"Unreal," Andrew said beside me. He stared out the window like a child, taking in everything. I forgot he hadn't been here before and a wave of guilt washed over me. It was my fault. I turned away from the window. I didn't need to see anymore.

When we pulled up to the hotel and the limo door opened, I said a silent thank you to Nicole for booking her festivities anywhere but at the MGM. The Mirage was beautiful, with dozens of palm trees lining the drive, and of course a spectacular volcano sitting on the strip. Ryan had wanted to stay a The MGM Grand because they had excellent wedding packages, but Nicole worked her magic and negotiated a great deal at one of their sister hotels instead. I don't think I could handle relieving my entire Vegas experience. She knew that.

Still, I couldn't stop the feelings that rushed through me as I followed the guys through the grand foyer. It was stupid. That was six years ago. It was a completely different place, with different people. This time, I was with my husband. That one detail, made the entire trip different.

Drastically different.

"So, is that okay with you, Lex," Ryan's voice snapped me out of my day dreams.

"Sorry," I said. "I didn't hear you. Is what okay with me?"

"I'm going to check in," Andrew said, "and take our bags up to the room. You can just go straight up and talk to Nicole. We'll meet both of you down here for dinner in a bit."

"Assuming you can calm her down," Ryan added. "You can calm her down, right?" The hope is his expression would've made me laugh if he didn't look so worried..

"Of course," I nodded. "What's the room number?"

Ryan breathed a sigh of relief and pointed me in the right direction. I left the guys to take care of the details and I went in search of Nicole. At least taking care of her drama would keep my mind off of the past.

***

1150, 1152, 1154. Nicole's room was at the end of a long hall. Instead of knocking, there was a doorbell. So I rang it. I rang the doorbell. Must be nice to have a room big enough to require a doorbell. But, she was the bride. She deserved it.

Moments later, the door flew open and Nicole burst out into the hallway. "Oh, Lexi. Thank God you're here." She wrapped her arms around me and started bawling.

I wiggled out of her grip enough to free my hands which I brought up to her shoulders and pushed her away just enough to look at her. Her pretty face was puffy and red from crying. Her hair was tied back in a pony tail. Strands that escaped the elastic were pasted to her face from the tears that soaked her skin.

"Nic. What's going on?"

"Everything is awful," she moaned. "I don't know what to do."

"What are you talking about? Calm down."

"Come in." She pulled me into the suite and closed the door behind us. "Where are the boys?"

"Downstairs, we'll meet them in a bit. But first, tell me what's wrong."

Nicole flopped onto a blue velour couch and started sobbing again in earnest. Clearly, this wasn't going to be easy. "Nicole," I prompted.

"I've made a mistake," she said. "This is all wrong." She sat up and waved her hands encompassing the stunning suite.

"No, this is beautiful," I said.

"Well, yes. This is nice," she conceded. "But everything else is wrong. What was I thinking?" She buried her head into the plush sofa again.

I pulled up a red leather ottoman and sat next to her. "In what way? Getting married? Or getting married in Vegas? Because there's a world of difference. Are you having second thoughts about this Vegas thing?"

She nodded but didn't look up.

"You're wishing you had your family? That you'd done it the old fashioned way?"

She nodded again.

"Well don't," I said. "It's normal to get scared and have cold feet, Nic. It's going to be great. The ceremony, the parties back home. Like you said, you get to wear your dress more than once and what could be better than having three parties in your honor? You're not a traditional kind of girl, I can't imagine you walking down the aisle, with the whole big white wedding thing. This is going to be so much more you. You and Ryan."

The sobbing stopped and she looked up. "You really think so?"

I didn't. I thought while good for some, getting

married without her mother was not a good idea for Nicole. But it wasn't the time for honesty, it was the time for lying to my best friend.

"But what about my mom? She should be here. I should have some family here. Did I make a big mistake?"

I grabbed her hands and held them tight. "You said yourself that your mom doesn't like to travel. She would've been miserable here. Besides, she knows you and what's best for you. She didn't try to stop you or convince you to do it differently, did she?"

"No."

"That's because she knows you and Ryan need to do this your way. Besides," I squeezed her hands again and gave them a gentle shake. "I'm family. I wouldn't miss this for the world. And I'm here for you, for everything."

"You really think it will be okay?" She wiped her eyes and sniffed loudly.

"Of course I do. It's going to be amazing. And I'm here now so I can help you with any last minute details."

I had been planning on spending the next day with Andrew walking along the strip and doing all of the touristy things Vegas had to offer, but he'd understand if I had to help Nicole. Besides, how many details could there be for such a small wedding?

"Oh, Lexi." She threw herself at me and I caught her in a hug. "What would I do without you?"

"Nic, you'd be lost without me." I laughed. "Now come on. We have to get you cleaned up. It's our first night here and we better get down to the boys before they drink the bar dry."

I waited while she had a quick shower and pulled her hair up in an elegant, funky twist. Nicole did her make up in record time, for her anyway, and it wasn't long before she came out of the room looking like she was ready for a night on the town.

Turning away from the view of the strip I said, "I thought we were just going for dinner. Why so dressed up?"

"Seriously, Lex. It's Vegas. Everything is an occasion here. Didn't we have this conversation last time?"

"Whatever." I looked down at my jeans and t-shirt. I wasn't dressed like a slob exactly, but next to Nicole I looked more suited to gardening rather than a nice dinner.

"You look...well, fine," she said.

Laughing I said, "Fine? I look fine?"

"Do you want to go to your room and change?"

I wasn't even sure where our room was and by the time I tracked down Andrew and went back up and changed, it would take forever. But, it would be nice to freshen up a little. The grumbling in my stomach made my decision for me. "No, I'll be fine like this. Besides, I think I'd be disappointed to see our room after this amazing suite. I'm sure ours doesn't even begin to compare."

"It is nice, isn't it?" Nicole glowed. "I just love it. I think it's nicer than our condo at home." She smacked her palm to her forehead. "Hey, I just thought of something. I bought the cutest wrap dress yesterday. It'll totally work on you."

"Don't worry about -"

"Don't be silly. Come on." Nicole grabbed my arm and hauled me into her bedroom.

***

She was right, the dress worked on me. Mainly because of the wrap style that I could tug tightly around my waist. I didn't fill out the chest area as well as Nicole's curves would have and due to our height difference it was much shorter than I thought decent, but I didn't really have a lot of options. My new black heels that I'd bought just for the trip worked too, although they did make my legs look indecently long.

"That color makes your eyes look crazy blue," Nicole said when she saw me. "Here, use my lipstick and for goodness sake get rid of the pony tail."

After a few more minutes and final adjustments, we were in the elevator headed to the lobby.

"This is how it should be, two sexy ladies out for a good time" Nicole said and admired herself in the full length mirror lining the inside of the elevator. "Just like old times."

Old times.

I flashed back to six years earlier. It had been just like this the night of her birthday party. The night I got to know Leo. The night I-

No, I wouldn't think of Leo.

I couldn't.

The bell sounded, announcing our arrival in the lobby and the doors slid open revealing a bustling scene. Nicole grabbed my hand and together we made our way through the casino floor.

"Where do you think they'll be?" I asked.

"Ryan and I had drinks at a place last night. Let's start there."

The lounge was decorated in luxurious woods and plush chairs. It felt very decadent and luxurious. And the guys were there. Andrew and Ryan sat in the centre of the space at a table for two. Andrew had changed and was wearing a fresh pair of black pants with a crisp white shirt rolled up to his elbows. He looked casual in a practiced put together way.

In contrast, Ryan wore dark jeans, and a black t-shirt. Even with stubble covering his cheeks and chin he still managed to look dressed up in a very rock and roll way. He spotted us first and got to his feet letting out a low whistle. "You two are a sight for sore eyes. Damn," he said and pulled Nicole close giving her a very passionate kiss.

Andrew swiveled around and popped to his feet. He looked me up and down and after a moment he leaned forward to give me a kiss on the lips. It felt cold and obligatory next to the passion going on beside us.

"Wow," Nicole said breaking away from Ryan. "That was nice."

"I'm just so glad you're feeling better, baby," Ryan said. He glanced at me and mouthed "thank you" over Nicole's head. "Shall we eat? I'm starving."

We all agreed and Ryan led the way out of the lounge, holding tight to Nicole. Andrew and I trailed behind them.

"You got our room alright?" I asked.

"I did," he answered his voice tight and controlled.

"Is something the matter?"

Andrew stopped short and grabbed my arm causing me to spin around and face him. "Is there some reason you're dressed like that?"

"Pardon me?"

"Why are you dressed like...like a..."

"Like a what, Andrew?" I jerked my arm away from him and stood up straight. "I happen to think I look pretty good. We're not at some company function. We're in Vegas. So what's wrong with dressing up a little bit?"

"It's just, don't you think you took it a little far?"

"No. I look good, and I'm pretty sure there are others that would agree. Should we ask someone?" I didn't want to ask some random guy if he liked how I looked, but I'd do it just to prove to Andrew that he was being an asshole.

"No," he said. "You don't have to do that. The dress just seems a little much."

"That's probably because you're drunk," I muttered under my breath.

"I've only had a few."

"Whatever, Andrew. Let's just let it go."

I really didn't want to get into it with him any more than I already had.

Andrew's face morphed, the anger gone. A sure sign he'd had too much to drink. He probably couldn't remember why he was angry in the first place.

"I'm just not used to seeing you like this," he said. "But I think I could get used to it." He reached an arm around me and his hand squeezed my ass.

"Cut it out," I said an smacked his hand away. It was confirmed. He was drunk.

Andrew released me and tried to take my hand.

I pulled away and said, "Come on, let's go eat."

I led him towards the restaurant on the other side of the black jack tables. The whoop of a winner at a table to my right caught my attention and when I glanced over I almost stopped breathing for a second. My feet stopped moving and Andrew, his reflexes slowed, ran into me.

"What's wrong?" he asked.

I didn't answer, just shook my head.

It couldn't be.

The man stood in profile, his dark hair a sharp contrast to his white shirt. I couldn't see his face but it was him. He looked the same. But no, that was ridiculous. I was just imagining things this wasn't even the same hotel.

"Lex?"

"Nothing," I managed.

"What are you looking at?"

The man turned his back to me. I knew that back. I knew how it felt under my hands. I knew...

"Nothing," I said again. "Let's go. I must be hungrier than I thought."

CHAPTER FOURTEEN

Lexi.

It was her. It had to be her. I hadn't thought of her in years. Oh, who was I kidding? I thought about her every bloody day, every time I turned around and caught a flash of long blond hair or stopped to watch the Bellagio fountain show.

I managed a smile at the pit boss who was looking my way and ducked around a bank of slot machines where I caught sight of her again. That thick blond hair, it was shorter. Her legs though, they were just as long and luscious as I remembered. There was no doubt that it was her. Nothing could or had compared to having those legs wrapped around me. I would never forget that.

What were the odds of having her here again? Would she remember me? Would she talk to me? I watched her disappear into the restaurant with a man. Probably her husband. Maybe the same husband she had separated from. But no, then she wouldn't have children and she wanted that too badly to give it up. I would have, could have given her children. The thought popped in my head so quickly it knocked me back.

No, she never called. She didn't want a future with me. Tamara, who took my phone from her when she handed it in, said Lexi took my note and crumpled it up.

No, she chose not to have anything to do with me.

So why was I still so damn hung up on her? I couldn't get her out of my head.

"Leo."

I twisted around and saw my assistant Roberta, standing with a clipboard.

"I've been looking for you everywhere. You told me you'd be back in five. I need to talk to you, we have a problem."

"I was just on my way," I said and with one last look, turned away from the restaurant. I tried to push the image of Lexi out of my mind. "Come on, let's go back to my office." I led the way through the crowd.

Lexi was here. She probably didn't even remember me. I looked down at the wedding ring on my finger and rubbed it without thinking.

"When are you going to take that ring off," Roberta asked as we made our way past the craps tables. "Hasn't it been two years?"

"Three actually."

"It's ridiculous," she said and strode past me heading to a door at the edge of the casino floor.

She was blunt. It was one of the traits I admired about Roberta. It was handy to have an assistant who got to the point. It was also annoying.

As we walked, heads turned in our direction. Roberta's striking looks always garnered attention. Her black hair pulled back in a harsh pony tail contrasted sharply with her pale skin and bright red lipstick. But it was her sharp eye and attention to detail that made her the perfect assistant to the Manager of Customer Affairs, although that trademark attention to detail could be another one of those annoying traits.

I rubbed the ring again and said, "I wear it because it's easier than dealing with bored housewives who are looking for a good time."

"Sure," Roberta said. She used her keycard to open a door off the casino floor that led to a web of hidden hallways. After a few minutes of me doing my best to keep up with Roberta's quick pace, we arrived at my office.

"What's going on? What's the crisis?" I said, only half listening for the answer. I sat in my chair and spun around to my computer. With a flick of the mouse the screen came to life. I clicked opened the guest database but stopped myself before typing in her name. It would only take a second to see if she was a registered guest.

"What are you doing?" Roberta said, pointing to my computer.

I pressed a button and the screen went blank. "No. I just thought of something, but it can wait. Tell me what's up."

Roberta wasn't stupid, she didn't buy my excuse but she was too smart to press me, for details. She flipped open her portfolio and produced a piece of paper. Sliding it across the desk to me she said, "This is the problem. Do you realize we've lost two staff members in the last week?"

"Two? Daniela moved to California with her boyfriend who's the other? Oh wait," I said just as the realization hit me. "Please don't tell me..."

"You got it. Andre finally fired Scott. Last night."

My head was starting to pound. Andre had been gunning for my best wedding planner for months. I kept telling him to keep business separate from personal but when Scott started working for me almost a year ago, Andre fell hard for him. They dated for a few months, if you could call it that, but Scott was young and the last thing he wanted was monogamy. Andre had other ideas and the split was messy. Andre may be a general manager, but he had no right to fire my staff.

"Dammit." My fist came down hard on the desk and Roberta jumped. She recovered in a second and tapped the paper in front of me again.

"You can yell at Andre later. But right now, I need help. With Daniela gone it was going to be tight, but now without Scott...well, simply put, I can't be in two places at once."

I looked closer at the schedule she was pointing at. We were always busy with weddings and I wasn't surprised to see two scheduled for this Saturday. It was pretty normal. What wasn't normal, was being so short staffed.

"I'm sure you can handle it, Roberta. You're the best. If there's anyone who can deal with this situation, it's you."

"Or you.".

"Roberta, I'm sorry, I can't help you with these," I said before she could weasel me into agreeing. "I have two major conferences happening this weekend. I can probably spare Josh for a few days. Will that work?"

She thought about it, and her pen tapped against the clipboard. Finally she said, "Fine. I'll give him the easy one," Roberta said. "It's actually a really small wedding. But she wants the whole deal. Flowers, music, cake. And a private dining experience on the pool deck next to the waterfall."

The small one? Suddenly I was curious. "What if I'd said that I'd help you out? Would you hand over the big wedding?" I raised my eyebrow, waiting for the answer.

Roberta tilted her head and shot me a look. "You? I don't think so."

"Do I have to remind you who's in charge here?" I pulled rank with a sudden rush of ego.

"No, sir," she said her voice was dripping with sarcasm but her smile told me she was barely holding back laughter. "But," she added, "If you were to take on such a large event with two big conferences going on at the same time, you wouldn't have the time to look up whoever it is that you're not looking for." She pointed a long red finger nail at my computer again.

"I told you-"

"You don't have to tell me anything," she said. "Here's the file. You can do it yourself or pass it to Josh. Let me know either way. It's the Lennox/Stewart wedding. Like I said, it's small, only two guests." She held up a finger at my protests. "But they want the whole shebang. And I know it's been awhile since you've done a wedding, but it's our job to make sure big or small, we make it happen."

"I'll be hiring next week."

"I know you will." Roberta smiled and stood. "If you need anything, or can't remember what to do," I shot her a warning glance and she changed tracks. "Any help at all or advice, let me know, boss."

I sighed and leaned back in my chair. "Thank you, Roberta. And just for the record-"

"I know. You're not looking for anyone. Not even that leggy blond you were eyeing." She winked at me and was gone.

I laughed. Attention to detail, that's what made her so good.

The file lay on the other side of my desk, which was empty of any family pictures, there was no family after all. I glanced at the computer but didn't power up the screen. Curiosity got the best of me and I grabbed the file.

I might as well get some work out of the way first. Maybe I would take on the wedding, not that I had any time to spare. But it might help keep my mind from driving me crazy with memories if I was run off my feet for the next few days.

I flipped it open. Only the basics were there.

Bride - Lennox. Groom - Stewart.

Number of guests - 2.

Two? Oh well, if there's anything that my years of experience in the customer service industry had taught me is that everyone deserved the same treatment. The names of the witnesses weren't listed; we'd need that for the marriage certificate. The bride had yet to confirm flowers and music. The wedding was two days away.

I sighed and picked up the phone.

Josh usually worked in parties and special events which meant he saw his fair share of stag and stagette parties. A wedding shouldn't be too much of a jump. He answered on the third ring and I relayed all the details to him. Told him the information would be in his in-box, and hung up.

I closed the file. The blank screen of the computer seemed to fill the room.

Why not? There wasn't any harm in looking to see if on the off chance she was actually here. Before I could change my mind I powered the screen back on. It flickered to life and I quickly punched in: Alexis Titan. Almost immediately the results were displayed in front of me.

The air rushed from my lungs and the words on the screen blurred for a moment.

"She's here."

CHAPTER FIFTEEN

Leo.

Just thinking his name affected me. And here? At the Mirage? He could absolutely not still be in Vegas, let alone the same hotel I was staying it. That was crazy. Beyond crazy. It was ridiculous.

But he was.

As I stood under the shower spray, my mind filled with images of him. Despite the hot water, I shivered at the thought of his kisses on my skin. My body responded to the memory and elicited a feeling in my belly I thought I'd never feel again.

But it had to stop. I cranked the tap causing the water to run icy so I could focus and finish my shower.

I hated rushing. I hated being late. And it would only get worse. I hadn't even told Andrew about the change in plans for the day. With any luck, he would still be passed out, sleeping off the hangover I'm sure he had and I could sneak out.

At dinner the night before, the guys had switched from beer to wine and the four of us split two bottles with the men drinking more than their share. By the time we left the restaurant, Andrew insisted on trying his luck at the craps tables where he promptly lost a couple hundred dollars, maybe more. I didn't want to think about it.

Instead of calling it a night, he was just getting warmed up and with Ryan feeding him booze, the two of them could not be talked out of playing blackjack as well. It was well after two by the time I was able to drag him back to the room.

Even though I was annoyed, I was relieved that he was too drunk to want to fool around. With thoughts of Leo occupying every spare moment, the last thing I wanted was to be intimate with my husband. And I knew that was wrong, on so many levels. Andrew was passed out on the bed before I'd even brushed my teeth.

But he must have slept it off because when I stepped out of the shower, Andrew was awake.

"Lex, come back to bed."

"Can't. I have to get going." I tied the robe snug around me and shook my hair from the towel.

"Going where?" he mumbled his voice thick with sleep. "You said you were going to show me the strip and it will still be there in an hour. Take that robe off and come back to bed."

"Oh, Andrew. I forgot to tell you." I combed out my hair before grabbing my moisturizer.

"Forgot what?"

"I promised Nicole I'd help her out today with some last minute things. I'm sorry I can't hang out with you today, but maybe-"

"What the fuck?"

I ducked around the mirror and faced him. "Excuse me? Don't swear at me. Are you still drunk?"

He probably was and I really didn't want to deal with any more of that. He was not only unpleasant when he drank, but down right obnoxious. Apparently that carried over to the morning after as well.

"I'm not swearing at you," he said. "I'm swearing at your total preoccupation with her. It's a wonder to me how she can function at all without you."

I took a deep breath. "Are you serious? This is her wedding. It's my job to be there for her."

"It's always something, isn't it," he mumbled but I still heard him. "Anything but me."

"You're acting like a child."

"No, if I was acting like a child, at least I'd get some attention." He sat up and the sheet fell from his body revealing his bare chest, reminding me that it'd been a long time since I'd seen him naked.

"What is that supposed to mean?"

"Nothing," he said but it was obvious that it was anything but.

I took a deep breath and decided not to push that particular issue. One problem at a time was more than I could handle.

Besides, Andrew was already back on the issue of Nicole. "Her wedding is tomorrow," he said, "Is it too much to ask that I spend one day with my wife?"

"You will," I said and grabbed a pair of khaki shorts and a black silky tank. I returned to the other side of the mirror, to change. "Just not today."

"What am I supposed to do all day?"

"Andrew, really. You're a big boy. You'll be fine on your own," I said and grabbed the hair dryer. His next words were drowned out by the white noise. I tried to ignore him as he got out of bed and stumbled past me into the shower.

I did my best to dry my thick hair but before long, gave up. The desert heat would finish the job. As soon as I clicked the dryer off, Andrew was ready to pick up the argument.

"You can't ignore it you know," he said from the shower.

"What are you talking about?"

"Lexi, this trip was supposed to be about us."

"No, it's supposed to be about Nicole and Ryan. I told you that." I swiped mascara on my lashes.

"And us," he insisted. "Maybe you haven't noticed, but we haven't been very close lately."

Was he kidding?

"You have to be kidding." I dropped the mascara tube into my makeup bag.

He clicked the water off and reached out for a towel. "When's the last time we had sex?"

"It's hard to have sex when..." I wanted to say it was hard to have sex when I resented him so much. But I didn't. "...when, you're working so much. You could come home and spend some time with us."

"Us?" His reflection filled the mirror as he stepped out of the shower with the towel wrapped around his waist.

"Yes, us. Your wife and child. Remember?"

My cell phone chirped. A text from Nicole.

Where r u?

The hard lines of his face melted and his voice softened as he said, "I want to spend time with you, Lexi."

And that was the problem right there. "It would be easier to be with you if you were home, playing the role of family man once in awhile."

"But would a family man do this? " He slid up behind me and wrapped his arms around my waist. He smelt like soap and I could feel exactly what he wanted through his towel. I shivered, not in a good way, before I could stop myself but he took it as encouragement and kissed my neck.

"Hmm..." he moaned. "Nicole can wait."

My irritation flared again and I shook him off. "You're unbelievable," I said. "It's not always about you, Andrew. Nicole needs me." I pushed past him and grabbed my purse off the dresser.

"That's right," he said the anger back in his voice. "Someone always needs you. What about me?"

"Please, don't do this now."

"So, you're going to choose her over me?"

"It's not about choosing."

"It's always a choice, Lex." He looked me straight in the eyes and I got the distinct feeling that we weren't talking about Nicole anymore.

My phone chirped again.

Hello? R u alive?

I grabbed my phone and punched in. *Coming*

"I have to go."

He ignored me and went into bathroom, shutting the door behind him.

***

It took forever to get around the stupid hotel. Even though I jogged through the halls and into the lobby, it was still almost ten minutes later before I found Nicole outside by the taxi stand.

"Finally," she hollered when she saw me. "I think he's going to start charging me by the hour. Get in." She pointed to a black limousine waiting at the curb.

"A limo? Again?'

"It's my wedding weekend. I'm traveling in style." Nicole flipped her hair and ducked her head as she slipped into the car. I followed, sliding along the leather seat until I was at the opposite end of the huge space.

"What's wrong?" Nicole asked.

"Nothing, I'm fine."

"No you're not. You're never late, ever. Something's wrong."

I sighed. "Andrew and I had a little argument this morning. It's nothing."

"Spill."

"He's mad because we never spend anytime together. We haven't had sex in ages."

"Like how long?"

"I don't know...a few months."

"A few months?" Nicole sat straight up in her seat. "Lexi, that's awful. No wonder he's grumpy. What's the problem?"

"Honestly, I have a really hard time being attracted to him sometimes."

"You have to be kidding me," Nicole said. "I mean, Andrew's hot, Lex."

"I know, he is. It's just..." I struggled to find a way to tell her that my husband's tendency to totally neglect our son was a complete turn off for me and was destroying our marriage bit by bit. "Maybe it's just me."

"It's definitely not you," she said. "Maybe it's-"

"So," I said, desperate to change the subject, "what's on the agenda today?"

A grin lit up Nicole's face. "Dirty lingerie."

"What? I thought we were shopping for the wedding."

"We are," Nicole said. "I need something fun for the wedding night."

"Right. We'll find you something pure and chaste." I grinned.

"Screw chaste," Nicole roared. "I want dirty."

We both broke into giggles while the driver closed the privacy screen.

***

Nicole wasn't kidding when she said she wanted dirty lingerie. After a quick trip to Victoria's Secret, she declared all the silky and lacy garments were "too pretty" and "not slutty enough." So we made our way to Fredrick's of Hollywood where, upon entering into the red and black store, Nicole announced, "Now this is what I'm talking about."

I tried to help her choose something wedding appropriate, but it soon became clear that her idea of wedding appropriate and mine were totally different. She steered clear of anything white or cream. Her color of choice was black, not red, because it would clash with her hair, but she selected a few items in various bold shades as well.

I found a plush chair outside the waiting room and settled in as she started trying things on.

"So, what's Ryan doing today?" I asked her through the curtain.

"I think he's hanging with Andrew. I got a text awhile ago that said they might go have a bit of a bachelor party," she said. "Oh, this one's hot!"

"Let me see," I said. "A bachelor party? What does that

even mean when there are only two of them?"

Nicole emerged from the dressing room clad in a black leather bustier and matching thong. "What do you think?"

She did look hot. "Maybe a bit too dominatrix for your wedding night," I said.

She glanced down. "You're right," she said and disappeared again. "I think Ryan said they were going to have some drinks."

"It's not even noon."

"It's Vegas. And I wouldn't be surprised if they went to a show or something. It's not really Ryan's style, but it's traditional."

"A show? Like strippers?" I couldn't imagine Andrew stuffing dollar bills into some girl's g-string.

"That's exactly what I mean," she said. "Ohh, I really like this one." She whipped the curtain open and revealed herself in an emerald green satin corset with matching panties.

"How did you even get that done up so fast?"

"Hidden zipper," Nicole grinned and spun around for me to take in the full effect.

The corset gave her a tiny waist and pushed her breasts up so they were almost bursting out of the cups. I had to admit, she looked hot. Dirty sex hot, not slutty.

"That one," I said. "Ryan won't be able to keep his hands off you."

Nicole beamed. "Perfect. That's exactly what I'm going for. Now, what about you?"

"Me what?"

"You should get something," she said as she twisted to admire herself in the mirror. "Maybe it will help Andrew forget about your little fight this morning."

I thought of the black negligee still in my suitcase. And the argument we'd had. The last thing I wanted to do right now was put it on for him. "I don't think so," I said.

As if he could sense me talking about him, my phone chirped with a text message.

Sorry. Dinner tonight?

"Is that Andrew?" Nicole asked through the curtain.

"Yup, he wants to have dinner tonight. He's sorry."

"There, he's sorry." Nic appeared redressed. "And we all know, it's always the man's fault, so go with it." She grabbed the green satin number, hesitated and then snatched the black leather bustier too. "For another night," she said and grinned. "Maybe tonight. Is it wrong to have sex the night before the wedding?"

I laughed. "You're doing everything so non-traditionally; I don't think it'll make much difference."

"Good. Then go to dinner with your husband. I'll be busy." Nicole swept past me on her way to the cashier. "I'll meet you outside."

I looked down at my phone, sighed and typed.

7 Steak place

A moment later, his response came through.

C u then

***

"We need to be back at the hotel by one," Nicole said leading me through the mall. "So, let's grab a quick bite and head back."

"What's at one?"

"Ryan got a call from our wedding coordinator last night. I need to finalize a few details."

"I thought everything was done."

"Well, that's the thing," Nicole said. "I'm having a little trouble picking out flowers and the cake and-"

"Nicole." I grabbed her arm, stopping her and forcing her to look at me. "Are you kidding? The wedding is tomorrow."

She looked down. "I have trouble making big decisions, you know that."

"There's only four of us. It's not like you have two hundred guests."

Nicole's head snapped up. "Just because it's a small wedding doesn't mean that I don't want everything to be perfect."

She looked like she might cry so I softened my voice. "No, of course not." The last thing I needed was for her to have another melt down. "It'll be perfect. Everything will be amazing."

"And you'll help?"

"Of course I'll help," I said. "Let's get going then. It might take awhile for the limo driver to get down the strip."

CHAPTER SIXTEEN

I was beginning to feel claustrophobic. All around me were pictures of weddings, flowers and cakes lining the walls of the tiny meeting room. Photo albums were stacked on the table and Nicole was flipping through one, stopping on every page to comment on some detail that I probably would never have noticed.

"With her hair twisted up, you can see her earrings," Nicole said pointing to the bride in the picture. "Do you think I should wear mine up?"

Before I could answer, she'd turned to the next page and was criticizing the bride's choice of flower arrangements. I grabbed a peppermint from a bowl on the table and popped it in my mouth.

Ignoring her, I glanced at my watch. It had been fifteen minutes since the concierge had brought us to the meeting room. The wedding planner was late.

"What time did you say she was supposed to be here?" I asked.

"One. And it's not a she," Nicole said not taking her eyes off the album. "The lady I was dealing with left. I have someone new. A guy I think."

I choked on the mint and started coughing. Nicole handed me her water bottle and smacked me on the back.

"Are you okay?" she asked after I took a few sips of water and the coughing subsided.

"I think so." I took another gulp of water. "A guy?" I asked.

"What?"

"The wedding planner," I said. "He's a guy? You have a guy?" My heart was racing out of my chest. All morning, every dark haired man I saw had made me take a second look I was being paranoid.

There was no way Leo was planning weddings now. Besides, this wasn't even his hotel. But he did work in customer relations way back when. And that must have been him I saw last night.

No, no way.

I dismissed the idea. It was too ridiculous to even think about. Besides, it could be anybody.

"Is that so crazy? Men can plan weddings, can't they?" Nicole was asking.

"What's his name?"

"I don't know. Ryan took the message and you know how he can be with details." She rolled her eyes. "So, I guess we'll find out. Why, what's going on? Why do you look so weird?"

I blushed and focused on a photo of a poolside wedding. "I just thought for a minute..."

There was a reason Nicole was my best friend. She knew everything, and what she didn't know, she could figure out pretty fast. "It's not..." she said, the realization hitting her. "No way. You don't think?"

"I don't know," I said looking at her. "It's possible, I guess. But it's dumb. Forget it."

"Is he even still here? After all these years?"

"I honestly don't know," I said, "but I thought maybe I saw him last night. It's stupid. It couldn't have been him though. This city has me acting all crazy."

Nicole stared at me. "That would be crazy."

"Crazy," I murmured.

"Well, I guess we'll find out won't we?" Nicole grinned.

I panicked. Any second the door would open and he could walk in. I'd die. What if he recognized me?

Worse, what if he didn't?

I pushed back the chair and stood up to leave.

"Lexi, you can't -"

A knock at the door.

I froze. We both stared at the door as it opened.

Too late.

***

A tall woman wearing a black pencil skirt and neat red blouse came flying into the room. She dropped her black leather portfolio on the desk and said, "My name is Roberta. I'm so sorry to keep you waiting. It's been one of those days around here. I'm going to help you take care of all the details today, Miss Lennox." Her gaze flicked between us trying to ascertain who the bride was. Her gaze landed on Nicole with the bridal album in front of her. "It's a pleasure to meet you," Roberta said and stuck her hand out. "Shall we get started? We have a lot to take care of and not a lot of time."

Roberta's no nonsense tone didn't leave much room for debate or discussion. I slid back into my chair and for the next thirty minutes sat, occasionally offering my opinion on flowers, cakes, and music choices. The decisions were made so fast, my brain raced to keep up but I gave up somewhere around cake flavors.

Finally after Nicole settled on the vows she wanted, Roberta snapped her portfolio shut and stood.

"It was very nice meeting you, Ms. Lennox. Josh will be handling your event tomorrow. He sends his regrets that he couldn't be here today, but like I said, it's just been one of those days." She moved to the door. "He'll be with you tomorrow though to make sure everything goes off without a hitch. It will be a beautiful ceremony and a day you will remember forever." She smiled a warm smile and slipped out the door before I could release the breath it felt like I'd been holding for hours.

Josh. Not Leo. Of course.

"Wow," Nicole said. "I feel so much better now." She stretched her arms over her head and let out a yawn. "But I'm exhausted. I think I'm going to head up to the room for a nap. Thanks for all your help, Lex. I swear, I couldn't do this without you."

We made our way out to the main lobby and Nicole asked, "You going up to your room too?"

I shook my head. "No, I think I'll walk around for a bit."

"Lex, are you okay?" Nicole put her hand on my arm. "I mean, being here and..."

"I'm fine." I did my best to offer a reassuring smile.

"And really, the wedding planner? That would've been nuts, right?" Nicole said.

"I don't know what I was thinking." I forced a laugh. "I was just being stupid."

"You sure you're okay?"

"Nic, it was a million years ago. I was a different

person, and like you said back then, it was just a Vegas fling. No biggie."

I could tell by her face she didn't believe me, but she didn't push the issue either. "Go," I said. "Sleep. I'll see you tomorrow if you don't need me any more today."

"Nope. You have the rest of the day off from wedding stuff. But I'll see you in the morning for some spa time. I have us booked in for pedicures, massages, the works."

"Sounds good." I gave her a hug and watched as she crossed the lobby to the elevator bank.

It wasn't a biggie. Was it? It was stupid to think that Leo could be planning Nicole's wedding. I knew that. But instead of feeling relived that it wasn't him, I couldn't help the disappointment that bloomed inside me as I headed outside to the strip to lose myself in the crowd of tourists.

CHAPTER SEVENTEEN

Thank God it had been a crazy day. I was so busy trying to sort out the conference room mix up between the life insurance group and the Pleasure Party ladies; I hadn't had time to think. Upgrading the life insurance stiffs had been much easier than trying to relocate the Party ladies and all of their *tools*.

I don't know how the overbooking happened, but I might be inclined to fire the person responsible if I ever found out. Or give them a raise. After all, the mess had allowed me a few hours of chaos that kept my mind off Lexi. But the crisis was over now and all I could think of was that it was a damn good thing I hadn't taken on that wedding. Small as it might be, I didn't have time.

It wasn't until I sat down at my desk at seven, that my mind had a chance to fill with images of her.

Lexi Titan. Here. In my hotel.

A sharp knock on the door announced Roberta's arrival. She strode into the room and dropped a file in front of me. "Here's all the information for the Lennox/Stewart wedding tomorrow. You got off easy."

"What do you mean?" I slid the file over. "Josh was supposed to be taking care of this."

"He had some sort of emergency with a group in town

for a stag party. I told him I'd take care of the details, but he promised he'd be there to take care of the event tomorrow. So here it is."

I raised an eyebrow. "A stag emergency?"

"I don't make this stuff up, Leo. I'm far too busy. I got the license too. It's on top there," Roberta said. "So, unless you need me for anything else, I'm off."

"Thanks, Roberta. I'd be totally lost without you."

"Remember that at bonus time," she said with a wink and was gone.

I rubbed my head. What a mess. I would need to phone up to HR first thing on Monday and start the recruiting process. We couldn't keep piecing together weddings. Thank God this was a small one.

I opened the file. I could use another distraction. Anything to keep my mind off the past and the fact that she was walking around my hotel.

Lexi Titan.

There she was, well her name anyway, staring up at me from the marriage certificate. She was the witness? I scanned the document, Nicole Lennox.

Of course, Nicole, the birthday girl. I scanned a bit further, Andrew Titan. The other witness. Lexi's husband.

Shit.

I closed the file.

"I can't deal with this." My voice filled the small office. "I need to..." I rubbed the ring on my finger. "I need to eat."

***

The casino floor was vibrating with life. Even with the

recession, people were still flocking to Vegas, an escape from their reality. But how did you escape when your reality was Vegas?

"Hi, Cindy," I said to the hostess who manned the door at our in hotel steak house.

"Leo," she purred. "Hungry?"

I ignored her implied question and said, "Famished. And looking for a steak."

Her pretty smile transformed into a pout. I was used to it. I made a point not to date anyone at work, and since I spent most of my time in the hotel, my options were dramatically limited. Which was probably why I had only dated a handful of times since the divorce.

"Go on up to the bar, Leo." She waved me away, having lost interest. "Sarah will get you some dinner."

"Thanks. Have a great night."

The restaurant was packed and it was only seconds before Cindy got back to orchestrating the dining room. I weaved through the tables and made my way to the bar where I told the bartender to tell Sarah, the head chef, that Leo was looking for the special.

While I waited for my dinner, I turned to survey the packed restaurant. There were tables of couples enjoying an intimate dinner. Others held groups of women, or business men. My eyes scanned the tourists and business people, some of whom I'd met earlier in the day. A group of Pleasure Party ladies were laughing and enjoying themselves in the corner.

At the table next to them was a lady sitting by herself. Her back was to me, but I didn't need to see her face to know who she was. My body's reaction told me that. My muscles tensed, the skin on my arms prickled, the clench in my gut and the twitch in my crotch, all told me that the woman I never thought I'd see again, but had dreamt about for almost six years, was sitting only a few feet away.

And she was alone.

It took a few minutes for me to regain my composure, but as soon as I was sure my body wasn't going to embarrass me, I gestured to the bartender that I'd be back, and before I could change my mind, I made my way to her table.

What was I going to say? I almost stopped. I almost turned around. What could I possibly say to this woman who I'd only known for a few days, but who'd made such an impact on me?

"Excuse me?" It was all I could think of.

She turned around. Her face, just the way I remembered it, only older, in a completely amazing way, gave away nothing.

"I'm not sure if you remember me-"

"Leo," she said and I released the breath I was very aware I was holding. She remembered.

"Do you mind if I sit for a moment?"

"I'm waiting for someone," her voice was even, controlled. But I thought I saw her shiver.

I had a strong feeling of déjà vu only this time I had a much better sense of who she might be waiting for.

"I won't bother you then." I didn't want her to see my disappointment, but I had no right to expect anything more. "Have a nice evening," I said and turned to return to the bar.

"Wait."

I took a deep breath forcing myself to stay in control. When I turned around I could see some of her carefully controlled composure had slipped. Her hand was outstretched to me. Instinct made me reach out to take it. I wanted to touch her again.

I craved it.

But she pulled away, gesturing to the seat across from her before I could reach her. "Please, sit for a minute."

Sitting across from Lexi with her blond hair, her eyes bluer then was possible, the physical ache to touch her grew stronger. "Lexi," I said.

"Leo."

"You look amazing." I could feel the smile grow on my face. "You haven't changed a bit."

She reached out and tucked a strand of hair behind her ear. I saw the flash from the wedding ring and felt the smile slide off my face. I pulled myself up so I sat straighter in my chair. I was acting like a fool. She was married, a stranger, what was I thinking?

She saw my reaction and glanced down at her left hand. She tucked it in her lap. "I'm married."

"Of course." I nodded. "Your first..." I stopped myself. It wasn't any of my business but yet, I needed to know.

She answered my unasked question. "Yes," she said her voice soft, making me strain to hear her. "We...we worked things out."

"I'm happy for you." I hoped for her sake that I sounded more genuine than I felt.

"Thank you."

We looked at each other for a few seconds. I drew a blank at what to say to her. More times than I could count, I'd dreamed about seeing her again. In the months after we'd met, I couldn't get her out of my head. The way she spoke, the way she moved, her lips, her naked body under my hands.

Time lessoned my fantasies, I moved on, I even got married. But there was something about this woman sitting in front of me. She'd pushed her way into my heart and my brain all those years ago and I could never seem to get her out.

"You're still-"

"I'm the-"

We spoke at the same time, our words tripping over each other. She laughed and the Lexi I remembered shone through her nervousness. Her eyes sparkled with life and her smile lit up her face.

She glowed.

"Sorry," she said. "You go first."

"No, I insist." I wanted to keep her talking. "Ladies first.'"

She took a sip from the water glass. A glass of red wine sat largely untouched. "I was just going to say that I'm surprised to see you. At the hotel I mean."

"I'm surprised to see you too. Pleasantly, though." I fought the urge to take her hand, and steeped my fingers together to keep from reaching for her. "I work here. I'm actually the Manager of Guest Relations now."

"For the Mirage?" She looked impressed. I didn't want to, but I couldn't help but wonder how it compared to her husband's job.

I nodded.

"That's great," Lexi said and I was treated again to her beautiful smile. "I remember that last time I was..."

She didn't finish her sentence but the blush that flooded her face told me that my job wasn't the only thing she was remember from her last visit. I couldn't fight it any longer, married or not I reached across the table and took her hand in mine.

"Lexi," I said. It's all I could say. She glanced down at our hands but didn't pull away. When her eyes met mine I knew for sure that I wasn't the only one that remembered everything about that night.

"I'm waiting for my husband," she whispered but her eyes didn't leave mine.

I nodded but didn't release her. I never thought I'd see her again, let alone touch her. I wasn't going to let go so easy.

"You didn't call," I said. "You got the note?"

"I didn't... I couldn't...."

"I've thought about you."

She blinked hard and her eyes glassed over.

"I'm sorry," I said rushing my words. "I shouldn't have said that. I just-"

"No, it's fine. I-"

"What the hell is this?"

Lexi jerked her hand away. I pulled back and looked up.

"Andrew, you're late," Lexi said.

"I see you got a replacement," Andrew said.

So this was the husband? He spoke with the concentration of a man who'd had too much to drink but was trying to hide it. I'd seen it more than once.

"Andrew," she said.

"I was just leaving," I offered and stood. At first glance he didn't look like the type of man to make a scene, but all bets were off when someone had been drinking. I didn't feel like risking it.

"Oh, don't leave on my account. It looks pretty cozy," Andrew said.

"We're just..." Lexi started and looked to me for help.

"I was actually the guy who helped her plan Nicole's birthday festivities all those years ago," I said without missing a beat. "What are the odds we'd recognize each other after all these years?" I added looking directly into her eyes.

What were the odds indeed?

"Is that right? Fascinating," Andrew said looking between us. He took a step forward and leaned down giving Lexi a firm kiss on her lips. When he righted himself he looked at me and asked, "Was there something else?"

I'd spent enough time in customer service to know when I was dealing with a man who was trying to assert his dominance. I also knew when to make my exit.

"Lexi," I said. "It was a pleasure running into you again." I didn't dare shake her hand. I wasn't sure I'd be able to let it go a second time. "Enjoy your dinner."

"Thank you, Leo," she said meeting my gaze. Was that longing in her eyes? Was there still something there? Did she feel it too?

Andrew cleared his throat.

I shook my head tearing myself away from her. "May I recommend the special? Sarah, the head chef, has a phenomenal palate," I said. I forced myself to turn away and walk to the bar where my Styrofoam takeaway was waiting.

I took my dinner, nodded to the bartender and left the restaurant without looking back to eat my dinner in my office, alone.

CHAPTER EIGHTEEN

The rush of water on my skin was a relief. I closed my eyes and let the shower cool me. I'd be a liar if I said that seeing Leo again hadn't affected me.

I was a liar.

Because that's more or less what I'd been telling Andrew for the last two hours. Dinner had been torturous. After Leo left, the tension between Andrew and I was palpable. I wanted dinner over as quickly as possible so we could leave. I ordered the special without bothering to look at the menu but Andrew pretended to agonize over his decision before he settled on his usual, prime rib. Over our meals, he continued to fire questions at me about Leo.

"How do you really know him?"

"I told you, he helped me with Nicole's birthday last time we were here."

"And?" Andrew said reaching for his wine glass.

I put my hand out to stop him. "Don't you think you had enough?"

He yanked away. "Don't you dare tell me I've had too much to drink."

It's not like Andrew had a drinking problem. In fact, he rarely drank at all which was a good thing because alcohol had a tendency to make him act like a completely different person and say things he didn't mean.

Or maybe he did mean them? Either way, he acted like an ass.

"Forget it," I mumbled and took a big bite of my steak. The faster we finished eating, the better.

"I think there's more to your story," he said and took a healthy gulp of his wine.

"What are you talking about?"

"The guy," he said. "You're not telling me something."

There's no way he could see through me that easily. Besides, even if he did know the truth, it's not like I cheated on him. We were separated. On our way to divorce. He had no room to get mad.

"There is, isn't there?" Andrew pointed his finger at me. "I bet you slept with him."

I dropped my fork and it clattered against my plate. Trying to avoid his gaze and accusing finger, I took a sip of my water.

"I'm right." Andrew sounded triumphant and a moment later angry, when he said, "Well, am I?"

"Are you what?"

"Don't play dumb, Lexi. You're not stupid. Tell me the truth. Did you sleep with that guy?"

"Andrew, I don't thin-"

"I think now is a damn good time to tell me who else my wife's been opening her legs to."

Anger shot through me and I worked hard to control my voice as I said, "I'm going to pretend that that was the booze talking and let it go. But if you ever speak to me like that again, you will live to regret it."

He sat back in his seat as if I'd slapped him, and his

face twisted in horror when he realized what he said.

Drunk enough to say it, but not too drunk to know he'd crossed a line. Perfect.

"Lex, I'm-"

"I don't want to hear it." And I didn't. I just wanted to get out of here and let Andrew sleep it off before he said something else. Or before I told him the truth. "Let's go."

***

After I signed the bill and got him up to the room I avoided any further conversation by jumping into the shower. I didn't want to deal with Andrew. I couldn't even look at him, let alone talk to him I was so angry. But if I had to be honest with myself, and I might as well be, I wanted, no, needed some time alone to process the whirl of thoughts and emotions at seeing Leo.

Now, I closed my eyes and let the water run over my face. It had been six years. He hadn't forgotten me. I sucked in a breath. I certainly hadn't forgotten him. The skin on my breasts and abdomen tightened in response to my memories. The way he touched me, the way he kissed me...

Stop! I couldn't let myself remember those things. I was married and he had a wedding ring on too. It certainly hadn't skipped my attention although I purposely hadn't asked about it. I didn't want to know. And it didn't matter anyway. I was here with Andrew. The point of this trip was to fix things. For Ben.

The water was still too hot; I adjusted the tap so cold water streamed down, cooling my skin and my memory.

Despite everything, when Leo touched me and held my hand, there was no denying the sparks between us. Andrew had seen them too. I groaned and turned the taps off. I couldn't see him again. It wasn't a good idea. Besides, it was a big hotel, I could avoid him. I had to.

Grabbing a towel from the rack, I wrapped it around my shivering body and went into the room. Andrew was lying across our bed, fully clothed, snoring.

Thank God.

I didn't bother with pajamas and slipped into the other bed, pulling the blankets tight around me.

There's no point. I can't see him again.

"I won't see him again," I whispered to myself.

***

I had gone to bed resolute in my decision. I wasn't going to see him again. It was the right thing to do. The responsible thing. Married women weren't supposed to respond to complete strangers the way I had with him. And after almost six years, he was a stranger. So the best thing was never to see him again. Then there wouldn't be any question of appropriate responses.

But my subconscious had different ideas. My dreams were full of visions of Leo. A mixture of past memories and my imagination combined to create vivid images that woke me more than once, my body on fire with the thought of him.

It doesn't count if I saw him in my dreams. After all, I couldn't control that.

Right?

So, since I'd already technically seen him in my dreams, it probably wouldn't make a difference if I ran into him by accident.

At least that's how I reasoned it to myself when I

changed into my bathing suit and slipped out of the room at dawn. Andrew was still snoring in our bed, oblivious to everything. Even if I hadn't have been extra quiet, he wouldn't have noticed my absence.

As soon as I pushed through the heavy glass doors leading from the casino to the deck, the difference in atmosphere was distinct. Cut off from the chaos inside, the gardens were an oasis of calm. Later in the day they would transform into a wet dance party. But for now, it was serene. It was only 6:30 but the air was already thick with heat as the sun worked its way up in the sky. The water would be a welcome relief.

There was only one other swimmer working his way across the pool with clean easy strokes. I took the lane next to him.

I didn't have goggles with me or even a proper suit for swimming laps. It had been years since I'd swam seriously so I hadn't bothered to pack anything. The green bikini I was wearing was a gift from Nicole last summer when we went to the lake for a weekend. She was still on her never ending quest to get me into something sexier than my black tank suit. I'd only worn it the one weekend, but this trip seemed like a good time to bring it out.

Conscious of my skimpy bikini, I sat on the edge of the tiles and slid into the cool water instead of diving as I once would have. I pointed my hands over my head and pushed off the wall with my feet.

I rocketed through the water and when I broke the surface, slipped into my old rhythm of front crawl. It felt good. More than good. The water streaming past my body, the slight burn of my muscles as they stretched and pulled, made me feel alive. Like I had finally woken up. At some point, I passed the other swimmer, approached the end, seamlessly took a breath, tucked under and executed a perfect flip turn, pushing off the wall.

I still had it.

How could I have ever given this up? I swam throughout my pregnancy because when I floated, I felt weightless and it gave my back a break from the heaviness in my belly. But after Ben was born, there was never any time to get to the pool. Andrew didn't like to be left alone with the baby. He said he didn't trust himself, that he wasn't good at the dad thing. And when Ben got older, life got busier. Somehow, swimming, like most things, took a back seat.

With every stroke I took, I increased my speed. As I approached the far wall, I took a deep breath preparing myself and dove under for the flip. But there was a body standing where I planned to make contact. In a rush of air, I blew out hard and bubbles spewed from my mouth. I pulled up and broke the surface coughing and spitting, directly in front of the man standing in my lane.

Leo.

"I'm sorry," he said. "I didn't mean to get in your way. Are you okay?"

"What are...what are you doing here?" I finished coughing and wiped the water from my eyes.

"I was swimming," he said with a glint in his eyes.

Of course he was; I knew he'd be here. Wasn't that the reason I'd come down to the pool this morning? I was hoping he would remember. And he had. Only I didn't expect him to be in the water let alone standing inches in front of me, naked from the waist up with drops streaming from his hard chest.

If time had affected his body, it was only for the better. The urge to run my hands across his stomach filled me. How was it possible that after six years he could look better than ever, while I...I crossed my arms over my exposed stomach.

I shook my head in an effort to focus. "I can see that," I said. "What I meant was, why are you swimming?"

"I swim every morning." It was stupid but I was disappointed. I wanted him to be there because of me. It must have shown on my face because he added, "For the last six years. I guess you could say that you inspired me."

"Really?"

He nodded. "I rarely miss a day. It helps me relax, and there's something about the water, it clears my head, puts everything into focus. Especially when I have a lot to think about." His eyes caught mine and wouldn't allow me to look away. Not that I wanted to.

"I know exactly what you mean," I said. "I've missed it."

"Missed it? You don't swim anymore? You told me once that you swam every day. It was important to you."

He remembered. The water between us heated up. The proximity of his bare chest stirred a conflict of emotions within me and I became very aware of the tiny bikini I was wearing. I wanted to reach out and touch him, feel his skin under my fingers. At the same time, I wanted to dive under the water and swim away from him and the swirl of feelings I was having.

"How do you remember that?" I asked.

"Lexi," Leo's voice dipped low. "I remember everything."

What was I supposed to say to that? We stood there, facing each other, not speaking, for a few minutes. A warm breeze floated across the water and I shivered.

"You're cold," Leo said. He moved toward me, like he was going to wrap his arms around me to keep me warm. I wanted him to. Despite myself, my body yearned to be held by him. He wasn't the only one who remembered everything.

I took two steps back and said, "No. I'm fine."

Leo moved back against the wall and I wanted to yank

him back towards me. With the distance between us, I did feel a little cold.

"You didn't answer me," he said. "Do you still swim everyday?"

"I don't actually," I said. "I was just thinking about how good it felt to be back in the pool after all these years."

"Why did you stop?"

I opened my mouth to tell him about Ben, the business of motherhood, how life changed and time seemed to slip away. Instead I said, "Things change." I looked down, uncrossed my arms and skimmed my hands across the surface of the water.

"They don't change that much," he said. Something in his voice made me jerk my head up to look at him. His dark features formed what I thought was a frown before morphing into a grin. It happened so fast, I couldn't be sure I'd seen the sad look at all. "That would explain the suit," he said. His eyes assessed me and my skin burned under his gaze.

"What's wrong with my bathing suit?"

"Nothing," he said holding his hands up in defense. "It's quite nice, but not really what I'd call a typical lap swimming suit."

I fought the urge to duck my head under the water and cool off my embarrassment. "I wasn't planning on swimming. But..."

I didn't need to finish my thought. I could see he knew exactly what I didn't have to say. I shivered again, but this time not from the breeze.

"Will you let me buy you breakfast?" he asked and before I could protest he added, "Right here by the pool. You don't even have to go change."

I nodded and pushed thoughts of Andrew, sleeping unaware, out of my head. It was just breakfast and suddenly I was starving.

***

Ten minutes later we were settled at a table next to the pool, partially surrounded by palm trees. Soft music floated on the breeze from hidden speakers. I had no doubt that later in the day loud dance music would be pulsing through those same speakers when the party began to pick up. But for now, Leo and I had the deck mostly to ourselves, with the occasional tourist wandering by.

Leo had made a quick call on his cell phone and before I knew it, a young staff member, her hair pulled back in a tight ponytail showed up with plush terry cloth robes, and a cart laden with coffee, fruit and a variety of fresh buns, croissants and other delicious looking temptations.

"Wow," I said after shrugging into the warm robe. "This is pretty amazing. I didn't even know there was a cafe out here."

"There isn't?" he said.

"I guess working here has some privileges. This is impressive."

"Sorry," Leo said and his confidence slipped. "I should have asked you what you felt like. I just thought-"

"Leo. It's fine." I smiled. "Honestly. It all looks very nice. I really am impressed." I took a seat and reached for the coffee he had just poured for me. "You must be doing very well here."

"I am," he said. "Vegas has been very good to me in a time when a lot of people haven't done well. Lady Luck must be on my side."

"I have a feeling it's more than luck," I said. I remembered what a hard worker he was all those years ago.

I could only imagine that his work ethic would have multiplied.

Leo shrugged and took a croissant from the platter. The pastry flaked as he tore it apart. "Maybe it's a bit of both," he said.

We looked at each other for a moment both of us trying to assess the other. What do you say to an ex-lover after six years?

After a minute I asked, "Are you happy?" I couldn't help but look at the ring on his left hand.

He saw my glance drift down and answered the question I really wanted to ask. "I only wear the ring to present a certain image. I'm not married."

"An image?"

"There are times when some of the female guests take a bit more interest in me than they should," he said. "The ring helps keep them at bay. Sometimes."

"It's a pretty nice ring for a fake." I grabbed a strawberry and popped it in my mouth.

"I was married."

The burn of jealousy flared up inside. It was ridiculous and unreasonable, but it was real. It was stupid to think he wouldn't have moved on. I could tell myself that we didn't mean anything to each other, but we did and the fact that we were sitting here now, confirmed it.

I swallowed the strawberry hard. "Was?"

"It didn't work out," he said and held my gaze. His eyes were every bit as dark as they had been six years ago. Only now they were framed by lines etched into his skin.

"I'm sorry," I mumbled.

"I'm not. She wasn't you."

My heart seized. Did he just say that? I took a sip of

coffee keeping my eyes averted.

"Lexi?" Leo's voice was soft.

I looked up but the expression on his face was so full of pain, and raw emotion that my first instinct was to look away again.

But I didn't. I matched the intensity in his eyes and didn't break his stare.

"I'm sorry," he said after a moment. He shook his head as if he'd been in a trance. "I shouldn't have said that."

"No."

"No, I shouldn't have said it?" he asked. "Or, no, I should have?"

"I don't know," I admitted.

His smile was so sweet, so genuine, it broke my heart.

He reached across the table and took my hands in his, and just as it had the night before, his touch sent a spark shooting through me. "Lexi, I know that some things change with time, but some things don't."

I nodded when what I really wanted to do was jump across the table and into the arms of the only man who'd ever lit me up.

"You're married," he continued, "he seems like... a good man." Leo swallowed hard.

The mention of Andrew brought me spilling down to reality. What was I doing? I shouldn't be sitting here talking this way with another man. Letting another man hold my hands this way. Letting another man make me feel the way I was feeling. I jerked my hands away and instantly regretted it. "He's not usually like that," I said. I busied myself adjusting my ponytail. Anything to keep from reaching for him again. "Andrew doesn't really drink much, he's ...Thank you for breakfast," I said and pushed up from the chair.

Leo jumped up and caught my arm. "Please, you don't

have to-"

"I do," I said and then softened my voice. "I should go, Leo."

He reached out with his other hand and cupped my cheek. I couldn't help it; I closed my eyes and sank into his touch. The feel of his thumb stroking my skin made me want to cry because despite the time between us, despite the separate lives we'd lived, this man knew me. He knew me in ways no one else could, or I feared, ever would. And he needed to know the truth. Slowly, I reached up and covered his hand with my own.

"Leo, I-"

"Leo!" The sharp voice broke the stillness of the moment and I jerked back, away from him. A tall brunette, Roberta, I recognized her from Nicole's wedding meeting yesterday, was approaching us at an incredible speed. Incredible because of the impossibly high heels she was wearing.

"I should go," I said and headed in the opposite direction before I could change my mind.

Before I slipped behind the palms, I thought I heard him say my name, but I couldn't be sure and I didn't turn around to find out.

***

I called after her. I needed to know if we could see each other later, but she didn't hear me. Or if she did, she didn't turn around to look.

It was too late. I was too late. She was married and I was being an idiot. The best I could ever hope for from her would be friendship, and even I knew that wasn't realistic. I could never be just friends with Lexi.

"Leo," Roberta's voice snapped me back to attention. "I need to talk to you."

I turned to face her and tried to keep the sadness out of my voice. "So, talk."

Roberta slapped her portfolio onto the table. "We have a problem. A big problem."

"You can handle anything. That's why I hired you. So handle it."

"I can't handle this," she said. "Not without your help."

There was something in her voice. I put my coffee cup down and focused on her. "What's going on?"

"I need you to take a wedding," Roberta said.

"Josh is doing the Lennox/Stewart wedding," I said and my eyes went to the palm trees the maid of honor had just escaped through.

"Focus, Leo," she said. There was no humor or teasing in her voice today. Roberta was pissed. "Josh is a mess. There's no way I'm letting him anywhere near a wedding today."

"What are you talking about?"

"Remember that stag party 'emergency' he had yesterday?" I nodded and she continued. "Apparently the big emergency was that his college buddy is getting married next month and the groomsmen surprised the groom by bringing him to Vegas for an impromptu party. Josh pulled out all the stops. Suite, limo, entertainment." She drew out the last word. "And of course, Josh participated. I doubt he even slept. He smells like a still, he can't walk straight and I'm sure he's still drunk. There is no way I can let him handle a wedding today. It would be a disaster."

I took a deep breath and ran my hands through my hair which by now was dry. "Sit, have a coffee."

She sat, but didn't touch the coffee.

"Look, I know it's been awhile -"

"I can do it. I used to be the best event coordinator around," I said and it was true. There was a time when I could organize and run a major conference, schedule three bachelorette parties and orchestrate the most beautiful wedding anyone had ever seen. All in one day. But I hadn't done a wedding in at least two years.

How hard could it be? "I'll take the big one," I said.

"No way. I'm sure you could handle it and all that," she said. "But I have a relationship with the bride. She's a real piece of work and will absolutely become unglued if you take over at this point. You need to do the small one." She pulled the file from her portfolio and handed it to me.

Nicole's wedding. With Lexi, dressed in some stunning gown no doubt. "No." I shook my head and pushed the file back to her. "I can't do this wedding."

"Why?"

"It's personal."

"Personal? Leggy, blond, personal?" Roberta's eyes challenged me. She knew me well. We'd worked side by side for four years. The woman knew me better than I knew myself some days. "I'm sorry, Leo. But whatever personal issues you have here, you have to put them aside. I know you're way too professional to let that mess up someone's special day."

She said the right thing and by the look on her face, she knew it. I wouldn't, no matter what was going on, let my personal issues screw up my career. Not again. I grabbed the file.

"Besides," she added, "it's not the blond getting married."

She was right. And it would give me a great excuse to see Lexi.

"It's all in there," Roberta said. "Everything should be

taken care of. It's really not too big a deal. If there was any one else... anyway, all you have to do is show up and make sure it goes smoothly."

"Right," I said as I scanned the file. "Smoothly. No problem."

CHAPTER NINETEEN

I was running late, again. It was starting to become a disturbing trend. By the time I returned to the room there wasn't enough time to shower so I threw on some clothes and slipped out to meet Nicole before Andrew even stirred from his bed.

Thank goodness. I didn't think I could hold a normal conversation with him when all I could think of was Leo and the way he looked at me, full of desire and longing. Was it possible to still have feelings for someone after six years? I needed to get a hold of myself.

But it was possible. I didn't need someone to tell me, I could see it. It was in the way he held my gaze and wouldn't let me look away. In the way he touched me, and stroked my skin with his thumb without even realizing it. It was in the sound of his voice, the way he said my name. But most frightening, it was in the way I felt when I looked at him.

The sharp ring of the elevator arriving interrupted my thoughts. It was Nicole's wedding day. The last thing I had time for was...whatever it was. Nicole was likely pulling her hair out with stress and I was obsessing about someone, something from six years ago.

I squeezed myself into the elevator with a handful of tourists and their giant suitcases and went down to the lobby to find her so I could play my role of maid of honor.

As it turned out, I was wrong. Nicole wasn't the frazzled mess I'd thought she'd be. In fact, she was waiting for me when I stepped off the elevator. She looked rested and fresh with her hair pulled back in a ponytail and only the barest of make-up on to compliment her features.

"You look fabulous," I said and meant it.

"Of course I do. I'm getting married today."

"Exactly. I thought you'd be...well, a little more..."

"Stressed? Obsessed? Freaked out?"

"Well, yes." I couldn't help but laugh. "You have to admit, Nic. You have a history of getting a little worked up before major events, and today's event rates pretty high on the major scale."

"That's just it," Nicole said. "There is nothing more major than my wedding. And I decided to try a different approach. Instead of pulling my usual freak out, I've decided to be Zen."

"You've decided to be Zen?"

"That's right, it's all mental," Nicole said and tugged on my arm. "Come on, we're going to be late. I've booked us in for the works. I love you, Lex, but seriously, when was the last time you had a facial?"

I touched my skin. "There's nothing wrong with my face."

"You're all red and blotchy. But don't worry, we'll get it fixed."

We walked through the main lobby, past a restaurant and through a bank of slot machines before Nicole led me down another corridor and into the spa. Stepping through the heavy glass doors was like walking into an oasis of calm. Trickling walls of water flanked both sides of the small reception area and gentle pipe music floated through the space. It was a very different world from the flashing lights, blaring top forty music and atmosphere of excess on the other side of the doors. I exhaled. This would be the perfect place to let my mind go blank and forget about Leo.

After checking in, we were led to an equally peaceful changing room with bamboo mats laid over polished pebble floors, the scent of vanilla incense filled the room in the subtle way only spas seem to manage.

"What are you going to do with your hair?" Nicole lifted my still damp pony tail off my back. "Ew. You smell like pool water." She dropped my hair and looked at me. "Were you swimming this morning?"

I turned away from her and pulled my t-shirt over my head. I was an awful liar, mostly because everything I was feeling, ever, showed on my face. "I went for a quick swim before breakfast," I said. I tugged off my shorts and slid into the thickest, plushest robe I'd ever seen. It was like being wrapped in a cloud.

"I didn't think you did that anymore. Swim I mean," Nicole said. "What made you decide to do that this morning? I assumed you were late because you and Andrew, well..."

"I don't know," I said ignoring her comment. "I felt like it. So I did." I stuffed my clothes in a locker and turned the lock before slipping the key into the pocket of the robe.

"Okay." Nicole took the locker next to me. "It just seems weird. But I suppose last time we were here, you saw-"

"So," I interrupted her before she could finish her thought. I needed to block Leo from my thoughts, not discuss him with Nicole in every detail. Which is exactly what would happen if I didn't change the subject. I grabbed her hand and led her out to the waiting area. "Tell me about this theory of yours. I think I could use some Zen calmness today."

It worked, once I got her talking about anything that interested her, she was infamous for forgetting about everything else. Which fortunately, kept the conversation firmly on her and off the topic of my morning swim. True to her word, Nicole had booked us in for the works and she'd asked for us to have the 'girlfriend experience' which meant we got to do everything together.

The topic of being Zen may induce calm in most people, but for Nicole it incited a wave of excitement. She chattered about the new meditation class Ryan had signed them up for a few weeks previously and how the breathing techniques helped calm her down and focus on her center. I couldn't help but wonder where those techniques were a few days ago when she'd freaked out. But I didn't think it was appropriate to ask.

Nicole is a hand talker which wasn't ideal for the manicurist who patiently waited with her nail file at the ready every time Nic needed to punctuate a point by waving her hand in the air. For two hours I listened to her as the conversation deviated from breathing exercises to her sex life with Ryan, to the paint colors she was considering for the condo they were redecorating. For awhile I was so thankful that we weren't talking about me that I didn't realize that what Nicole wasn't saying was more important than what she was saying.

"Nic," I interrupted her before she could start in on the tile samples she was considering. "Have you talked to your mom today?"

Nicole looked down and lifted her freshly manicured hand for inspection. She didn't answer me.

"Nicole," I tried again.

"No," she said dropping her hand and looking right at me. "She didn't call."

I thought she might cry or get emotional at the

mention of her mom. She did neither. Maybe there was something to all this relaxation and Zen talk. "It was pretty early when we left," I said. "And your phone is in the locker. She probably tried calling a few times already."

"Ladies." Two tall, willowy blonds stood in the doorway of the treatment room. "If you're ready for your massages, we can take you now. Unfortunately, we will have to use separate rooms if that's okay?" one of the ladies asked.

I nodded and looked back to Nicole. "It doesn't matter," she said, adjusting her robe as she stood. "I told you, I'm totally okay with this. And mom is too."

"Okay, but-"

"No, buts. Go relax, Lexi. I'll see you after," she said and disappeared with one of the blonds. I followed the other down a hallway and into another tranquil room, this one with a massage table in the center.

As I lay on the table, covered by the softest sheet that had ever touched my bare skin and waited for the masseuse to come back, I tried to concentrate on relaxation. A massage would be perfect. I needed to clear my head. All of Nicole's babbling had done a good job of distracting me from my thoughts but now I was ready to let my mind go blank.

There was a soft knock on the door and the therapist slipped into the room. "I've been told to give you a full relaxation massage," she said in a soothing voice. "I just want you to close your eyes, let your body relax, and allow yourself to surrender to the experience."

"Okay," I said, my voice muffled by the table.

"No more talking," she said and began to run her hands along my back, warming up my skin under the sheet. "Close your eyes."

I did as I was told, even though I couldn't help but

wonder how she knew they were open. She continued to speak to me in a low, melodic voice. It reminded me of how I used to talk to Ben when he was a baby and I was trying to get him to sleep. It was working though. She started to rub my shoulders and I could feel myself loosening up, slipping into sleep.

***

The massage didn't last nearly long enough and before I knew it the relaxation portion of the day was over and it was time to get the bride ready for the ceremony. Andrew had taken Ryan back to our room, so we had the suite to get beautiful.

As I worked the comb through Nicole's mass of curls I thought, not for the first time, that we should have hired a professional hairdresser to give her a proper up do. I was in no way trained to deal with thick, wavy hair. Or any hair at all really. The extent of my own hair dressing skills included a pony tail or maybe a braid; Nicole's red locks were way out of my comfort zone.

"Nic, are you sure you want it up?" I twisted it into a loose bun and held it against the nape of her neck.

"Of course, I have to have it up. If my hair's on my shoulders, it will take away from the embroidery of the dress."

I didn't think so at all but I dropped the hair I was holding and let it fall against her back. In fact, I thought there would be nothing more beautiful than her red hair contrasting against the milky white fabric and blue embroidery of her gown. I didn't bother telling her. I'd already mentioned it at least four times.

I sighed, grabbed a handful of bobby pins and stuck them between my teeth before gathering the hair in one hand, twisting it up as neatly as possible and securing it with as many bobby pins as I could jam in. I finished the look off with half a bottle of hair spray, pulled out two tendrils to frame her face and stepped back to check out my handiwork.

"Not bad," I said mostly to myself.

"Not bad? I look frickin' gorgeous." Nicole leaned in towards the mirror to admire herself and then spun around into my arms. "Lexi, thank you."

"Nic, anything for you," I said and hugged her tight. "You know that."

"No, Lex," her voice was muffled in my shoulder, "I really mean it. Thank you. For everything."

I laughed at her drama and it took a second to realize she wasn't laughing back. She was crying. And not just, pre-wedding tears of joy, but full fledged sobbing.

Oh no.

I snuck a look at the clock on the night stand. 1:40. We had only just over an hour to get dressed, get beautiful and get downstairs.

Shit.

"Nic, what's wrong?"

"Oh, Lex. Everything is wrong. Everything." Her body shook with sobs as she clung to me.

"Nicole, look at me," I demanded with as much kindness as I could. We were running out of time for sweet and gentle, I needed to fix this, fast. "Nicole," I commanded when she didn't look up.

She pulled away. I don't know how she managed it but her eyes were red and swollen, and her tear stained face was already blotchy. All this in only thirty seconds of tears. Thank goodness I hadn't attempted the make-up yet. "What's going on? Talk to me."

She snorted and wiped her nose with the back of her hand. "I can't get married," she wailed and threw herself onto the bed.

Her sobs ratcheted up to full scale as I watched her let loose. After a moment, I took a deep breath. "Nic," I said and moved to the edge of the bed. "This isn't very Zen. Maybe you should try taking a deep breath or some relaxa-"

"Screw Zen!" She flipped around and sat up clutching a pillow to her chest. "My life is falling apart and you're talking about being fucking Zen?"

"I just thought, well, maybe..."

"Oh, Lexi," she wailed, her anger dissolving into tears again. "What was I thinking? I can't get married without my mom. The wedding's off."

Of course. Her mom. I knew this was a bad idea.

"Do you want to call her again?" I reached for my cell phone. Nicole's mom had phoned shortly after we got out of the spa, and she'd had a light, breezy, very un-Nicole like conversation with her. It was time for a real mother to daughter chat.

"She won't want to hear from me now," Nicole said. "Not like this. I'm a horrible daughter. What was I thinking running off to get married without her? I'm awful. I'm an awful daughter." She curled around the pillow and resumed crying.

"Nic," I tried.

"Call it off." She pulled her head up long enough to yell at me.

I thought about saying something, about telling her to quit being so dramatic, about telling her that Ryan loved her, and this was their special day. That it wasn't about her mom, but I closed my mouth. I remembered very well how I'd felt on my wedding day when I thought about how much it would have meant to have my mom there with me.

And for me there hadn't been a choice.

I watched her for a moment and then left her lying on the bed, went into the living room, and made a phone call.

***

"I know it's last minute," I said into the phone for at least the tenth time. "But it's an emergency. I have a bride in distress. Surely you can understand that?"

"Ma'am, there's nothing I can do, I'm sorry," said the lady on the other end.

I sighed and looked up at the bedroom door where Nicole was undoubtedly still bawling. I took a deep breath and said the name I didn't want to say.

"Leo Mendez. Do you know him?"

"Of course I know him, Ma'am. He's the manager of customer relations here at The Mirage."

"He's a friend of mine," I said. "I'm sure he'd consider a personal favor if you could help me out with this today." I held my breath but it didn't take her long.

"For a friend of Mr. Mendez, anything. I'll have it up to your room right away, Ma'am. Is there anything else?"

"No," I said releasing my breath. "That will be perfect."

I hung up the phone, made another quick call back to Canada and went into the bathroom. I'd give Nicole another minute, she needed to cry. Once she got some emotion out of her she'd be in a better state. Then I could talk to her. There was no point now.

I looked at in the mirror and grabbed the make-up bag Nicole had supplied me with earlier. My experience with make-up was very basic; I never had the chance to dress up.

On the few occasions that Andrew wanted me to come to a work function, I usually muddled my way through, and the result wasn't too bad. Maybe with a little luck, I could do that again today.

I unzipped the bag; there was a photo of a model lying on top with a sticky note covered in directions. I smiled. I should have known better. Nicole wouldn't leave my make-up to chance. I picked through the bottles, powders and lotions and did my best to simulate the colors in the picture. When I was finished, I looked up and evaluated the results.

"Not too bad," I said to my reflection. Nicole would be impressed.

There was a knock on the door. Perfect timing. I sprinted to answer it. We didn't have much time.

"Come in."

The bellhop rolled a cart into the center of the room. And pulled off a large white cloth revealing the lap top I'd requested, complete with video camera.

"Everything is here, Ma'am," he said. "Would you like me to plug it in for you?"

"No, thanks. I got it." I handed him a ten dollar bill, hoped it was enough, and turned my attention to the cart.

It didn't take me long to click open the right program and dial the number. The room filled with the sound of a phone ringing and then, "Hello? Is there anyone there?" Nicole's mom, Cathy said. All I could see was pink and what looked like a nose.

"Mrs. Lennox," I said. "I'm here. It's Lexi. Hold on." I adjusted the camera on top of the laptop and my image showed in the bottom corner of the screen. "Is that better? Can you see me?"

"Oh, Lexi," she said. "There you are. This is just so crazy. When Sarah called and told me about this, I have to tell you, I was a little concerned. I mean, I didn't think I could actually see you so far away."

I laughed. Nicole's mom had always been afraid of computers; she used to say it was a fad that would pass and refused to go near one. I got lucky when I called Sarah, Nicole's sister-in-law, and told her my plan. She agreed to pick Cathy up and take her back to her house a few blocks away where we could use the video conference software.

"Mrs. Lennox, sit back a bit from the camera," I said.

"Oh." Her face came into clear view. "Is that better?"

"Yes." I smiled. "Much. Hold on a moment, I'll get Nicole."

When I opened the bedroom door, the quietness took me off guard. Nicole was sitting up in bed, hugging the pillow to her chest and staring at the door.

"You left," she said.

"Yes, I did." I sat next to her on the bed. "You needed to get it out. Feel better?"

She shrugged and sniffed. "No, I feel like shit."

"You're going to marry Ryan today."

"I know. But I wish my mom was here," she said and blew her nose. "I can't believe I thought it would be okay to do this without her."

I wrapped her in my arms and said, "I think I can help you with that. Come with me." I pulled her off the bed and gave her a gentle push out of the bedroom into the suite where she came face to face with her mother. Or at least her mother's face, larger than life on the over sized computer screen.

"Mom?" Nicole rushed to the computer. I thought for a minute she was going to hug the monitor.

"Hi, Honey," Cathy's voice cracked.

"What?" Nicole looked back to me, then back to her

mom. "How?"

"It was Lexi's idea," Cathy said and Nicole faced me again.

I shrugged. "You have to have your mom on your wedding day, right?"

Nicole flew into my arms. "You're the best friend ever."

"I know, I know. Now go talk to your mom for a minute and then she can help us get ready. We're running out of time."

***

While Nicole and her mom shared some private moments, I went and rounded up the hair dressing supplies and make-up and set up on a table in the living room. I gave them a few minutes of privacy, but that's all I could afford. We needed to move quickly.

After dragging her away from the screen, I situated Nicole so her mom could witness the proceedings. I brushed her hair out again and refastened it in the loose bun. As soon as the last bobby pin was secure a voice came from the computer screen.

"Nicky, come over here so I can see you better."

Nicole moved in front of the computer screen. "What do you think?"

"Turn around, let me see the back," Cathy said.

Nicole did what she was told. "Well," she said.

"What do you think?"

"I don't like it."

I sighed and sat on the couch.

"I should wear it down, right?" Nicole asked her mom.

"Of course. With your hair, you shouldn't tie it up and hide it. Show it off, for god's sake," Cathy said. "Lexi, I can't believe you would let her tie it back."

"I'm sorry, Mrs. Lennox." There was no point arguing now. "Come here, Nic."

Nicole returned to her chair and we let the bun down. I brushed until her red waves shone, reflecting the light. I finished it off with a beautiful rhinestone studded barrette.

"Okay, now your face," I said and with lots of direction, and input from both her and her mother, I managed to cover the redness in her cheeks and eyes and transform her into a stunning bride.

One more thing," I said. "Wait here Mrs. L. We'll be right back."

I took Nicole into the bedroom where she slipped out of her robe and into her gown. When I zipped up the dress I had to swallow hard to keep from crying. "Wow," was all I could manage.

"Oh, don't start." Nicole turned away from me to look at her own reflection. "No tears today, Lex."

"You're right. I think we've had enough already and something tells me there'll be more," I said and gave her a kiss on the cheek. "Come on. Let's go show your mom."

As soon as Nicole stepped into the view of the camera her mother let out a gasp.

"Oh, Nicky," she gushed from the computer. "You're so beautiful."

"Don't make her cry again," I warned only half joking. "I'll give you two a minute. I need to make a call and then we have to start heading downstairs."

Closing the bedroom door behind me I slipped on my bridesmaid dress. The blue fabric shimmered in the light and caught the sparkle in my eyes. I twirled in the mirror admiring my reflection.

I wonder what Leo will say?

As soon as the thought popped into my head, I cursed myself. I'd managed not to think about him for the last hour, well at least most of that time. I twirled again, and tried to reframe my thoughts.

I wonder what Andrew will think?

He was my husband, I should care about his reaction. But even when I made a serious effort in my appearance, I couldn't remember a time when he'd ever looked at me with as much longing and desire as Leo had this morning.

I didn't have time to think about it. A quick glance at the clock made that clear. We only had fifteen minutes. I grabbed my purse and went to collect the bride.

"Are you ready to become an old married woman?" I asked and started gathering up our purses and necessary things.

"I don't know about you, but I'm never going to get old," Nicole said and we all laughed.

"Time to go, Nic," I said. "We don't want to be late."

She turned back to her mom. "I guess this is it." Her voice started to shake. "I'm so sorry, Mom. I wish you could be here."

"Nicky, I'm there with you in spirit, baby," Cathy said and started to cry.

"Stop it," I said before the tears could start flowing everywhere. Nicole turned and looked at me as if I was the most insensitive person in the world. "You will be there, Mrs. L," I said ignoring her, "we'll connect again as soon as we get downstairs."

"Really?"

"Of course. I will not allow you to miss Nicole's

wedding. "

"Lex, you are the best." Nicole threw her arms around me.

"I know, I know," I said with a smile.

CHAPTER TWENTY

Stepping onto the terrace was like walking into the pages of a fairy tale. The already lush space had been transformed with even more flowers, if that was possible. It felt as if we were in a secret garden in the middle of a tropical forest. The aisle was carpeted in petals, and given that no guests expected, potted palms and large hibiscus plants flanked the edges. The altar was situated under an arched vine covered in more hibiscus blossoms. In the corner was a three tiered cake which I thought was a bit of overkill, but it looked delectable, decorated simply with sugar-covered flowers.

The guys weren't there yet, so I left Nicole in a small waiting area and rolled the cart containing her link to her mother down the aisle. I scanned the area amongst the palms and foliage for some sort of outlet in so I could get Cathy back online.

There had to be something.

I caught a glimpse of an extension cord snaking through the leaves. There didn't seem to be any help for it. I took a quick look around, pulled up my dress and dropped to my knees. Crawling under the plants, I saw what looked like an outlet and I burrowed deeper, dragging the computer's power cord with me.

"Lexi?"

Are you kidding me?

I swatted a leaf out away from my face and took a deep breath before abandoning my search. Taking my time, I backed out, turned, and from my position on the floor, looked straight up at Leo's smiling face.

"Hi, Leo."

He extended his hand in aid which I took. "Can I help you find something?" he asked as he hauled me to my feet.

I adjusted my dress and smoothed the fabric back into place, trying unsuccessfully to look poised.

His eyes took their time traveling up my body, assessing me. "You look amazing."

My stomach flipped. "I need to plug this in," I said and held out the cord.

"Of course," he said. "Let me take care of that for you." Leo took the cord from me but his fingers lingered on my hand.

"I don't want to keep you," I said. "You probably have a million things to do."

"Actually, this is exactly where I need to be right now," he said. His eyes held mine. "You have a little..." he reached out and plucked a leaf from my hair, "got it," he said.

Leo let the leaf drop to the ground but his hand still hovered near my face. For a crazy minute I thought he might kiss me. I couldn't tear my eyes away from his. He moved his hand and with a gentle touch, tucked a strand of hair behind my ear. His fingers trailed across my cheek. My eyes fluttered shut. I couldn't bear to look at him.

"Lexi?"

My eyes snapped open at the sound of Andrew's voice and I took two steps back from Leo. I felt like a kid who'd been caught doing something wrong. Which I suppose, I had.

"Andrew," I said. "Are you guys ready?"

Andrew's face was hard as he looked slowly between us. His gaze locked on Leo, his fists clenched at his sides and I was afraid he might try to hit him. Instead, he spoke to me his eyes not leaving Leo, "We're ready. Ryan's at the alter."

"Okay," I said grateful for an excuse to leave. "We just need to power up the computer, then I'll get Nicole and we can get started."

"Excellent," Leo said. "I'll take care of the computer and cue the music when you're ready. Just give me the signal."

"Pardon me?"

"What?"

Andrew and I spoke at the same time.

"I'm filling in today. I'll be taking care of everything for Nicole and Ryan's nuptials," Leo said. "I meant to tell you earlier."

"Earlier?" Andrew asked. The lines in his face grew deeper and his skin turned a deep shade of red.

I ignored him and turned back to Leo. "What do you mean, you'll be filling in today?"

"I'm sorry. I meant to tell you," Leo said.

"When? You meant to tell her, when?" Andrew demanded.

"But you didn't." My eyes were locked on Leo. "Fair warning would have been nice."

"There didn't seem to be a good time. Whenever I saw you, I just-"

"What the hell is going on here?" Andrew grabbed my arm and spun me around. "Someone better tell me what's going on."

I blinked hard, stunned as I looked at my husband remembering he was standing there. Had he seen the way Leo looked at me? The way I looked at him?

"Lexi, are you okay?" Leo asked. He stood behind me, so close I could smell his cologne. If I turned around, I would be in his arms. If I-

"She's fine."

"I'd like to hear that from her if you don't mind."

They squared shoulders with me between them and still I couldn't move.

"You better back off," Andrew said and pulled me to him. I hit his chest with a soft thud and looked up at him. My husband. His face was red and a bead of sweat lined his forehead.

He was jealous. Of course he was. I was his wife and all this was wrong.

I glanced behind me to Leo and my heart lurched.

No.

"Stop," I said. "Please. I'm fine." Turning back to Andrew, I forced a smile and squeezed his hand. "We should get started. Nicole will be freaking out."

The color in Andrew's face returned to normal, but he didn't return my smile as he watched me. His eyes were searching mine for something. I kept my expression as benign as I could manage.

"I'll plug this in," Leo said behind me but I didn't dare turn around. Andrew shifted his gaze up but I kept my eyes on him and I knew when Leo had left because he finally looked down at me again and said, "I'll get Ryan." His voice was hard. "We can get started."

He moved to leave, but I reached out to stop him. "Andrew."

When he turned around, the expression on his face almost broke me. He knew.

"Not now, Lexi," he said and disappeared down the aisle.

***

"Where have you been?" Nicole flung herself on me the moment I walked back into the alcove she was hiding in. "Is everything okay? Did Ryan show up? You got my mom hooked up, right? She'll be there?"

"Nic, chill." I tried to smile and shake off what had just happened. "Everything is going to be perfect."

"What's wrong?"

"Nothing. Everything is right on schedule. It will be beautiful."

"You're lying," she said. "Tell me what's going on."

I didn't have to answer, because in that second, Leo turned the corner holding an incredible bouquet of lilies and orchids. "Here are the gorgeous flowers for the most gorgeous bride," he said, handing them to Nicole who took them, her mouth dropping open.

"And for the stunning maid of honor," Leo said as he handed me an equally beautiful if only slightly smaller bouquet. Our hands touched as I took the flowers and I fought the urge to lace my fingers in his and hold on. Instead, I pulled away and held the flowers to my chest. The pungent smell of the lilies filled my senses.

"Oh, I see exactly what the problem is," Nicole said and smiled a smug smile. "How come you didn't tell me?"

"What? Is there something wrong?" Leo's brow furrowed. He consulted his clipboard and began checking items off a list. "I think we have everything. Did I miss something?"

"Oh, I think you missed something alright," Nicole said. "But it doesn't have anything to do with the wedding."

Leo looked up at her and gave her a strange look before looking to me.

I looked away and asked, "Are you ready, Nic?"

Nicole's smile lit up her face. She tucked a strand of hair behind her ear and leaving no room for question, said, "Absolutely."

***

I was supposed to be detached, impersonal, with just the right amount of objectivity to make the wedding sparkle, without getting personal. That's what I taught my employees. It's what every event coordinator needed to know. You needed to be involved enough to make the event special and memorable without showing emotion. I knew this. It's what made me good at what I did.

But when the music started and I saw Lexi walking down the aisle, the orchids and lilies, her shimmery blue dress showcasing the body I still dreamt about, I lost all the objectivity I was supposed to have. I forgot about staying detached, keeping a healthy distance and focusing on the event and the details I was supposed to be orchestrating. Instead, all I could think about was the extreme good fortune that had brought this amazing woman back into my life and how I would be a complete fool to let her walk away again. With every slow step she took, I listed the arguments in my head, the reasons I would give her for staying with me forever.

And then she reached the altar, and took her place across from the man who did have a claim to her. Her husband. My list disintegrated in my head and I watched him look at her with a possessiveness I knew I didn't have a right to.

I looked away and pushed the button that cued the wedding march. Nicole stepped out from the alcove and began her procession down the aisle. Turning, I saw the look on her groom's face. His bride was radiant, and by the look in his eyes, he knew how lucky he was. Love, mixed with a healthy dose of lust, oozed from him as he watched; mesmerized by every step she took toward him. My eyes shifted to his groomsman, Lexi's husband. He wasn't watching the bride, he was staring directly at me, and he didn't look happy. Our eyes locked.

He challenged me and I smiled in return. Purposefully, so he wouldn't miss it, I let my gaze slide to the left and land on Lexi. There were tears in her eyes as she watched her best friend reach the on the aisle and take Ryan's hand. I didn't care if her husband was glaring at me. I couldn't take my eyes off her.

The raw emotion in her eyes struck me. Was she thinking of her own wedding day? Remembering the love between her and her husband? The thought made my stomach burn with jealousy. But there was something about weddings. It didn't matter how many I witnessed, there was always a part of me that flashed back to the day when I too exchanged vows.

Looking back, I know it should never have happened. I never loved Tamara, not enough to marry her. And unfortunately for her, it didn't take her long to figure that out herself and become just as miserable as I already was.

Watching Lexi as Nicole and Ryan exchanged their vows, I was painfully aware that I didn't have a right to her despite the fact that she would always have a part of me. The Justice of the Peace declared the couple husband and wife and I watched as they locked in a passionate embrace before sneaking another glance at Lexi. She was staring directly at me, tears streaking down her cheeks.

CHAPTER TWENTY-ONE

I raised my glass in a toast. "To my best friend and her handsome new husband. Congratulations to you both. May your lives together be blessed with a lifetime of happiness and love."

"Cheers," Ryan said and everyone reached to the center of the table and clinked glasses.

The newlyweds kissed. They'd always been a showy couple, but matrimony had taken their passion to the next level. I felt a little like a voyeur sitting across from them, so to distract myself, I took a roll from the bread basket and broke it in half.

"It was a beautiful ceremony," Andrew said to me. He sat tense, uncomfortable. I couldn't be sure if it was because of the amorous display across the table, or the tension between us.

"It was." I put a piece of bread in my mouth.

"Look, Lex." He shifted so he was facing me. He was calmer, but I could see the anger from earlier simmering just under the surface. "Are you going to tell me what the deal is with the wedding planner?"

I swallowed the dry bread hard and reached for my champagne. After a sip, I cleared my throat and whispered, "I don't really think this is the right time to talk about that."

"Fine," Andrew said and then turned to the couple and said, "Do you two want to cut this dinner short or what?"

They broke apart, Nicole made an attempt to fix her hair and they both adjusted themselves in their seats.

"Sorry, guys," Ryan said. "I just can't believe this stunning creature finally agreed to be my wife. And there's just something about knowing that she's mine for the rest our lives that makes it hard to keep my hands off her. You must know how it is?" he asked Andrew.

Andrew flicked a glance at me and said, "Yeah. I remember those days."

"Let's have cake," I declared eager to change the topic. Andrew and I both knew how long it'd been since we'd had sex, let alone been in a stage when we couldn't keep our hands off each other.

Had it ever been like that between us? My thoughts flashed to Leo, the way it felt to look at him and yearn for his touch. The way my body reacted with a heat that was almost violent when he kissed me. Yes, it had been like that for me. Once.

"Lexi." Nicole's voice jerked me from my thoughts. "We haven't even finished our meal yet."

"Right," I said. I hoped my confusion wasn't obvious to everyone, but a quick look at Andrew confirmed that he at least thought I was acting strangely. He raised his eyebrow at me in question. I ignored him. "I just thought maybe you two were in a hurry to get on with your wedding night," I said to Nicole.

They both laughed.

"I think we can wait a little while at least," Ryan said.

Everyone turned back to their meals. I poked at my steak a little bit, before spearing a piece of asparagus.

The conversation turned to the details of the

ceremony. Nicole and Ryan each toasted each other, and even Andrew stood and gave a short but thoughtful speech to the happy couple. The champagne flowed and I probably drank more than my share. But it was Nicole's wedding and the alcohol muted my feelings. I kept thinking that with one more glass I might stop thinking about Leo.

The champagne made it worse. He occupied every thought.

Moments after the servers cleared our dinner plates, the object of my distraction came into the room, wheeling the cake we'd seen at the ceremony.

"How was dinner?" Leo asked.

"Everything's been awesome," Ryan said and wrapped his arm around his new wife.

When Andrew's hand squeezed my thigh, it was so unexpected that I let out a small squeak which I tried to cover by coughing into my napkin.

"Jesus, Lex," Andrew said under his breath.

"Are you okay?" Nicole said.

Andrew's hand slid further up my leg.

"I'm fine," I said and reached for my champagne. I took a sip and the bubbles hit the back of my throat. Leo looked at me, his face was worried with concern. When Andrew's thumb began stroking lazy circles on the silky fabric of my dress. I almost choked, but swallowed hard instead.

I turned to my husband. "What are you doing?" I hissed.

"Showing you some affection," Andrew said. "You're my wife." He emphasized the second word.

So, that's what this was about. Possession.

"Cut it out."

"Lex, there's nothing wrong with letting you know I care."

"That's not what you're doing and we both know it."

Andrew removed his hand and I breathed a small sigh of relief but then he moved his chair so it was closer to mine. "That's exactly what I'm doing," he said as he dropped his arm lazily over my shoulder. His finger tips dangled along the crest of my breast.

With his back turned to us, Leo had positioned the cart with the cake next to the table and was unwrapping a silver knife from a cloth napkin.

He was close. Andrew was too close.

I pushed back my chair, ducked under Andrew's arm and stood. "You can't cut the cake here, Nicole."

Everyone looked at me as if I'd lost my mind.

Maybe I had. Having Leo and Andrew in the same room, my marriage spinning further out of control, was making me crazy.

"Let's move it over to these flowers, without the table in the background," I said.

"I think it's fine," Ryan said.

"Of course it's not fine. You need flowers for the pictures," I snapped and grabbed the cart.

"I've got it," Leo said. His voice was a soothing balm that covered me. I looked into his eyes and felt calm settle over me. "It's okay. You can let go."

"Thank you," I said. His eyes held me and I didn't move.

Nicole broke our connection. "I think that sounds like a fantastic idea, Lex." She put her hands on my shoulders and pulled me upright, forcing me to let go. I turned and looked at her. "It's a good idea," she said again, but I don't think she was talking about the cake.

I nodded.

Nicole leaned in and whispered in my ear, "You need to calm down. Do you need a minute?"

I shook my head. "I'm fine," I said.

"Lexi, you don't seem fine. Take a breath."

I gave her a quick kiss on the cheek and pulled away. Her pretty face was crumpled with concern. "Honestly," I said. "Everything's fine."

"Is Andrew-"

"It's fine," I repeated but when Nicole gestured towards the table I turned.

Andrew's seat was empty.

I turned back to Nicole. "I'm sorry," I said. "I don't know where-"

"Are you ready, Nic?" Ryan called.

Leo had already moved the cart and the cake was now framed by tropical flowers and palms. Ryan was waiting, the knife in his hands.

***

Later, after she'd happily smooshed cake in her husband's face, Nicole wrapped me in a hug.

"That seemed so silly," she said. "It's not like anyone saw it."

"I saw it."

She laughed. "You know what I mean."

Her happiness was contagious. "It doesn't matter if anyone saw it. Your wedding wasn't about anyone else. It was totally for you guys. That's what I loved about it."

"You really think so?"

"Absolutely," I said. "It was a beautiful day."

Nicole unwrapped herself from my arms and pulled back. "Are you okay? I mean, Leo? I had know idea he worked here. It's so crazy and I know you said you're fine, but-"

"Nic, I'm okay." I forced the smile on my face to stay put. "Stop worrying about me."

"Andrew was acting weird. And where did he go? You didn't tell him about...well, things? I mean, that would be pretty hard to hear. Leo was, is...what I mean is, I remember how you felt back then. How are you feeling now? You don't still feel..."

My smile slipped.

"Lexi. You can't be-"

"Oh, stop it. I don't have feelings for him," I said. "That's crazy. It was a lifetime ago. Besides, we only had one night together. It's not like it was a relationship."

Nicole shook her head. "I don't buy it, Lex. There was always something more between you two. And then there's Ben..."

"Ben has nothing to do with this," I said trying to control the tremble in my voice.

"Yes, he does, Lexi. It's okay. I know."

"There's nothing to know," I said.

"But...you and Leo, you-"

"You and Leo, what?" Andrew said having chosen that moment to reappear.

Nicole's face turned an unnatural shade of red and with her back turned from Andrew, she mouthed, "I'm sorry."

"Come here," I said and pulled her into a hug. "Don't

worry," I whispered into her ear. "Go. Enjoy your wedding night."

I gave her a gentle push and with a slight wave to Andrew, she slipped away and into Ryan's arms.

"Are you ready to tell me what's going on?" Andrew asked. His face was a carefully controlled mask of fury. "I think I have a pretty good guess."

I turned so I was facing him head on. "There's nothing going on."

"Don't lie to me," he said through clenched teeth. "Do you think I'm stupid? That I can't see the way he looks at you. Like he's imagining you naked in his bed."

"Andrew."

He ignored me. "But what's worse is the way you look at him. Like you *want* to be naked in his bed."

"That's enough."

"Is it? Because I thought this weekend was supposed to be for us," he said. "So we could reconnect. But instead you're lusting after some hotel employee and not even bothering to hide it."

"Andrew, stop."

"Not until you tell me what's going on between you two. Did you sleep with him, Lexi? Is that it? Is that why he looks at you like that, because he's already had you in his bed? Tell me Lex. Did you fuc-"

My hand flew out and slapped him across the face. It was a solid contact and my fingers stung from the force.

Andrew clutched his cheek. His green eyes narrowed and blazed with anger. He brought his right hand up and for a moment I thought he might hit me.

He dropped his hand and started to stay something. Changing his mind, he shook his head and turned on his heel leaving me standing alone.

***

I let him go. It was best if I didn't talk to him right now. Besides, what would I say?

Ryan and Nicole were gone. Probably back to their suite to celebrate. Leo was gone too. Just the bus boy, clearing the table and the photographer who was packing up his equipment, remained. I grabbed my purse from under the table and slipped away.

I walked as quickly as I could in my heels. I needed to get away but had no idea where to go. Could you ever really be alone in Vegas? There were people all around me. Laughing, celebrating, having fun. My head was spinning. I couldn't get the image of Andrew's face when he asked me about Leo out of my mind. What could I tell him? What was there to tell? I needed to calm down.

Ben.

I needed to talk to Ben. I stopped in the middle of the casino floor and dug through my purse for my cell phone but before I could dial the number, I noticed the time. He would be asleep. With the hour time difference, I would wake him if I called. And for what? To tell him that his mother was doing a terrible job of keeping their family together? Hot tears pricked at my eyes and I blinked hard, forcing them back.

"Lexi?"

Leo's voice, warm like my favorite quilt, wrapped around me from behind. "Lexi, are you okay?" Reaching me, he touched my shoulder and it took everything I had not to collapse into his touch. The need for him to hold me overwhelmed my senses.

I shook my head, pulled just out of his reach and turned to face him. His handsome features were creased in concern and hurt.

He pointed to my phone. "It can be hard to get reception inside. Do you need to make a call?"

"No," I said. "I shouldn't disturb him."

"Your husband, you mean?"

I sighed and said, "I can't talk about this right now."

"Then when, Lexi? What's going on?"

I turned away so I couldn't look at his face and see the raw emotion there.

"There's nothing going on," I said. "Everyone needs to stop asking me that."

He reached out and touched my bare arm. The touch was tender, loving, more than friendly. "Okay, I won't ask anymore," he said, his voice only a little more than a whisper. "Come. You look like you need some fresh air."

I couldn't argue with that. There was nothing I wanted more than to get out of this casino. The lights, the noise, the smells and the people made me want to scream. I couldn't think surrounded by all of the activity. And I needed to think.

I nodded my response. He led me out the front door of the casino, his hand just hovering, not quite touching on the small of my back.

Leo spoke to the concierge who hailed a limousine for us and I got in without a word. We didn't speak as the car inched through traffic down the strip, eventually turning off and pulling into a small parking lot.

I was numb, and my feet moved automatically as Leo led me into the restaurant. It was the complete opposite of anything I'd seen on the strip. Instead of the over the top flamboyance of everything else I'd seen in Vegas, this place was tiny and dark. There were no pretentious waiters strutting around, or artsy walls made out of water. Each table was decorated simply with a white table cloth, and a candle. Black and white photos of landscapes dotted the walls.

The maître de led us through the dining room and outside to a patio area where there was a table tucked in the corner. The fountain burbling nearby, managed to block out what little noise there was from the other tables. There were mini-lights strung through potted shrubs and vines that created an easy atmosphere, and I could feel myself starting to release some of the tension I'd felt earlier. Leo asked for a bottle of red wine and then we were alone.

"I hope it's okay that I brought you here," Leo said. "I don't want to cause you anymore trouble."

I shook my head. "Don't worry about Andrew."

"I can't help it, Lexi." He reached across the table and took my hand. I let him. "I know I shouldn't be with you like this. I know I shouldn't be thinking the things I'm thinking. If I were your husband, I would be insane if another man was feeling this way towards you."

But you're not my husband, I thought. "It's okay. Honestly it is."

"When I saw you in my hotel again," he said. "I thought I was dreaming."

"I can't believe you remembered me."

"I haven't stopped thinking about you." Leo's gaze was so intense I believed him.

"Excuse me," the waiter said, breaking our connection.

Leo released my hand and we waited while two glasses were poured and the waiter retreated leaving us alone again.

"Tell me, Lexi, are you happy?"

I took a sip of my wine, letting it warm my throat as it slid down. I couldn't answer him.

"I can see the answer. You don't have to say it," he said. "But if you tell me I'm wrong, that you're happy, I'll leave you alone."

"It's not that easy, Leo."

"It is. You deserve to be happy, you deserve everything. Does he make you happy?"

His eyes were full of question and something else, was it hope? I could've lied to him. Maybe I would have if I thought he'd believe me.

"No," I said.

He picked up his glass of water, leaving his wine untouched. "Then leave him."

"It's not that simple, Leo."

"It can be. Life is to short to be unhappy. You deserve so much-"

"We have a child," I said quietly. "His name is Ben."

I held my breath, waiting for his reaction. Would he remember how badly I'd wanted a family? What it meant to me? I couldn't read his expression. I waited.

Finally, Leo said, "A son. You have a family."

I nodded and tried to smile. "Yes."

"I remember," he said to my unspoken question. "That's why you were here, besides Nicole's birthday of course," he added.

"We were separated. Andrew didn't want children."

"I guess he changed his mind," Leo said with a tinge of regret.

"When I went home. He was there, waiting. He wanted to-"

Leo shook his head. "You don't have to explain. I get it. I was just a fling. A diversion while you were in Vegas. I get it, Lexi."

Hurt marred his features. I could see the struggle on his face, but he didn't look away from me. My heart felt like it was cracking in two; the ache in my chest was so real I had to fight back tears. I reached for him across the table and cupped his strong hands in mine. I held them tight feeling the heat from him.

"No," I said. I stared straight into his eyes, willing him to understand. "It wasn't like that and you know it. I can't explain it any more than you can. But do you really think I'd be sitting here with you right now if all you were six years ago, was a fling?"

He didn't answer and when he tried to look away, I squeezed his hands again.

"So that's why you stay? For your son."

I swallowed hard. "He's the only father Ben knows," I said. "I was trying to keep my family together, but..."

"What?"

"He's not the father I imagined for my son. That's the problem, he's not-"

I broke off when Leo turned away from me again.

"Leo?"

"Can I see him?" he asked. "Do you have a picture?"

I pulled my hands back and twisted them in my lap. "I do," I said cautiously. "Why do you want to see a picture?"

"I want to see this little man who has captivated your heart to such an extent that you would sacrifice your own happiness," Leo said with a sad smile. "He must be pretty special and...well, he's yours."

My heart hammered in my chest. I could feel the beads of sweat on my forehead and I dabbed at my face with the napkin. My hand was shaking and it slipped from my grasp back to my lap.

"Lexi, are you okay?"

I reached for my glass of wine and took a long swallow. When I replaced it to the table, the glass bobbled and sloshed onto the white linen cloth. I watched the stain spread, bleeding into the fabric.

"I'm fine," I said after a moment.

I reached for my clutch that was sitting on the table and in slow motion, withdrew the photo of Ben from its sleeve in my wallet. It was a school picture taken in Kindergarten a few months ago. He was smiling a wide, toothy smile. His dark eyes sparkled with mischief.

I slid the picture across the table where Leo picked it up and stared directly at his five-year-old self.

CHAPTER TWENTY-TWO

"How old is he?" Leo asked. His thumb slid over the photo absently.

"Five."

Leo looked away from the picture to meet my eyes. "Five," he repeated.

I nodded.

"When's his birthday?"

"November 24," I said.

I couldn't look away as he lowered his gaze, concentrating. Fine lines appeared on his temple as he did the math in his head. I knew the exact moment he realized the truth. He shot straight up in his seat, his dark eyes shone and they burned a hole straight into my heart when he looked at me.

"Ben," Leo said. "Ben is his name?"

"Yes." I squeezed my hands together under the table to keep them from shaking.

"You've always known." It wasn't a question.

"Not for sure, but...yes, I always knew," I admitted.

"Does he know?" With the emphasis on 'he', I knew he was talking about Andrew, but couldn't bring himself to say the name.

"No." I could feel the sting of hot tears as they started to build. I blinked hard. "Nobody knows. What was I going to say?"

Leo didn't answer; he just looked down at the picture again. A smile grew on his face illuminating his features. The silence built, but still he didn't speak.

"Leo, I'm sorry. By the time I realized, it was too late. There was nothing I could do. My child needed a father and Andrew, well...I didn't know what to do." The tears that threatened spilled onto my cheeks. "I was scared. And you didn't want me, you stood me up, left me waiting. I know I should have told you, found you somehow...but there didn't seem to be any point. There hasn't been a day that's gone by that I haven't thought about you. Every time I look at Ben, I see you. I think about you and wonder..."

I couldn't finish. Instead I gave myself over to sobbing. I couldn't look at him anymore. I closed my eyes and let myself cry. I didn't care who saw. I'd made such a mess of everything, it didn't matter anymore.

When I felt the heat of Leo's strong hands on my shoulder, and then his arms as they wrapped around me, I let myself fall into his embrace. He held me and rubbed my back but didn't say a word while I exhausted the pent up emotion. When I'd pulled myself together enough to look up, he handed me a napkin and I wiped my eyes. Leo stood from his crouch and pulled his chair around the table so we were sitting side by side.

"I can't imagine how you must have felt," he said when I had regained my composure.

"You're not mad?"

"I'm feeling a lot of things right now." He scrubbed his hand over his face. "But I don't think anger is one of them. I'm confused though."

"Why?"

"You said I didn't want you." He took my hand and held it so gently I thought I might start crying again. "Nothing could have been further from the truth, Lexi. I left you a message with my number but you never called."

"You didn't leave me a message."

"I did. With the same girl that you gave my phone to. I told...Dammit!" He dropped my hands and I had to stop myself from reaching for them. "I'm so stupid," he said and pushed up from his chair. "I left the note with Tamara," he said as he paced in front of the table. "How could I be so dumb? Of course she wouldn't have given it to you. Oh, God, Lexi. I'm so sorry. I couldn't meet you that day, the chance of a lifetime came up with work. I had to take it...I thought you would understand...I...I should've turned it down." He stopped pacing and sank back into the chair dropping his head into his hands.

"Leo." I reached out, touching his shoulder. He had wanted me. He'd tried. My stomach flipped and for a minute I was afraid I might be sick. It could have been different.

It should have been different.

As if he read my mind, Leo sat up and turned to me. "This shouldn't be happening. This...us...it should have-"

"I know," I whispered. "I know."

He pulled me into his arms and this time instead of letting him comfort me, his body shook with sobs of his own, our tears falling on each other's shoulders.

When I pulled back, seeing the tears in his eyes and on his cheeks created a physical ache in my chest for all he'd missed.

"I have a son," he said.

I didn't bother to wipe the tears that continued to stream down my cheeks. "You have a son."

***

I have a son.

I couldn't stop saying the words over and over in my head and out loud. It was exhilarating, and unbelievable. A son.

Lexi's son.

Thinking about the time we'd lost was making me crazy. Things should have been different. I was so stupid to think that Tamara would help me. But I didn't know then how self centered she could be. That wasn't until later, when she was my wife.

I couldn't change the past and get that time back. "Tell me everything," I said to Lexi. I needed to focus on the future, on this child I didn't know yet. If I didn't, the regret and anger would consume me. "Does he like sports? Is he smart? What's his favorite color? I want to know everything."

She laughed her sweet smile, but there was sadness in her eyes too. "I'll tell you everything I can and I'll show you pictures too."

"Do you have more with you?" I knew I sounded eager but dammit, I was.

She shook her head. "No, not with me. This is just my evening bag. I didn't expect..."

"To tell me." I finished for her, then asked, "Were you ever going to tell me about him, Lexi?"

It was the wrong question. Her smile faded and she looked as if she might cry again. For a split second I wanted to take back the question. But I needed to know. I deserved to know.

"Were you?" I prodded.

She shook her head. "I didn't think I'd ever see you again. I didn't see how. It's been almost six years and Andrew-"

"Don't say it." That man had my life, the woman I'd always loved and now, my son. I couldn't bear to hear her tell me that Andrew was Ben's father. "For now," I said and held her hand, "just tell me everything you can about Ben. I want to know it all."

A tentative smile returned to her face and she said, "Where should I begin?"

For the next hour, Lexi told me what Ben was like as a baby. How he started walking at ten months and refused to nap after his first birthday.

I nodded and smiled. He sounded just like the stories Grandma used to tell about me as a toddler. Getting into everything, never sitting still. When Lexi started telling me about Ben in preschool, and in his junior soccer league, I couldn't relate. I didn't have either experience.

"Does he play baseball?" I asked, interrupting her story of Ben's first goal.

She turned her head and raised an eyebrow.

"I've never played soccer," I explained. "To be honest, I've only ever watched a few games. Baseball was my sport. Has he tried it?"

"No. He's never tried it."

"We'll have to fix that," I said. "Maybe I can teach him how to throw a ball."

After the words left my mouth I could feel Lexi's hand tense. It was the question we'd both been avoiding. What would happen now? What part would I have in Ben's life? In Lexi's?

We sat in silence for a moment until she let go of my hand to take a sip of her water, the wine had been abandoned long ago. The unanswered questions burned in my mind.

A waiter walked by with a platter of steaming food. The aroma of rich cream sauces mingled with roasted garlic floated through the air and my stomach growled.

"You're hungry," Lexi said. She looked relived for a distraction.

"I didn't get a chance to eat earlier. It's been a crazy weekend. Should we order?"

Lexi's face took on a mischievous grin and her eyes flashed brighter. "Not here," she said. "You know where I want to go?"

I shook my head although I had an idea.

"Does that burger place still exist?"

"Our burger place?" I smiled. "Absolutely. Let's go."

***

Sitting across from Lexi, still in her bridesmaid dress, in the vinyl booth with two big baskets of oversized burgers and greasy fries in front of us, I couldn't wipe the smile off my face. I should've been upset, or angry, or, well, a million emotions besides deliriously happy, but I couldn't help it. I knew there were so many questions to ask her, so much we had to figure out still, but right then, at that moment, I was just happy in a way that I hadn't been for years.

"Why are you staring at me?" she asked. I wasn't aware I was.

"I'm not."

"You are. You've been holding that burger for so long

it may decide to make a break for it before you get a chance to eat it. Now cut it out."

"If I'm staring at you, it's because you're so beautiful and I can't help that."

She blushed and the flush in her cheeks reminded me of what she looked like laying in my arms after we'd made love.

"Stop it," she said and waved a french fry at me before taking a bite.

"I'll try." I took a mouthful of burger and chewed slowly. Making a point not to look in her direction, I turned to stare at the pictures on the walls instead. They hadn't changed in six years.

"Leo?"

I turned back to her. "I can look at you now?" I teased.

"Stop it," she said laughing, then her voice grew more serious. "Tell me about you. You know what I've been up to in the last few years with Ben. It's your turn. Tell me what your life has been like."

I swallowed hard. I couldn't tell her.

"I've been working," I said after a long sip of coke.

"Obviously. But what else? You must have left the hotel. Had a life. Done something."

"Nope." I took another large bite and busied myself chewing. I sent a silent prayer that she would drop it. She didn't know it, but she didn't want to push me for details. She didn't want to hear what I would say. But looking at her pretty face, hard with determination, I knew she wasn't going to drop it.

"Leo, what are you afraid of? Why won't you tell me?"

I took another sip of the coke and forced the burger down my throat. What am I afraid of? What a great question.

Only everything. I just found out about my son and if I tell her the truth about myself, she won't want me to be a part of his life. How could she? Would she even want me to be part of hers?

"Leo?"

I looked at her. Really looked at her. Her long blond hair had been released from its pins and was lying loose around her shoulders. But it was her ocean blue eyes, the same eyes that had haunted my dreams for the last six years that made me admit, "I'm terrified that once I tell you, you'll walk out of my life again."

CHAPTER TWENTY-THREE

I didn't want to make him false promises. I didn't want to tell him anything I wouldn't be able to stay true to. But looking at him across the table, touching him, sharing the knowledge of Ben with him, I wasn't lying when I said, "I'll never walk away from you again."

At that moment I couldn't imagine my life without Leo in it. But at the same time I had no idea what the future looked like for any of us. I had a child to think about and he already had a father, no matter how absent he was, Andrew was the only dad Ben knew. But he deserved to know his real father too, didn't he?

Before I could think about it further, Leo brought me out of my own thoughts and directly into his. "Okay," he said. "I'll tell you about my past, but please know that that's exactly what it is, the past. I'm not that man anymore."

A chill ran through me and I couldn't stop the shiver that I knew he saw. I swallowed. "Okay," I said. There was nothing he could tell me that would change my opinion of him.

"I'm not proud of my past," he said, "but after you left, it's strange, but things kind of fell apart for me. I think you'll understand if I tell you that even after knowing you for a few days, I knew I loved you."

I nodded. I understood all too well.

"The worst thing I ever did was not meet you in the lobby."

"But your career," I said. "I know how important that is to you. I remember you telling me about your dreams. I understand why you had to go."

He reached for my hand. Nothing felt more natural.

"That's just it. My career was always the most important thing in my life. To the point that I sacrificed love." He squeezed my hand before continuing. "And then, I almost threw it away. In fact, I think I did I everything I could to throw it away."

"What are you talking about?"

"It was a dark time in my life. I'm not proud of it, but I can't hide it. Especially from you. You need to know everything about me, even the bad stuff. It's part of who I am and I'm a different person now. But my past is part of me."

I felt the room starting to spin and I was glad for Leo's hold on me. What was he going to say? did I really want to hear it?

"Lexi, please, look at me."

"Tell me."

"I was married," he started. "To Tamara. The woman-"

"At the front desk." I didn't have to ask. I knew. I was shaking, vibrating, but I didn't realize it until Leo's grip on my hands loosened and his thumb started making slow circles on my skin, calming me.

"I think I always knew she was interested in me, but I never thought of her that way. Until, well, it was after you left. She said you dropped the phone off and didn't want to take the note. She said you laughed and played it like we were just a Vegas fling."

"But you knew-"

"I thought I knew. I should've known. I didn't trust in us, that's something I have to live with. And when I needed someone to turn to...well, Tamara was there. I guess I mistook lust for love. The whole relationship was a mistake from the beginning and we both knew it."

"What did she look like?"

He seemed stunned by the question. "What? Why?"

I couldn't explain it but I had to know. I tried to remember the girl at the desk that day, but I couldn't. As much as I tried, I couldn't conjure her image in my head and for whatever reason, I needed to know. The ball of jealousy burned in the pit of my stomach. "Please, just tell me."

He shook his head but said, "She's petite. Dark hair, green eyes."

The opposite of me.

"Nothing like you," Leo said. "I think that's why I turned to her at first. But then it became the problem. She wasn't you."

I forgot that I was supposed to be upset with him and found myself leaning across the table.

"She had me convinced that you'd blown me off. That you wanted nothing to do with me. But you weren't easy to get over, Lexi. That was the whole problem. We started dating, if you could call it that, right away. But I couldn't stop thinking about you. Even when she asked me to get married, it was you I really wanted."

"She asked you?"

He nodded. "I wasn't thinking about marriage at all. Looking back, I don't even think I loved her. It was all wrong."

"But you got married anyway," I said.

"We did. At a little chapel off the strip. Just us, no

witnesses. We'd only been together about a month."

Right around the time I discovered I was pregnant.

"It was bad from the start," he continued. "We fought all the time. Badly. I hated who I was with her. I don't know why I expected marriage to be any different."

While he spoke, Leo was looking at me, but I don't think he saw me. His eyes had a faraway look as if he was picturing his wife. "She was wild," he said. "She loved the night life of Vegas and the constant party. And sure, it was fun for awhile. We'd go out after work, even if it was two in the morning. And we'd drink, a lot."

I flinched at the thought of this Leo I didn't know, this other Leo. His grip tightened on my hand and his eyes came back into focus on mine.

"Please," he said, his voice pleading.

When I nodded, he continued. "I only drank when we were out. It wasn't a problem for me then, but it was a problem for Tamara. And there was more than just alcohol."

"Drugs?"

He nodded.

"Did you?"

He nodded again. "Like I said, I'm not proud of who I was. I always said I'd never be like my mother, but there I was, doing my best to be just like her."

"No."

"There was cocaine," he said as if he hadn't heard me. "I resisted it at first, and tried to keep Tamara away from it too. But, after a few drinks...anyway, partying started to take over my life too. There were times I'd come into work without having slept. I don't know how I managed it, but I did."

"And Tamara?"

"Things were different with her. I don't know if I was too drunk or high, but I didn't see the real her. Even if I had wanted to, I don't know if I would have. Our schedules didn't always merge and on nights that I was working, she'd go out anyway. We'd been married about a year when I realized she wasn't always alone on those nights."

"She cheated on you?"

Leo laughed but the sound was hard and cold. "If you could call it that," he said. "Tamara's definition of marriage was much looser than mine. There were a lot of men."

"Did you leave her?"

"No," Leo said and shook his head. "I don't know if you remember me telling you, but I never knew my dad."

"I remember."

"I grew up with a strange sense of family, and all I ever wanted was what I never had when I was little. In my head, marriage was supposed to be forever."

"But you didn't love her."

"No, but....I was married."

"So you tried," I said. I could picture a younger Leo trying desperately to hang on to a marriage that never really was, and my heart hurt for him.

"I tried. In my own messed up way. For awhile we even stopped partying so much. At least, I did."

"So what happened?"

"As I'm sure you can guess, drinking on the job, let alone using, is completely forbidden. And as a general rule, I tried not to party at the casino at all. I thought it was best to completely separate the two. Despite everything, my career was still important to me."

He fell silent for a minute. "That's why I don't understand why I did what I did. Looking back, it didn't seem like a big deal at the time. Tamara wasn't working that night. In fact, one of the blackjack dealers was getting married, so there was a huge party with a lot of the staff at the hotel. And by luck of the draw, I was in charge of the event. Everything started out great at first, all the details I'd arranged went off without a hitch. And all our friends were there. People Tamara and I regularly went out and partied with. Everyone was having a great time. It was definitely one of my finer events and when I was offered a bit of coke, I didn't think it would hurt. After all, these were my friends.

"Just when I thought everything was going well, I noticed Tamara on the dance floor. She was surrounded by men and there was no doubt that she was loving the attention. I wasn't enjoying it as much, so when she came to get another drink, I took her aside and confronted her. Of course there was a scene. She yelled at me and said I was boring and no fun anymore. She told me that if I wanted to keep her I would need to prove it to her. Then she downed a shot and went straight back to the dance floor and into the arms of some guy. Right in front of me."

"Leo, that's awful."

"Not as awful as what I did."

"Tell me."

He wouldn't look at me as he said, "I went to the bar and took three shots. Tequila. Then I went out on that dance floor and proceeded to show my wife and the rest of the crowd just how much damn fun I could be. It worked, at least for Tamara, but my boss didn't think it was so great that I drank almost an entire bottle of the customer's booze, and proceeded to get so smashed that I ended up crashing in one the suites with ten of my closest friends. But not before we completely trashed it."

"Oh my goodness, Leo. Really?"

"The worst part is, I don't remember a thing after doing the shots."

He looked at me then and I could see the worry lines

etched in his face. "I'm not proud of it, Lexi."

"Tell me what happened next."

"I was fired and Tamara left me."

"She, left *you*?"

"She didn't want to be associated with me. She was afraid she would lose her job too. I let her go. I realized that I didn't like who I was with her. Who I had already become. I started going to meetings right after and I haven't used since."

"That's good. Really good." It was turn to squeeze his hand but he wouldn't look at me.

"Three weeks later," he said, "they offered me my job back on the condition that I pay for the damages, go on probation for six months and of course, change hotels. I jumped at the chance. The divorce was finalized and I haven't looked back."

"And Tamara?" I had to know.

Leo shrugged. "Last I heard she was still a party girl. She doesn't work for us anymore. The rumor was that she got caught stealing, but I don't know. I don't care. That's a chapter of my life I'm not very proud of, and I'm not that man anymore."

"It doesn't sound like you."

"It wasn't me," he said. "It was me trying to forget who I really was, and I'll never make that mistake again."

Releasing his hands, I leaned over the small table and brushed at a piece of hair that had fallen over his forehead. "Good," I said and let my fingers linger on his skin. "Because I like who you really are and I wouldn't want you to change for anything."

Leo took his free hand and pressed my palm against his cheek, turned and placed a gentle kiss against my wrist that felt scandalous and perfect all at the same time. "So, now that you know..."

I shook my head. "It doesn't matter one bit."

He leaned forward and I closed my eyes. I knew what was coming and every fibre in my body yearned for the feel of his lips on mine. For the taste of him. The second his mouth made contact with mine, a shock flew through me landing in my core. I opened my mouth, ready for more. His hand reached out to my cheek and his thumb stroked gentle circles on my cheek while his lips worked gentle kisses on mine.

It felt perfect, it felt right, it felt like, Leo. With one kiss, everything I'd been missing for six years became clear. It was sweet, there was no pressure behind it, but I couldn't deny the intensity there.

"Leo," I said when we finally broke apart. "I..."

I couldn't finish the sentence. There were too many unknowns.

"Please don't say that you shouldn't have done that," he said. "Because if you felt even a fraction of what I just felt..." His thumb resumed the slow circles on my cheek and for some reason, the sensation made me want to cry. "Lexi, I am fully and completely in love with you. I always have been. So please, don't tell me that you shouldn't have kissed me. I don't know if I could bear to hear it."

"But," I said fighting back tears, "Andrew. I can't do this to him."

"Do you love him?" Leo whispered. "Like I've always loved you? The way I think you love me?"

"No," I whispered through a veil of tears. "No."

Leo drew me forward and met my lips again. This time both his hands held my head, and the intensity behind his kiss was clear. When he pulled back, he used his fingers to wipe my tears and said, "Then what, my dear, are we going to do, because I can't let you go again. I won't."

CHAPTER TWENTY-FOUR

I left Leo in the lobby. I knew what I needed to do. What I'd needed to do for years.

It was time. We parted with a hug, but as much as I wanted to, I couldn't kiss him again. Not until I spoke to Andrew. It wasn't fair. And despite everything between us, Andrew wasn't a bad man. He loved me, and he didn't deserve this.

I took one more look at Leo before the elevator doors closed. I didn't bother memorizing him; this wouldn't be the last time I'd see him. I knew that now. I'd call him when I was done talking to Andrew. I just didn't know when that would be. For all I knew, Andrew was still wandering around the casino or gambling somewhere.

It was two in the morning by the time I slid the key card in the lock of our room, but time didn't mean anything in Vegas.

I opened the door slowly, afraid to find him up waiting, more afraid that he wouldn't be. But the room wasn't dark as I'd expected. The bedside lamp burned and illuminated Andrew, and our suitcases which were packed and sitting on the bed. He jumped up when he saw me.

"Where have you been?" he asked. He didn't sound angry and he looked exhausted. No longer wearing his wedding clothes, he had changed into jeans and a polo shirt, but they were rumpled, like he'd slept in them. His eyes were red with dark circles under them. Had he been crying? Maybe he already knew.

"I'm sorry, Andrew. I-""

"Lexi, we have to talk," he said and took my arm. His touch was gentle as he guided me to the bed.

"I know we do. I have so much I need to-"

"You didn't take your cell phone with you," he said as if he hadn't heard me at all. "I didn't know how to get in touch with you and I've been waiting, hoping you would get back in time, we have to go now or we'll be late." He spoke fast, and his voice was thick, with emotion or exhaustion. It took me a moment to register what he was saying.

"Go where? Be late for what?"

Andrew stopped and looked me in the eye. Despite the obvious sleep deprivation, his eyes were clear, he hadn't been drinking. "Lexi, we have to go home," he said much slower.

I looked around the room for the first time, at our bags, our coats lying on top of them. Everything was packed.

What was happening? Panic began to seep through me, causing the hairs on the back of my neck to stand up. "Andrew, what's wrong? Is Ben okay?"

He scrubbed a hand across his face and his eyes glistened with unshed tears but he didn't answer right away.

Andrew didn't cry. Ever.

I hopped off the bed and yanked his hand away from his face.

"Andrew! Tell me," I yelled. "Tell me my baby is

okay."

***

Waiting wasn't easy. I felt that part of me, the most important part, the part that remembered how to breathe, had gone with her. I was empty.

It had been four hours since Lexi left. I knew she wasn't gone forever. I knew it was only four hours. Four hours where I should have been sleeping, resting for the busy work day ahead. But I couldn't sleep. How could I when I knew she was upstairs with her husband? When I knew she was telling him about us? Telling him the truth. In only a few hours my life would change.

Of course I couldn't' sleep. Instead I was in my office, mindlessly moving papers around and staring at the details of a jewelry convention for next weekend. I hadn't read a word. I glanced at my Blackberry and checked for the hundredth time that it was on and receiving messages. There were messages.

None from Lexi.

What was taking so long? I should've heard something by now. Anything.

Frustrated, I pushed away from my desk and looked for something to take my mind off the phone that wasn't ringing.

Moving the mouse, my computer screen came to life. I flicked through some emails but didn't read anything. Not really.

"Focus," I said.

"Talking to yourself, boss?" Roberta appeared in the doorway looking perfectly put together as always. She probably slept.

"What are you doing here in the middle of the night? Go home. You don't have to work all the time."

She laughed. "It's six o'clock, Leo. I have a million things to do today." She walked into my office and dropped a paper in front of me.

"What's this?"

"The ad for a new event planner," she said. "You told me you would start looking right away but you seem a little preoccupied, so I thought I'd help you out a little bit. All you have to do is approve it and it'll be online by noon."

My eyes flicked down to the paper then back up at her. "I'm sure it's fine. You know as well as I do what we need."

Roberta took the paper and tucked it into her portfolio.

"Is there anything else?" I asked when she didn't move away.

"Yes, there is," she said. "You look like shit. Are you okay?"

"I'm fine."

"Have you slept?"

"Not lately."

"Leo, go home."

"No can do, Roberta." I clicked my computer off, aware that I hadn't even looked at it, and stood. "I have things to do."

"Would those things involve a certain woman?"

Roberta rarely mentioned my personal life, and I never inquired about hers. It was an unspoken rule we had and an arrangement that worked well. I raised an eyebrow at her and said, "I think you know that's none of your business." I grabbed my Blackberry off my desk as I stood. "I have a meeting with the banquet coordinator in an hour about the conference this weekend."

"I can handle it," Roberta said. "You need some rest and if you don't mind-"

"I do mind."

"It's just that, if this is about that woman, you should know-"

"Roberta," I warned, "this isn't your business. Drop it."

"It's just, you should kn-"

"Enough," I barked at her and before she could say another word, I pushed past her and left her standing in my office.

***

I should've let Roberta take the meeting. It took forever. The representative for the jewelry group couldn't decide between cold or hot finger foods for cocktail hour and despite both the head of catering and myself urging her to choose a selection of both, she waffled for over an hour before finally selecting cold appetizers. Then details about the rest of the food needed to be worked out and it was a quarter to nine by the time I escaped the meeting room.

As soon as I was on the casino floor I powered up my phone and checked messages. Lexi was probably wondering where I was. There were four messages. All from Roberta. Lexi hadn't called.

Something was wrong. It couldn't possibly take so long to tell someone their marriage was over. Unless...no...I wouldn't go there.

My stomach churned and for a moment I thought I was going to be sick. What could've happened? Andrew didn't seem like the violent type, but no one could predict what a man would do faced with the news Lexi was going to deliver. I should have insisted on going with her. She should never have gone alone.

My first instinct was to phone her room but I stopped short of dialing the number. If her husband answered what would I say. And if I went upstairs myself...no. There were other ways to handle this.

I dodged and swerved through the black jack tables and approached the front desk.

"Nancy," I said to the concierge on duty. "I need you to send housekeeping to a guest room please."

"Hi, Leo," she said and immediately turned to her computer screen. "What's the room?"

"2634."

She dutifully tapped away on the keyboard before turning to me. "That room is vacant, Leo."

A chill ran down my spine. "No, they aren't due to check out until tomorrow. Look again."

Nancy turned back to the computer. "Sorry, Leo. It seems they checked out this morning."

"No." I put my hands to my face and pushed my thumbs into my eye sockets in an effort to relive the building pressure.

She wouldn't have left. Something must be wrong. She wouldn't leave again. She wouldn't.

"Leo? Do you need me to call someone? You don't look good. Are you feeling okay?"

"I'm fine," I said and pulled my hands away from my face, smoothing my hair. I tried my best to hide my rapidly increasing panic. "Thanks, Nancy."

I left her and crossed the tiled floor. The sounds of the busy lobby were muffled as if I were underwater. Bruce, the desk manager, was busy checking customers into their rooms. I waited as patiently as I could while he handed a couple their keys and gave them a quick explanation on how to get to the proper elevator bank. As soon as they turned to leave I grabbed Bruce's sleeve.

"Were you working this morning?"

"Hey," he said and removed his arm from my grip. "Nice to see you too, Leo and yes actually I worked the graveyard shift, I'm just covering for Susan this morning, she's at a doc-"

"Sure, whatever," I said trying to keep my voice level. "Did you happen to notice a couple checking out a day early?"

Bruce raised a bushy eyebrow.

"It's important," I said trying to use a professional voice. "They were at a wedding I hosted last night and I think the woman may be in some kind of trouble."

Bruce narrowed his eyes, but he sighed and said, "What room were they in?"

"2634. Titan."

He nodded. "I remember them. They checked out in the middle of the night."

"When?"

"Must have been almost four in the morning. He said they had a flight to catch."

"Did he say anything else? Did you see his wife?"

"What's this about?"

"Did you see the woman?" I yelled.

"No," Bruce answered tightly. "I didn't see her."

I turned and walked past the other desk clerks who had all stopped what they were doing to stare at me. Weaving through the guests who were waiting to leave for tours in the lobby, I crossed the marble floor, and pushed my way into the men's bathroom where I found a vacant stall and promptly threw up the contents of my stomach.

When I was finished, I let the water in the sink run cold before splashing it on my face. It wasn't until my skin was sufficiently numb, that I looked up at my reflection.

Roberta was right, I looked like shit. I doused my face again letting the cold water drip off my skin where it soaked the front of me. I needed a fresh shirt. I hadn't changed since being with Lexi last night.

Was it really only hours ago that I tasted her lips, felt her body in my arms.

"She's gone," I said to my reflection.

"Brutal, man, lost love in Vegas is the worst," a man said coming out of a stall. He stood at the sink next to me. He reeked of cigarette smoke and stale alcohol. The stench of him made my stomach flip again. "Happens all the time, buddy. It's just that kinda town."

I turned back to the mirror.

"It's just that kind of town," I repeated to myself.

"Like I said, happens all the time. By the look of ya, she was probably somethin' special, huh? Hurts more when they're special."

"She is very special," I said. I turned off the water and faced him. "It's just, I didn't think she'd leave again."

"Again? Man, she left ya before? You got it bad," he said and picked something out of his teeth with a grubby fingernail. "Ya want my advice?"

I don't know why, but for some reason I did. I nodded.

"Go get her." The man smoothed his sparse locks across his bald forehead.

I stared at him.

"You thought I was gonna say something else, didn't ya?"

I nodded dumbly.

"Normally I would," he said. "There are millions of broads in this town and I don't see the point in chasing just one. But you... you look different." He smiled a grey, nicotine stained grin. "Ya got anything else to lose?"

"No." I shook my head. "I don't have anything to lose."

"Then what are you doing yakking at me? Go."

CHAPTER TWENTY-FIVE

I hesitated outside the door I'd been directed to by the nurse. She'd looked at me with a mixture of pity and sympathy. It wasn't a good combination. She might as well have told me how sorry she was, or to prepare myself for the worst.

I put my hand on the smooth, cool handle and pushed down. With a click, the door opened and I was in the room. As soon as I walked in, I wanted to turn around and run. I probably should have spent some time thinking about what I'd see when I got here or prepared myself in some way. But Andrew had given me a sleeping pill on the flight home so I could rest. When I'd woken up right as the plane touched down, I was angry at him for slipping me the pill. But in hindsight, I had needed the rest. It was going to be a long day. I had slept, but I had not prepared myself.

Not for this.

The monitors, tubes and wires. Tears sprang to my eyes but I blinked them back. He couldn't see me like this. Not now.

"Lexi," Uncle Ray croaked. His voice just above a whisper. "It's okay. Come here."

I left the sanctuary of the doorway and walked to his bedside. He looked so small. Uncle Ray always seemed to fill a room, but hooked up to the life saving machines, he seemed to have shrunk. I took his hand. His skin was paper thin, a washed out grey and it felt like it would dissolve with my touch. How could things change so much in three days? How was it even possible?

"Uncle Ray," I said. "What...how...I don't understand."

"It's okay. My old ticker just decided it wanted a little break is all."

"Did Ben see? Was he there?"

"Such a brave boy. He called 911," he said and managed a smile. "He's a good kid."

My thoughts flashed to Ben who'd rushed to give me a hug as soon as he'd seen me walk through the hospital doors. He'd been waiting with Sara Beth. They were watching for us in the lobby. I'd held on to him, inhaling his little boy scent, feeling his warmth. I didn't want to let him go, but when Sara Beth pulled me away, I watched as he went next to Andrew, slower this time. But Andrew scooped him up and squeezed him tight before piggy-backing him to the cafeteria for hot chocolate. All I'd ever wanted was for Andrew to be that kind of dad. But not like this. Watching them together, walking away, my heart splintered a little more if it was even possible. But I couldn't dwell on it. There was no time. Sara Beth hadn't wasted any time filling me in on the details of Uncle Ray's heart attack. It wasn't good. As if any heart attack could be good. But this was bad and I said as much to him now.

"It's not good, Uncle Ray. Sara Beth told me you need surgery."

He nodded.

"A quadruple bypass," I said and the tears I'd been fighting began to fall. "That's big. Really big."

"It's okay, Lexi." He tried to squeeze my hand but the result was pathetic.

"Is it?"

"Yes. It's going to take a lot more than a little blockage to get rid of me. Don't worry, I'm going to be here for a long time to come. The doctors tell me it's just a matter of a little surgery. It's routine. They'll clear up my tubes and I'll be good as new."

I looked at him sideways and tried to wipe my tears.

"I will," he said. "And maybe now you'll actually be able to convince me to eat some of that rabbit food you're always trying to push on me."

"It's lettuce, Uncle Ray." Despite myself, I smiled.

"That's what I want to see," he said. "No more tears now. I don't want to talk about this anymore. It's boring and there's nothing to say." He tried to wave his hand but the effort seemed to exhaust him. "Tell me about Vegas and the wedding. I want to live vicariously through you."

Dutifully, I obeyed. I filled him in on the details of Nicole's meltdown before the ceremony and how her mother was able to attend via the internet. He smiled when I told him about the battle with Nicole's hair. But he fell asleep before I could tell him the rest.

I didn't let go of his hand. I know it was stupid, but I had the strangest feeling that he could draw energy from my body if only I could stay connected to him.

I didn't know if I should tell Uncle Ray about Leo. I'd always told him everything but what would he say if he knew the truth? I watched the lines on the monitor, the rhythm of his heart. If I lost him I'd be alone. Except for Ben of course. And Leo? But what about Andrew?

My thoughts flashed back to what I'd been about to do the night before, when I went back to the hotel room. I couldn't tell him now, not with everything else going on. But what about Leo? I never said goodbye. He was probably still waiting for me to call him. Oh, God he probably thought I'd left again. I needed to talk to him.

I didn't even have to close my eyes to feel his lips against mine. To remember the way his arms felt wrapped around me. No, my body didn't need any prompting to recall the way Leo made me feel. I needed to call him, now.

"Mrs. Titan?" A voice startled me from my thoughts and I turned toward the nurse standing in the doorway.

"That's me."

"I don't want to wake him," the nurse whispered. "Can I borrow you for a moment?"

I nodded and slipped my hand out from Uncle Ray's. I stood and kissed him on the cheek before joining the nurse in the hall.

"It's nice to meet you, Mrs. Titan. My name is Patricia. I've been looking after your uncle."

"Call me Lexi." The nurse, Patricia, appeared to be in her late forties or early fifties. She was kindly looking, like she should be wearing an apron over her round middle and baking cookies instead of caring for patients. I liked her immediately.

"Lexi." Her smile was warm. "Have you spoken with the doctor yet?"

I shook my head.

"They're very busy, so you may not see Dr. Wallace for awhile. But I can answer any questions you might have. Ray is stable now, but we'll need to monitor him closely until surgery."

"When will that be?" I twisted my hands together.

"Hopefully tomorrow."

"That soon?"

"He has a pretty severe blockage," Patricia said. "The longer we wait, the higher the risk will be."

I swallowed hard. "The risk for surgery?"

"No, the surgery itself is not without risks, but generally it's fairly routine. The real risk is that Ray will have another heart attack before we can operate. His heart has been weakened. I'm sure you can see the change in him." I nodded and she continued, "If he were to suffer another heart attack, his heart may not be able to withstand it."

"You mean?"

"Let's not think about that right now," she said and patted my hand. "Why don't you go sit with him for a bit. I'll be in to check his vitals soon and we can talk more when he's awake."

It was all so much to absorb. Like a robot I returned to Uncle Ray's side and picked up his hand.

"You're going to be fine," I said, my voice barely more than a whisper. Tears blurred my vision and burned my eyes, but I didn't bother to wipe them away. "You can't leave me, Uncle Ray. You can't."

***

I used the staff showers to clean myself up and changed into the spare set of clothes I kept in my office. I didn't have a razor, but I felt better at least. The water helped revive me and clear my head a little bit. When I entered the lobby again I didn't feel quite so out of control anymore.

Pulling out my Blackberry, I tried to call Lexi again but it went straight to voicemail. I didn't bother leaving another message. I wanted her, no, needed her to call me back.

"Leo!"

I turned to see Nicole waving from across the lobby. She looked beautiful. Just like a woman should the day after her wedding. I tried my best to put a smile on my face and crossed the floor to her.

"Mrs. Stewart," I said and accepted her hug. "How are you this morning?"

She giggled. "It's going to take a while to get used to being called that."

"Where is your new husband?" I asked.

"He's checking out," she said. "I'm glad I saw you, Leo. I wanted to thank you for everything yesterday. It was a beautiful day and having my mom there, even through the computer, it was special. Thank you."

"Well, you are definitely welcome, but it was Lexi," I tried not to let my voice change when I said her name, "who had the idea for your mom." Nicole's smile turned down at the corners. She'd noticed my reaction. Hoping to avoid the subject, I asked, "Why are you checking out? I thought you were booked in for one more day."

Nicole shifted her purse on her shoulder and touched my arm. "You didn't hear?"

I stood tall and pretended I didn't notice her pity. "If you're referring to Lexi checking out, then yes. I heard."

Nicole tilted her head and narrowed her eye. "You do know why they left, don't you?"

The idea of anyone, even Lexi's best friend, knowing she had broken my heart again was more than I could handle at the moment.

"It's really none of my business what Lexi does, is it?" I crossed my arms in front of my chest causing Nicole's hand to fall.

She stared at me for a moment and then, as if a fire had sparked to life inside her. She glanced from side to side before grabbing my arm. Leaving her bags on the floor, she pulled me over to a bench with surprising strength and pushed me down on the hard leather. She stood over me, her red hair flashed against the lights and her eyes pinned me to the spot. "Drop the tough guy act," she hissed. "That crap, might work with someone else, but I'm not falling for it. Do you think I'm stupid, or just blind?"

I didn't answer her. I was a still a little stunned to be handled so forcibly by this petite woman.

"Well?" she demanded.

"Neither," I managed.

"Lexi is my best friend and I know everything there is to know about her, but that doesn't mean that she doesn't try to keep secrets from me."

"What do you mean?"

"Leo," Nicole said. Her stance softened and she didn't look quite so much like she was going to hit me. "She doesn't have to tell me for me to know what you mean to her."

I tried to wrap my head around that convoluted sentence. "Come again?"

"Leo, you're special to Lexi. You always have been."

Despite myself, my heart soared like a grade school kid rewarded by his first crush. "What do you mean? Special?"

Nicole plopped her tiny frame next to me on the bench and I twisted to look at her.

"Look," she said. "I blame myself that she went back to Andrew all those years ago."

Whatever I was expecting her to say, it hadn't been that. "Pardon me? You what?"

"That time, after she met you," Nicole said waving her hands in the air. "She tried to tell me about your special connection or whatever."

"No, not whatever," I interrupted. "What did she say exactly?"

"I don't remember her exact words, it was years ago." Nicole shot me a look before continuing. "But basically, she liked you. A lot."

I smiled. I couldn't help it.

"But I told her it was pointless. Just a fling, that relationships didn't happen in Vegas," she said.

My smile fell and my stomach twisted as I remembered hearing those exact words myself. "You told her that?"

"Well, come on, Leo," she spoke quickly. "You have to admit, Vegas isn't really the place to meet your soul mate, right? I mean, I was just trying to be a good friend."

"But, I...Lexi..."

"I know," Nicole said. Her voice was soft and she put her hand on my arm. When I looked up I could see the hurt in her own eyes. "I know that now. Hell, I think I knew it then. But then Andrew was there, and he wasn't awful, he just...and then when Ben was born..."

My thoughts fled to my unseen child.

"I knew," she said.

"You knew what?"

"I'm not blind, Leo. I've always known."

"That Ben is my son," I whispered.

"He's the image of you."

I couldn't help it, I smiled. "I've only seen the one picture." I pulled the photo out of my pocket and showed her. "Lexi told me last night. Did you ever talk to her about it?"

She shook her head. "No. It was one of those things," she said. "Lexi never brought it up and to be honest, I think it took her a long time before she admitted it to herself. She tried so hard to create the perfect family for Ben."

I looked at my son, and a longing to meet him filled me. I tore myself away from the picture. "What do you mean?"

"Leo, you have to understand something about Lexi. She's not the type of woman to have a one night stand."

"I know."

"Do you? I mean, I'm not trying to pretend that I understand what kind of relationship you two had or have, or whatever, but do you really know her? Do you have any idea how totally unusual that was for her? Lexi isn't the type of person to do that, and it affected her. A lot. I thought she might even leave Andrew again, but then she found out she was pregnant."

"She still could have left."

"No, she couldn't. You know that."

I nodded. I did know. Lexi would have done what she thought was right. She sacrificed everything to give my son a family. "Does he know?" I asked.

"Andrew?" Nicole shook her head. "Not that I know of. But he's never been the most attentive father. He said he'd have children, but he never wanted them. That's more than obvious."

"But, he never guessed? I mean, Ben, he looks..."

"Nothing like him?" She laughed. "Ben doesn't look anything like either of them. Except for-"

"His smile. He has his mother's smile." I ran my thumb across the photo again.

"Yes, he has her smile." She rested her hand on my arm again. "Leo, you being here after all these years, I have to think that it's some kind of sign. Clearly you were meant to be part of Lexi's life."

"It doesn't really matter, does it?"

"What are you talking about?"

"She left again." The words came out bitter, and I wanted to take them back. Nicole didn't deserve my anger, but I couldn't stop. "She went to tell Andrew the truth, and she never came back. She left with him and didn't even call to tell me her choice."

I looked down and it's a good thing I did because I didn't see Nicole as she wound up and punched me in the shoulder.

"Ow! What was that for?" I rubbed the spot she hit. She was remarkably strong for such a small person.

"For being an ass," she said. "Lexi's uncle had a heart attack, Leo. That's why they checked out. Andrew was able to get their flights changed so she could be with him. He practically raised her and he's in the hospital. She's beside herself."

"What?" Of all the scenarios that had played out in my head over the last few hours, that had not been one of them. "Is he going to be okay?"

"We don't know." Nicole looked like she might cry too. She glanced away and waved. I turned to see Ryan approaching, lugging the bags behind him.

"Hey, Leo," Ryan said when he got close enough. "Ready?" he asked Nicole.

She rose, leaving me sitting alone on the bench. "I'm ready," she said to Ryan. "Can you grab a taxi? I'll be right there." Nicole kissed her husband on his cheek.

"Sure," he said and then turned to me. "Thanks for everything, man."

I nodded but couldn't say anything. I didn't take the hand he extended and I only vaguely noticed him walk away. It was a few moments before I realized Nicole was still standing in front of me. I raised my head to look at her.

"Leo," she said. "I don't know what you're going to do, but can I tell you one thing?"

I nodded.

"Lexi needs you. She's unhappy. Andrew doesn't make her happy."

My heart leaped in my chest.

"Uncle Ray's been telling her for years that life's too short to spend with someone that doesn't give her everything she needs. And I think I'm just starting to realized how much she gave up."

"Do you think she loves me?" I muttered.

"I've seen the way she looks at you even when she thinks no one is watching. And in all the time I've known Lexi, I've never seen her look at anyone else that way. Ever." Nicole's words hung between us and she added, "Besides, you are the father of her child. Don't forget that." She bent down and kissed my forehead. "I'll see you soon." And she was gone.

I stared after her, replaying her words in my head. When she vanished from my sight, I looked down at the picture I still clutched in my hand.

"You're the father of her child. Don't forget that."

As if I could.

CHAPTER TWENTY-SIX

I looked around the small room, bursting with life. It was totally at odds with the situation we were in. The monitors, wires and alarms hooked up to Uncle Ray seemed to fade into the background as my small family took center stage. Ben was only marginally more restrained than usual as he bounced up and down on the floor peppering us with questions.

"They're gonna cut you open, Papa? For real?"

"For real, buddy," Uncle Ray said. The bed was propped up so was sitting up in a reclining position. His skin was still washed out and grey in a way that reminded me of cold winter day, not of the ruddy faced man I knew. But he was enjoying Ben's questions and twice had told me to leave him alone when I'd tried to get my son to sit down. I didn't take my eyes off him though, I was terrified with all his bouncing, he would trip over a cord or fall on the bed and hurt Uncle Ray.

Sara Beth sat in a chair by the window. She was working on a project from her ever present knitting bag. The needles clacked as they worked, but she wasn't paying attention to her work. Her eyes were fixed on Uncle Ray; the worry in them evident.

In all the three years that Sara Beth had been part of our lives, I'd never known her to look tired or lacking in energy in any way. She was always dressed in a track suit or some other clothing that would allow her to stay active and keep moving. Even at sixty, she prided herself on running 5-10 kilometres a day. I'd taken her up on her invitation to join her for a run only once. Keeping up with her pace left me gasping for breath and clutching my chest, but she'd never left me behind. Her supportive words of encouragement kept me from quitting.

Sara Beth was the most positive person I knew, and not in that fake, syrupy way. She had a genuine kindness about her, and I don't think I'd ever heard her utter a negative word. When I watched her, sitting in the corner of Uncle Ray's room, she didn't say a word, but I could see that she was just as terrified as I was.

"Tell me how they're gonna do it," Ben pleaded and hopped closer to the bed knocking the table on his way.

Andrew caught the dinner tray before it crashed to the floor. It was still full of food, if you could call what they were allowing Uncle Ray to eat, food. He put the tray out of harm's way on the counter on the other side of the room and said, "Ben, for god's sake-"

I shot him a look and he changed tracks. "Come here, Ben," Andrew said, his voice much softer. Ben did as he was told and walked over to where his...where Andrew sat. Much to my surprise, and probably Ben's too, Andrew scooped him up and sat with him on his lap close to the bed so he could see Uncle Ray without jumping up. Ben let Andrew hold him. For the moment he was content to sit still.

Watching them together, the way I'd always wanted them to be, I wanted to cry. Or scream. Why now?

I couldn't deal with it. I couldn't deal with anything. I needed to get out of there. The walls of the room seemed to grow even closer if that was even possible in the tiny space. I turned in a circle, trying to think of a reason to leave.

"Mrs. Titan? Lexi?" Patricia, the nurse, poked her head in the room.

"Yes?"

"You have a phone call."

"A phone call? Where?" I glanced at the crowded table next to Uncle Ray's bed. It was covered in tissues, magazines and flowers, but no phone.

"At the nurses station," Patricia said. "We don't usually accept personal calls, but the gentleman insisted it was important."

Leo.

I turned around to look at Ben who was deep in discussion with Uncle Ray about one of his monitors. Andrew however was watching me intently, his eyes full of questions I couldn't answer.

Not now.

I turned again and followed Patricia out of the room.

***

I'd almost given up hope when Lexi's voice came on the line.

"Leo?"

She knew.

"Of course," I said. "How are you? Is your uncle...is he okay?"

"He's okay right now. But he needs surgery." I could hear the tremble in her voice and I longed to hold her, to be there to comfort her. "Leo, I'm sorry I le-"

"No. You have nothing to be sorry about. You need to take care of this."

"I meant to call, there just never seemed to be a good time. And I can't have my cell phone on here. It's just...something always came up and..."

She started to cry. I could hear her sniff and swallow as she tried to control herself.

"Lexi, I'm coming." I hadn't planned it, but as soon as I said it, I realized I need to be with her.

"I don't think that's a good idea right now."

I swallowed hard. I couldn't push her. She had too much to worry about. "I want to be there for you. I want to support you through this. You shouldn't be alone."

"I'm not alone."

Jealousy flared through me. "Of course," I said, "you have Andrew."

"Leo, don't. Please. Don't do this. Not now."

"I'm sorry. I shouldn't have said that."

My body ached with the need to touch her. To reach through the phone line and hold her close, and let her cry.

"I can't do this right now, Leo," she said and I could hear the pain in her voice.

"What are you saying? You can't do this now? Or ever?"

The silence on the line grew. For a moment I was afraid she'd hung up. "Lexi?"

"Leo, I ca-"

"Lexi," I rushed the words out. "I love you. I..." My voice cracked. "I love you," I repeated because it was all I could do.

"I just can't think about this right now. I need to focus on Uncle Ray, it's just not a good time. It's too much. Everything is...I'm sorry, Leo."

"Don't, Lexi...please," I said.

But it was too late.

She was gone.

***

I walked down the corridor stunned. I couldn't feel my feet, but the kept moving. The walls seemed to be closing in around me.

Had I really just hung up on Leo? I'd said I couldn't deal with it, but...could I deal without him?

The door to Uncle Ray's room was open, so I slipped inside. Andrew looked at me and started to rise but I shook my head and he settled back into the chair. I stood against the doorway and took a deep breath.

"The first thing they do is knock me out," Uncle Ray was saying to an enraptured Ben.

"They hit you?" Ben asked.

"No, they use these cool drugs to make me fall asleep."

"Won't you wake up?"

"No way, they make sure I'm really asleep. And then, when they're sure that I'm sleeping, they cut me open."

"Cool," Ben said. "Where?"

"Right here." Uncle Ray drew a line with his finger down his chest. "Then they take these big things, they look like nut crackers and they split my -"

"Okay," I said. "I think that's enough of a description for right now, Uncle Ray."

"Aw, come on, Mom."

"Come on, Lexi," Andrew said mimicking Ben's tone.

"Ya, come on." Uncle Ray joined in.

Fresh tears sprang to my eyes. I swiped at them and turned away before anyone could see, but it was too late.

"Hey, Lex," Uncle Ray said. "We were just kidding."

"Well it's not funny." I whirled around. The tears were coming hot and fast.

Andrew stared at me and looked for a minute like he wanted to say something. Instead he looked down at Ben who was staring open mouthed at me and said, "Hey, buddy. Let's go find some hot chocolate."

"Hot chocolate!" Ben jumped down and ran for the door, pausing long enough to wrap his arms around my legs for a quick hug before racing out into the hall.

"I think I'll join you," Sara Beth said and put her knitting aside. She gave me a quick kiss on the cheek as she passed and whispered in my ear, "Spend some time with him, honey. You need this. You both do."

Andrew stared at me from across the room and again looked again like he wanted to say something but he only shook his head and walked past me without saying a word.

I stared at the door after everyone left. I knew Uncle Ray was going to say something about my tears. He'd probably tell me everything would be okay and not to worry and all the rest of the crap that people tell you when they don't want to see you cry.

"Lexi?"

Here it comes. I ignored him but the sound of his voice only started another round of tears.

"Lexi," he said, softer this time. "Come here. I'm a dying man, don't make me beg."

I whirled around flew to the side of his bed. "You're not dying," I said. "You're going to be fine."

He laughed but the sound lacked its usual heartiness. "I just said that to get you over here."

"That wasn't nice." I smacked his shoulder, just hard enough to make my point. "Don't ever do that again."

"It worked didn't it? Now sit."

I did as I was told and pulled a chair close to his bed so he wouldn't have to turn his head to look at me.

"Are you going to tell me what's going on, or do I have to guess?"

I shot him a look and grabbed the corner of the bed sheet.

"It's not like I have a lot of time here, Lexi." He gestured to the wires coming off his chest.

"Stop it. I told you it's not funny." I focused on twisting the sheet around my fingers until the tips turned purple.

"I'm serious," he said. "Now talk to me. What's going on?"

"You're lying in the hospital waiting for major heart surgery, isn't it obvious?"

"Stop." He took hold of my hand forcing me to stop twisting. "This you can handle. You're tough. A little heart attack isn't going to derail my Lexi. No," he said. "There's more. Now spill."

I looked up at him. "How do you know?"

"I know you, Miss Muffet." Unshed tears shone in his eyes when he used my special name. He hadn't called me that in years. Not since the early years after my parents death. He started using the nickname when I first went to live with him because for some reason it made me smile when almost nothing else would.

It still worked. I smiled, then opened my mouth and told him the story of Leo, from the beginning.

He didn't say a word as I spoke. On one occasion, I thought he might actually be sleeping. His eyes were closed with only his chest moving up and down. When I stopped talking for a moment his eyes snapped open, and I knew he was listening. When I got to the part about telling Leo the truth about ben, I started to cry again but didn't bother to wipe the tears away, there was no point.

"Well," Uncle Ray said when I was done. "That's quite the pickle you've put yourself in. But I have to say, Lex, I just don't under-"

"Understand how I could be so reckless? How I could do something totally and completely irresponsible like get pregnant on holidays and then hide the truth from my husband? I'm such a fool. You must think I'm awful."

"No," he said. "I don't think you're awful. In fact, I'm wondering what I did so wrong in raising you."

"Pardon me?" I pulled back and stared at him.

"Lexi, did I teach you to deny yourself love?" he asked, but didn't wait for an answer before adding, "Maybe it was my fault. I tried so hard to do right by you, to give you all my attention. But I never did give you the example of a proper loving relationship. I guess I always thought it was enough that your mother and father had that."

What was he saying?

"This was not your fault, Uncle Ray," I said. "I know how to love, I didn't give it up."

"Didn't you?" His question pierced me. "Isn't that what you're doing again?"

"No." I shook my head.

"Lexi?"

"It's not," I said. "It's different. I just can't deal with all of this right now." I tried to block out the memory of Leo's voice on the phone. "It's too much."

"Then when? You can't put off living forever. One day it'll be too late."

"Don't say that."

He chuckled, but the sound was weak. "I don't me mean me." Uncle Ray rubbed my hand and his touch inspired a fresh bout of tears. "One thing makes sense though," he said.

"What's that?"

"I've been asking you for years why you stay with Andrew when you're both so obviously unhappy. Now I know."

"He's not a bad man."

"No, Andrew's a good man," he said. His voice was soothing and calm, a sharp contrast to my own. "But just because a man is good, doesn't mean he's good for you."

I turned away.

"And now that I know the truth, it makes more sense. You're a good girl, Lex." He patted my arm but still I didn't look at him. "You're raising a great boy. And you didn't do anything wrong when you met his father."

I swallowed hard.

"But you did do wrong when you lied to your husband. And you've done wrong to Ben's father and to your own heart. You don't need me to tell you what you already know. It's time to make it right, Lex."

I knew Uncle Ray would tell it to me straight. He never minced words. I turned back to him and took his hand.

"And, Lexi?"

I nodded.

"It's okay. You don't need to punish yourself anymore."

"I don't know what you're talking about."

"Yes you do. It's clear to me that this man Leo lights a

spark in you. I can see it when you say his name. You don't have to deny yourself that love because of a mistake you made many years ago. Take it from me, Miss Muffet, life is shorter than you might think."

"Don't talk that way." I adjusted the sheet over his chest so I wouldn't have to see the electrodes fixed there.

"Well, what good am I if I can't impart my wisdom on you?" he smiled. "I waited too long to find Sara Beth. She's a good woman, and she makes this old, clogged up ticker sing." He released my hand to pat his chest. "I haven't had as long with her as I'd like and I wouldn't trade any of it. But if I have one regret, it's that I waited too long to let myself find love. Don't make my mistake, Lexi."

"But, Ben."

"Ben's a strong boy," he said. "And he deserves to know the truth. You can't deny that boy a real father any longer."

"And Andrew," My throat clenched at the thought of what I needed to do.

"It's not going to be easy..."

"But it's necessary," I finished for him. "He deserves the truth too."

He nodded, waited a beat, and then smiled. "I did do a good job," he said. "Now tell me about this Leo. Does he love you the way I think you love him?"

"Lexi, I am fully and completely in love with you. I always have been."

"There isn't a doubt in my mind," I said remembering.

"Then, I think you know what to do. For all of you."

I nodded.

"Don't let your life pass you by, Miss Muffet. Please," he whispered the last word and when I looked up I saw tears shining in my strong uncle's eyes.

I pulled my chair as close as I could and wrapped my arms around him. Careful of the wires and tubes, I snuggled next to him, as close as I could, and like a little girl, I let him hold me until both of us had exhausted our tears.

CHAPTER TWENTY-SEVEN

Two days later I picked out the suit Uncle Ray would be buried in.

Only a few hours after I'd left his bedside, and only six hours before he was scheduled to have his life-saving surgery, he'd suffered a second massive heart attack and died in his sleep. I felt the loss even before Sara Beth called from the hospital to give me the news.

Andrew helped me tell Ben who asked a million questions before breaking down into tears when he realized his Papa wouldn't be coming home. A little boy's heart breaks hard and I held him tightly while he cried angry, loud tears. When Ben had sobbed himself to sleep, Andrew carried him to bed and then settled me on the couch with a soft blanket and a cup of tea. He sat in the chair across the room. Even in tragedy, the gulf between us couldn't be breached.

"How are you doing?" he asked me.

"I don't know if it's hit me yet," I said. "But I'm okay. More okay than I thought I'd be. We had a good talk and I'm glad I had that time with him."

"When you want to talk about it, you know I'll be here, right?"

I nodded. My eyes fixed on the crystal vase Andrew

had filled with tulips, Uncle Ray's favorite, and brought into the living room for me. "You're a good man," I said echoing Uncle Ray's words.

"But not the one for you," Andrew said. It wasn't a question.

It wasn't the right time to talk about this. Not today. I focused on the vase. It represented love, real love.

Uncle Ray's words rang in my head. *"Don't let your life pass you by."*

No, it was the right time.

"I'm sorry," I said.

"Don't be," he said, resigned.

I took a sip of my tea letting the warmth fill me. "Ben," I said after a moment forcing myself to look at him, "he's not yours."

I was ready for him to yell at me. I was ready for him to scream, rage, cry, get up and walk out. I was ready for anything. I held my breath and waited.

"I know," he said quietly. "I've always known."

"Andrew, I...what? What did you say?"

"Lexi, I've always known Ben's not mine," he said the words calmly and looked me in the eye the whole time he spoke. I would know if he was lying, making up a story to hurt me but there was only truth reflected there.

"How?"

"Well, he looks nothing like me," Andrew said and laughed a little.

Did he think this was funny? I felt detached from my body, like I was floating above the couch. I clenched the mug, needing to feel the burn of heat on my skin.

Andrew's face changed; the moment of levity gone. "I know because I can't have children, Lexi. When you told me you were pregnant, I knew that there was only a very slight chance that the baby could be mine. And when he was born, well...I think it's obvious he's not mine."

"Why didn't you say anything?"

"I loved you. You know how much I wanted to be with you. I would've done anything."

"But if you knew the baby wasn't yours..."

"I assumed it was just an indiscretion on your part," he said. "We all make mistakes."

I shook my head. "No," I said. It wasn't like that. I refused to think of Leo as an indiscretion. And Ben? My baby? He was not a mistake. Trying to steady myself, I focused again on the crystal vase.

"Well, if it-"

"Wait a minute," I said. My mind raced over what Andrew had just told me. "You said you knew Ben wasn't yours because you can't have children?"

"That's right." Andrew shifted in his seat.

"And you knew that when we got back together?"

He hesitated then nodded, just a little.

Taking care, I put my tea on the side table. "You lied to me." I pushed the blanket off my lap and swung my legs to the floor. "When I came back from Vegas, you agreed to try for children," I said trying hard to control my voice. "You said you'd changed your mind. That we could try."

"As it turned out, you were already pregnant."

"That's not the point." I waved my arm. "Why can't you have children, Andrew?"

"Lexi," he said. "I don't-"

"Why?"

"I had a vasectomy."

Bile rose in my throat. I swallowed hard. "When?"

"After we split up."

"So when you came to me, begging for me to take you back, to make our marriage work, when you told me you were ready to start a family, you already knew you couldn't? Is that right?"

He nodded. "I didn't want children. I wanted you."

Anger clouded my vision. "How could you do that to me?" I spoke through clenched teeth. "You knew how badly I wanted a baby. You knew what it meant to me. What were you going to do when we didn't get pregnant?" I was yelling now, the battle for control lost. "Were you ever going to tell me or were you going to let me go through fertility treatment and years of heartbreak?"

He stood from his chair and stood in front of me. "Well," he said his voice laced with bitterness, "that wasn't an issue after all, was it?"

Before I could stop it, my arm flew out and my palm made contact with his cheek. The crack of my skin on his flesh echoed in the room. He didn't touch the flaming red mark on his cheek just narrowed his eyes at me and said, "I'm not the bad guy here, Lexi. You can stand there and pretend that what I did was awful and heartless and everything else you want to call it. But try to remember your role here."

"Get out."

"You're the one that screwed around and got knocked up." I didn't recognize him, the venom in his voice.

"I want you to go."

"You're no saint, Lexi."

"Get out," I said again.

"Opening your-"

I couldn't listen. I needed to shut him up. Before I

could think it through, I reached forward, grabbed the vase and heaved it as hard as I could. With a crack, it hit the wall, missing its mark.

We both stared at the mess.

"Lexi," Andrew's voice shifted.

"Just go." My voice shook but I stood my ground.

"I need to know for sure. Is he Ben's father?"

I could hear the pain in his question and I hated myself for it.

I turned away so I wouldn't have to look at him. "Yes," I whispered. "Leo is Ben's father."

I kept my eyes fixed on the sofa and traced the pattern in the fabric with my eyes, following the thread until I heard Andrew's footsteps and the gentle click of the front door as he left.

CHAPTER TWENTY-EIGHT

Surrounded by boxes, I didn't have time to think about the mess I'd made out of my life and I was grateful for the distraction of sorting through Uncle Ray's things. Sara Beth had helped for awhile, but it quickly became clear that she wasn't ready. With a flood of apologies and tears, she made her exit earlier that morning, leaving me on my own to sort through the condo and Uncle Ray's few possessions.

I was almost done with the bedroom, which was pretty easy since I'd decided that most of Uncle Ray's clothes were going to goodwill, when I heard the front door open.

"Lexi?" Nicole called.

"I'm in here." I pulled myself off the floor just as she poked her head in the room.

"Hey," she said. "How're you doing? You handling everything okay?"

I nodded. Ever since the funeral yesterday, when I cried more than I thought possible, I'd done a pretty good job of keeping it together.

"I'm doing okay," I said honestly. "What're you doing here? Shouldn't you be with Ben?" Nicole and Ryan had been wonderful, giving up their honeymoon to help me out. With Ben. I didn't feel right asking Andrew to take time off work. Especially after everything. Nicole had hardly left my side until today when she insisted on taking Ben to give me a chance to take care of things.

"Ryan and Ben decided to go to the zoo."

"More like Ben decided and dragged Ryan along," I said. "Will he be okay?"

"Are you kidding? Ben loves Uncle Ryan." She smiled. "Besides, it'll be good practice for him."

"What? Are you?"

Nicole blushed. She never blushed. "Well, not yet. But soon hopefully. We're trying."

"Nic, that's awesome news."

She stepped over the garbage bags full of clothes and I pulled her in for a hug. "You'll be a great mom," I said.

"Well, I'm not yet." She rolled up her sleeves. "Right now I'm going to be a great best friend. What do we need to do?"

"Thanks, Nic," I said. "I mean it. Thank you for being here. "

"There's nowhere else I'd rather be."

We worked together, bagging clothes and sorting items. Every once in awhile, something would trigger a memory and I'd break down. So much for holding it all together.

"Do you want to keep this?" Nicole asked and held up a bulky sweater.

"I made that for him," I said. "I was thirteen and I didn't have enough money to buy him a present, so I bought yarn, needles and a learn to knit book." Nicole handed me the sweater and my vision blurred with tears as I looked at the uneven rows, and dropped stitches. "He wore it too," I said. "He even wore it last winter."

"It's a great sweater," Nicole said. "Let's put it over here." She took it gently out of my hands and put it with the fishing vest I'd set aside to keep for Ben. She grabbed a box of tissues and worked her way back through the clutter to where I was sitting.

I wiped my eyes and Nicole got back to work.

"Ben's doing pretty good," she said as she stripped the sheets from the bed. "All things considered."

I wiped my tears. "He has his moments. Sometimes I think he's still waiting for his papa to walk through the door. He doesn't totally understand."

"Give him some credit," Nicole said. "He's smart kid and a good kid. He'll be okay."

"I hope so," I said. "He's got a lot more changes coming."

Nicole sat on the mattress. "About that, what's going on with Andrew?"

"We haven't had a lot of chances to talk about it."

"No, I guess you wouldn't," Nicole said. "The timing kind of sucks, doesn't it?"

I nodded. "But it had to happen. And in a way, Uncle Ray gave me the courage to confront Andrew. He basically told me to make it right and that life's too short."

"He was right."

I looked away so I wouldn't start crying again.

"So, what now?" Nicole asked. "I'm assuming you've talked about divorce."

I nodded.

"What did Leo say?"

"Not much," I said and it was true. When I'd called him the morning after Uncle Ray died, I started the conversation by asking him to please not ask about us, and he'd respected that. Just hearing his voice made me feel better, it soothed me, but I couldn't make any decisions about the future. Not yet.

"But you told him about Andrew, right?"

I nodded. "I told him everything."

"So when is he going to be here?"

"It's not that easy, Nic," I said and grabbed another bag from the pile. "Leo has a life there. A successful career. He can't just pick up and leave."

"Are you seriously telling me that he's not coming?"

I didn't answer her because I didn't know. Leo told me he'd be on the next plane to be here for me. He wanted to come, and I knew he would. But I wouldn't ask that of him. I knew how important his career was to him. After all, hadn't he chosen it over me once before? I wouldn't ask him to make that choice again.

"It doesn't' matter," I said and busied myself putting socks in a bag.

"It absolutely does matter, Lexi," Nicole said. "You know it does."

I didn't look up.

"Lex?"

I put more socks in the bag.

"Lexi, why isn't he coming?"

When the socks were gone I tied up the bag and moved to the closet.

"Lexi." Nicole's voice rose an octave. "Cut it out, right now."

"What do you want me to say?" I slammed the closet door and turned to face her. "Are you waiting for me to say that I called Leo and he can't wait to drop everything and be with me? That we're going to live happily ever after and everything will be okay?" I looked at her hurt expression and felt a stab of remorse but I couldn't stop. "Because if that's what you're waiting for, don't hold your breath. It's not going to happen. This isn't a fairy tale where everything turns out the way you want it."

"Lexi..."

"Nicole, don't." I held up my hand.

"Have you even discussed it?"

I whirled around. "No," I said. "We haven't discussed it. I can't ask him to give up everything for me. He's worked so hard for what he has there. Besides, what would I say, Nic? I mean, come on. It's not like this is your regular everyday relationship."

"It doesn't have to be hard."

"Pardon me, if I don't share your optimism. Not everyone's life is so easy."

Nicole reeled as if I'd slapped her. "I didn't deserve that."

"No." I softened. "You didn't. I'm sorry."

"Besides, it's not optimism," she said. "I've seen you two together. He loves you, Lexi. God, I wish Ryan loved me like that."

"What?"

"I mean," she remedied. "Ryan loves me, I know that. But it's different. Lexi, the way that man looks at you. The way his eyes go somewhere far away whenever he says your name...that's something else. That *is* a fairy tale. You don't find that every day."

"I don't know what you're talking about," I said. I turned away from her so she couldn't see my face.

"The hell you don't," Nicole said grabbing my arm and forced me to look at her. "You know exactly what I'm talking about because you're the same way with him."

"Nicole, don't."

"You know what?" she said. "I think I will." She stood in front of me and her five foot four figure seemed to fill the room. "I think I'll say exactly what I need to say."

"Pardon me?"

I don't think she heard me.

"I need to say this, and you need to hear it, Lexi Titan. Leo is in love with you like I've never seen before. He's the kind of in love that you read about in romance novels. The kind you tell your daughters about in the hopes that they won't settle for less. He's the kind of in love that means nothing else matters. Not jobs, not countries...nothing. Leo is in love with you in the way that women around the world dream about at night. And *you* are throwing it away."

"You're crazy."

"Am I?" she said still standing with her arms crossed in front of her. "Am I really?"

"Yes," I said swiping at my eyes. "Because you're forgetting one very important thing, Nicole. Fairy tales aren't real. And romance novels? They're fiction too. This..." I waved my arm around the room. "This is reality."

CHAPTER TWENTY-NINE

I was tired of playing by Lexi's rules. If she didn't want to talk about us over the phone then I'd just have to go to her. She was going through a lot, a whole lot, but I'd be damned if I was going to let her push me away. I wouldn't go that easy. Hell, I wouldn't go at all.

That's why I'd taken a leave of absence from the hotel, and was now sitting in a rented SUV, driving towards the mountains. It hadn't been hard to get time off. I hadn't taken a sick day in years. When I told Roberta I'd be gone for awhile, she just smiled and nodded as if she'd been expecting it. Knowing her, she probably had from the moment she saw me watching Lexi.

Once I'd made the decision to come and find her, everything fell into place. I found a flight, packed a bag and was jetting towards Canada in less than a day. It was once I landed, that things started to get complicated.

The last time I spoke to Lexi she sounded more upset than ever. I'd phoned to hear her voice and to see how she was holding up with the stress of dealing with her uncle's funeral and of course, things with her husband. I wanted to lend support, even from a distance. It wasn't that easy.

"Nicole and Ryan have been great," she said. "They're helping out with Ben, he's so sad and..."

"I should be there with you," I said.

"No. It's fine, Leo." I could hear the strain in her voice. "I think it's better if you don't come right now."

Was she lying? Or did I just not want to hear what she was saying?

"Lexi, I miss you. I..."

I stopped myself. It wasn't fair to make this about me. She had too much going on. I needed to be there for her, not demanding more.

"I'm going to take Ben and go out the lake for awhile," she said. "I think it'll be good for us to get away and just be together, the two of us."

The two of them?

"I can get on a plane today."

"No, Leo." Her voice was thick with pain and I wanted nothing more than to make it go away for her. "Don't come right now, please."

I'd promised her I wouldn't, but after I got off the phone I couldn't get her voice out of my head. She needed me and I loved her. Of course I would go to her. I can't believe it took me so damn long.

I didn't have much of a plan. Heck, I didn't have any plan except to get to Canada. Once I landed, I tried Lexi's cell phone but it went straight to voicemail so I called Nicole, thankful that I'd thought to swipe her number out of the customer database before leaving. She'd been more than happy to give me directions to Lake Lillian and Lexi.

That was three hours earlier. It had taken longer than I thought possible to secure a rental car and get on the highway after getting lost in the city a few times. After a few turn arounds, the open road was finally in front of me, I could see the mountains in the distance and I was on my way.

The clerk at the rental company said Lake Lillian was a four hour drive. So, barring any more navigational issues, I'd be there by dinner. I hadn't decided if I was going to go straight to Lexi's cabin or if I would wait until morning. I had to think of Ben and even though I couldn't wait to see him, I didn't want our first meeting to frighten or confuse him.

I had four hours to think about it, so I settled into the drive, set the cruise control and found a radio station to keep me company.

The scenery leaving the city was fascinating. I'd never been north of Arizona. There wasn't the opportunity or need, so I'd never seen anything like what I was driving through. The houses gave way to farmer's fields that were in various stages of harvest. Piles of what might have been wheat lay in rows across the rolling fields. But it wasn't long before the fields became hillier, with trees and large rocky outcroppings replacing the long rows of grain. The mountains that had seemed so small from the city limits now loomed in front of me. The closest I'd ever been to a mountain range had been Mount Charleston, outside of Vegas, when a tour group I was in charge of wanted to go for a hike. Faced now with the towering Rockies in front of me, I realized that the 'mountain' I'd crawled to the top of huffing and puffing was a mere hill.

Pulling the car to the shoulder, I got out and stood on the side of the road. I looked straight up and as soon as I did, had to grab onto the jeep to steady myself from the sudden rush of vertigo. The day was clear, and with the blue sky behind them, the mountains popped, their tips dusted in white gave them a surreal dominating presence. There was no snow where I stood; after all, it was only the end of August, but the air felt cooler than it had in the city. Not enough for a jacket, but I was glad I had a sweater in my bag.

I got back in the car and continued driving. Slower this time, due to the tight twists and turns of the road. Occasionally I had to pull over and stand in wonder at a waterfall crashing down the side of a cliff or an icy blue river that wound its way through deep valleys below the road. In all my life, I had never seen such wild, unbridled beauty, and despite my hurry to get to Lexi, I allowed myself the opportunity to absorb my surroundings. Turning the radio off, I unrolled the window and let the crisp air fill my senses.

***

Walking up to the door of the Lake Lillian Inn, I wasn't even sure if it was open. My rental car was the only vehicle in the parking lot, and the potted plants on the porch didn't look like they'd seen water in weeks, but the woman at the grocery store, Enid was her name, said this was the only place in town to get a room. She hadn't mentioned anything about them being closed. I tried the door, expecting it to be locked, but it swung inward and revealed a cozy sitting room. The focus of the room was a huge stone fireplace, with a fire laid inside, but not started. A stack of logs sat on the hearth. Two inviting, overstuffed chairs stood in front of the fireplace and just beyond that was a small reception desk. A large tabby cat stretched on one of the chairs and hopped off to greet me. There was no one in sight.

"Well, hello," I said to the cat and bent down to scratch its ears. "Aren't you friendly?"

"Chester's my door staff," said a scratchy voice and I looked up to see a man appear from a doorway. "What can I do for ya?"

I straightened and went to shake the man's hand. He looked to be in his late sixties or maybe seventies, with white stubble covering his chin. His plaid shirt was untucked and his hand shook as he extended it. "My name's Leo," I said. "I was hoping you had a room."

"The name is Dex," he answered. "And I have lots of rooms. In fact, there ain't nothing but room at the inn."

"So you're open?"

The man nodded and said, "Yup, I'm open. Although I see how you might not think so."

"It is pretty quiet."

"Quiet," he scoffed. "It's dead. Not a lot of visitors here this time of year. Or any time, it seems." Dex's eyes took on a faraway look for a moment. He moved to the desk and flipped open a register book.

"So you need a room," he said. "What brings you to Lake Lillian? Fishing? Hunting? Or you running away from something?" Dex looked up from the book and eyed me suspiciously. "You ain't one of those cons I hear about on the TV?"

"No sir," I said and held up my hands. "I promise, I'm not a con and I assure you, I'm not running away from anything."

He shrugged and returned to flipping through his book. "What you here for then? We don't get a lot of visitors around here anymore."

"I'm looking for someone. She has a place out here."

Dex opened a drawer and took out a key. "Why aren't you staying with her then?"

"Well." I debated for a moment on how much to tell the man and settled for a variation of the truth. "She doesn't know I'm coming so I thought it might be best to get my own room."

He narrowed his eyes at me under his bushy eyebrows. He stared at me for a moment before showing his lopsided grin and saying, "Probably a good idea. Women can be funny."

I returned his smile. "Yes, they can."

Dex showed me to a room at the top of the stairs, which he said was the best one he had. When I opened the door to the small space, furnished modestly in hand crafted pine furniture I couldn't help but compare it to the rooms in Vegas. It certainly wasn't luxurious and posh like the hotels I was used to, but the rustic space was decorated nice and it was clean. When I pushed aside the thick curtains to reveal sliding glass doors that lead to a small patio, I saw why Dex said it was the best room he had. The view was spectacular. The patio overlooked the lake with an unobstructed view of the water and the mountains. With the sun directly overhead, the lake sparkled, mirroring the mountains in perfect detail on its surface disturbed only by the occasional ripple from a distant boat or jumping fish. No, there was no way even the fanciest suite in Las Vegas could rival this room. There was simply no comparison.

I didn't bother to unpack. I wanted to find Lexi soon. But I still wasn't sure today was the right day. If she just got here, like Nicole said, she needed time. The thought of another day going by without seeing her was unthinkable to me, but I couldn't push her. She was broken right now; I wouldn't be the one to shatter her.

Heading back downstairs I took a minute to look around. The inn wasn't in bad shape. Sure, it could use a coat of paint, and the wood floors would benefit from a polish, but it was really a nice place. The location couldn't be better and with a rustic log home feel, it would be a great destination for couples wanting to get away for a romantic weekend or even families looking for some time in the woods.

I found Dex in the dining room which was just off the

main entry way. He was carrying a tray with a thermos and a few mugs on it.

"I thought you might like a cup of coffee after your trip," he said.

"Only if you'll sit and have one with me."

I took the tray from him and followed him to a large covered deck out back. There was a huge sloping lawn that led to the lake with a dock sticking out into the water at one end of the sandy beach.

"I don't think I could ever get sick of looking at this view," I said putting the tray on a small table. I settled into a wooden deck chair and poured two cups of coffee.

"Just black," Dex said as I handed him the mug. I added two sugars to mine and sat back.

He took a sip of his coffee despite the steam coming from the mug. "This friend of yours. A woman, you said?"

"That's right."

"Hmmm."

"Is there a problem?"

"I'm gonna be straight with you," he said.

"Please do."

"This here is a small town. We stick together. If you're gonna cause trouble..."

"I promise you," I said turning so he could see my face, "the last thing I want is to make trouble."

He examined me for a moment then nodded. "Yup, I see that. You don't seem like the trouble maker kind." He turned back to the lake. "The woman, she doesn't know you're coming?"

"No. But I think...I hope she'll be happy to see me."

"If there's any trouble..."

"There won't be," I assured him again.

"Good."

He seemed satisfied and his protective duty for the community done, we fell into silence.

After a few minutes I asked, "Why aren't your rooms full, Dex? With this location, I would think you'd be booked out for months."

The old man sighed and the sound came from deep inside. After a moment he spoke. "It used to be like that. When my Jessie was alive, we were full every weekend and most weeks through the summer too. But when Jessie passed, the heart of the place went with her. It fizzled and died after that." He took a sip of coffee and stared straight ahead.

"I'm sorry to hear about your wife," I said and I meant it. The sadness permeated me. "Can I ask, why didn't you sell the place then?"

Dex continued to stare straight ahead but he said, "At first I didn't have the heart. This here was Jessie's place, her dream. Then some young upstart, John Jackson was his name, said he would, "take it off my hands." He offered me a good deal, said he wanted to turn it into a re-sort. But I couldn't do it. Everywhere I looked, there was Jessie. She was everywhere, everything. The gardens were bright all summer with plants she'd tended. The cook still mixed up her recipes, and the guests she'd booked, they kept a comin'. It was like she was still here and if I didn't dwell on it, I could pretend that she'd done and gone to the city to visit her sister and she'd be coming on back soon. But then the flowers died and the garden done got weedy. The guests stopped coming and without any new bookings, I had to let the cook go. Pretty soon, it was just me and the occasional guest."

I drank some coffee and let the heat of it warm me. "Then why didn't you sell?"

"Couldn't."

"You still couldn't bear to leave?"

"No," Dex said and turned to me. "I couldn't sell it. I tried. That John Jackson, when I turned down his offer he'd gone off to Wasa Lake just about two hours further East and built up a fancy re-sort there. I called him, told him I was ready to sell. He laughed at me, called me a stupid, sentimental old man. He made me an offer though."

"Really?"

"I can't even call it that really," Dex said. "The pissant offered me less than I owed on the place and he knew it too. There was no way I could take it."

"So why not make a go of it again?" I sat up in my chair, excited by my own ideas. "With a little work this place could be booked up in no time. You could offer honeymoon packages, fishing trips, ladies' retreats and even family getaways. I'm telling you, Dex, you could make the Lake Lillian Inn a destination and show that John Jackson just who he's dealing with."

Dex laughed, but it was a tired sound. "You got dreams, Leo. You're a young man."

"Maybe I could give you some ideas? I'm kind of in the hotel business myself," I said. He arched a brow in question and I added, "Vegas."

"Well, son, this here ain't Vegas. It's Lake Lillian and that John Jackson did just what you're talking about down in Wasa Lake. He bought up some shoreline property and built a monstrosity. It even has a pool. Why you need a pool with a perfectly good lake steps away, I never understood. It's one of them commercial jobs. No life in it. I can't compete with that." Dex looked out over the lake again. "Even if I wanted to," he said. "Which I don't. Just don't have the energy no more. Now if Jessie were still alive, things would be different. The love of a good woman, well, it just makes you want to be a better man. You know what I mean?"

I nodded. More to myself than to him and we fell into silence sipping our coffee.

CHAPTER THIRTY

The clouds hung low on the mountains, obscuring their peaks. Wisps like white cotton candy clung to the tree covered slopes. But it wasn't a solid grey covering which gave me hope for the day. Being so deep in the mountains, the weather could go either way this late in the summer. Patches of blue broke free from the gloom. I walked to the water's edge and tested the water. Still warm. For Lake Lillian anyway. It was a glacier fed lake, so warm was really a relative term. The cool air made the water feel less frigid than it really was. For now. All it would take is one cold day and swimming would be done for the season.

A loon's call fractured the quiet of the afternoon, and then, sneaking out from the trees, the glassy surface of the lake was broken by the smooth movement of the bird. I watched its progress in front of me and waited until it moved to the other side of the dock jutting out into the lake. The water settled in the loon's wake and once again the surface was glassy. Gentle waves lapped the shore and licked at my feet. I dug my toes into the smooth pebbles and the cool mud below. I glanced behind me at the cabin that was still mostly closed up.

Ben had tried to stay awake for the entire drive but he'd succumbed to the sleep he so desperately needed about a half an hour earlier, so when we pulled into the gravel drive, I'd left him in the car to sleep. I didn't take the time to turn on the water or electricity and open the house up. I went straight to my bedroom, grabbed the bathing suit I kept there, and headed out the back door to the lake.

I turned back to the water. There was one boat at the far end pulling a skier, but on my end, it was peaceful. The cabin was nestled in a small cove with only a handful of other homes. Most of them were seasonal, with only a few residents living at the lake all year long. The ebb and flow of the waves mesmerized me and drew me forward. With one last quick glance behind me, I took two long strides putting me knee deep in the cool water, pointed my hands over my head and dove in.

Being surrounded by water was a feeling I never grew tired of. The sensation of being swaddled and protected by a force that could be all at once soothing with the underlying threat of menacing, relaxed me. I held my breath longer than necessary, waiting until the pressure built in my lungs and the fire started burning before I kicked hard and propelled myself to the surface.

"Mom!"

I wiped the water from my eyes and say Ben running from the house and towards the dock.

"Mom!"

I cupped my hands around my mouth and called, "I'm here, Ben. Hold on." I put my head down and swam as fast as I could back to the dock. I didn't realize how far I'd managed to get from shore, but my muscles knew what to do and I reached the ladder and climbed up onto the dock only a moment later.

"I thought you were gone," Ben cried. "I woke up and you weren't there and..." His body convulsed in sobs and he shook.

I wrapped my arms around him, not caring that I was soaking wet. Out of the protection of the water, the air was cool and bit at my skin. "It's okay, honey. I'm right here. It's okay," I murmured into his hair.

"But you were gone."

"No, baby. I just went for a swim I didn't want to wake you. I'll never leave you."

Ben pulled away and wiped his nose with the back of his hand. "Papa left," he said.

I didn't have the words that would make his pain go away so I pulled him close again and hoped that he would mistake the moisture hitting the top of his head for the water dripping off my body.

***

"Okay, try it now," I called up to Ben from the basement utility room. After hastily getting changed and hauling in our bags, I had been attempting to get the water started for the last ten minutes. The problem was, I couldn't remember which tap to turn. It had been a long time since I'd come out to the cabin alone and it didn't seem to matter how often I'd done it over the years, I still had to try all of the taps before finding the right one that would restore the water to the pipes.

I heard a rush followed by Ben yelling, "It worked, Mom! Cool, it's red."

Red? Of course. Rust in the pipes. I smiled and turning off the lights in the utility room, went to find Ben.

I found him standing on a stool next to the kitchen sink with the water still running.

"Buddy, you can't let the water run."

"But it's...aw, it's not red anymore," he said and shut the tap off before jumping down from the stool.

"Did you really want to drink red water?"

"Well," he said, "probably not."

I laughed; it was good to see him smiling again. Everyone kept telling me how resilient little boys were, but that didn't make it any easier to help him grieve. I hoped coming out to the lake would help both of us say goodbye. The peacefulness of the mountains always soothed me and gave my mind a chance to be still. Besides, with things so strange between Andrew and me, there weren't a lot of options left. Andrew had gone to a hotel for a few days, but he couldn't stay there forever and we both knew there was nothing left between us. I finally understood his detachment from Ben, but I didn't forgive it, and I'd be damned if I was going to subject my son to that type of indifference again. There was only once choice for me. I packed up everything we could fit into my SUV and came to the only place I could think of. Watching Ben now, running across the lawn towards the lake, an expression of joy on his face, I knew I made the right choice.

I opened the door to holler at him to come in and unpack and then changed my mind. It could wait. I had enough food for a day or two; we could head into town to provision properly later. For now, this was all we needed.

CHAPTER THIRTY-ONE

The next morning, I wrapped myself in an old afghan and settled into the porch swing on the back deck with my mug of tea to watch the sun rise. The old chains protested and creaked with my weight. All of the living took place at the back of the house. The wide wood planked deck was in good condition and held my favorite spot, the swing, as well as a variety of other chairs meant for lounging and relaxing. A cedar table, hand crafted by Uncle Ray, stood at one end of the deck surrounded by chairs. It had been the center of many family meals as we watched the sun set behind the mountains. My chest tightened to think there would be no more dinners with Uncle Ray at his table.

My gaze travelled off the deck to the lawn. We were lucky to have such a large piece of lake front property. Uncle Ray used to say so, until he had to cut the grass with his manual mower. Secretly though, I know he enjoyed taking care of the property. He never really loved the small house that we lived in when I was growing up in the city. He did the bare minimum to keep the place maintained and looking good, but he never put the time and attention into it the way he did the cabin. It wasn't until I was in my late teens that I realized just how much he loved it at the lake. He used to talk about retiring here, but never did. I blamed myself. He was so worried about me and Ben. He couldn't leave.

I blinked back tears. I would have to show Ben how the manual push mower worked. He would probably like helping me with the lawn.

The lake was starting to come to life. Birds I couldn't see chirped from their nests hidden in the trees, and I watched a sandpiper pick its way across the rocks in the shallows, pecking at insects or small fish. Soon, they'd be gone for the season. Uncle Ray always left well stocked feeders out for the birds that stayed all year round. And ever since he'd had the cabin winterized ten years ago, he himself had spent more time out here, escaping the city even in the dead of winter when the tourists and summer people stayed away. I hadn't visited in the winter since I was a kid when we used to come up and go ice fishing and skating on the lake. But when I got older and busier with school, I hadn't bothered to make the trip.

What would it be like to stay here? To spend a winter here? I was still mulling over the thought when Ben, bleary eyed and still smelling of sleep came outside and climbed up onto the swing with me.

"Good morning, buddy."

He snuggled under the blanket with me. "There's no orange juice, Mom."

"I know." I kissed him on the top of his head. "We'll have to go into town today and stock up on a few things."

"So we can stay?" His voice held a trace of hope.

I looked out again to the lake and listened to the gentle lapping of the water. "Yes," I said. "I think we can stay for a bit."

"A bit?" Ben twisted to look at me. "What about school? Do I have to go to school? Jake said we'll be in the same class for grade one, but I don't want to, he's bossy sometimes."

I smiled. "You don't have to be in the same class as

Jake."

Especially if we stay, I thought and made a mental note to check out the local elementary school. And figure out a job.

***

"Mom, look at the puppies." Ben had radar for the cardboard box on the edge of the covered porch of the general store. I followed him and peered inside the box. There were three golden retriever type dogs curled together on a blanket.

"Oh, Mom, look at them. They're so cute."

They were cute, but I knew where this was leading.

"Can we-"

"No."

"But they're all alone," Ben said.

"They're not ours." Thankfully, he couldn't read the sign taped to the box, not yet anyway.

"F-f-fr-ee," he sounded out. "Free. Free! Mom, the sign says free!"

I sighed.

"Mom. Please?"

"I'll tell you what. You can stay out here and pet them while I get the groceries. Deal?"

Satisfied for the moment, Ben settled in, cross legged on the porch to play with the puppies while I went to do my shopping.

The store, much like the rest of Lake Lillian, hadn't changed much. Despite the fact that there wasn't as many visitors to the lake in recent years because of the new mega hotel in Wasa, the town's main industry was still tourism, mostly from the summer people who'd been coming here for generations. The small population almost doubled in the summer months. Fortunately, not all of those people were concentrated within a few streets. The unofficial town boundaries stretched to encompass the entire western side of the lake. The railroad tracks ran along the east side, so there were very few homes there. Many of the houses and cabins were scattered along the waters edge or tucked up into the trees with an amazing view. Our place was on a small dirt road, with only four other homes, each one surrounded by trees and very private. Andrew always thought it was a pain having to drive ten minutes into town, but I didn't mind. It was a small price to pay for privacy.

Driving in, I'd noticed many businesses starting to shut down for the season already. It seemed a little early. Jensen's fruit stand was boarded up with a sign that said, "See you in the spring!" The Putt-Putt mini golf course was advertising discounts until Thanksgiving when it too would close for the year, assuming that the snow stayed away until then. I'd have to take Ben for a round. Mini golfing had been one of my favorite things to do with Uncle Ray on warm summer nights, but I don't think I'd ever had the chance to take Ben.

I took one last look at my son now, with a puppy in his lap and went inside the store. A woman stood with her back to me, stocking the shelves. She looked up at the sound of the chimes on the door.

"Enid?"

"Lexi, is that you?" The woman put down the box of cereal she was holding and came to greet me.

"Enid," I said, letting her hug me. "It's so good to see you."

Enid and I had spent a few summers playing together when we were kids. I was always envious that she got to live in Lake Lillian year round while I had to go home. It was good to see a friendly face.

She released me, grinned broadly and stood back. When we were young, she'd always been chubby and that hadn't changed. Her long black hair was tied in a braid down her back. She wore overall jeans and a t-shirt, and I couldn't help but think how beautiful she looked.

"Look at you," she said. "The city girl has returned. You look fantastic."

"I was just thinking the very same thing about you."

She wiped her hands on the legs of her jeans and laughed. "You must be crazy."

"I'm totally serious. How've you been?"

Enid flung out her left hand. "I just got married," she squealed.

"That explains why you look so radiant."

Enid blushed and then hooked my arm leading me up the aisle. "Come, I'll talk to you while you do your shopping so we can catch up. I haven't seen you in years."

I grabbed a cart from the corner and started to fill it with the necessities while Enid caught me up on her life. She'd moved to the city, fell in love and only recently moved back to Lake Lillian to run the store with her new husband. When her parents decided they wanted to retire and head south with the Jensen's during the winter months, it was the perfect opportunity.

"I couldn't be happier to be back," Enid said. "There's something about the lake and the mountains. I can't believe I ever left."

"It's true. It's very special here."

"So, tell me about you. Mom said you were married and you have a son."

"I do have a little boy, Ben," I said avoiding the rest of the statement. "He's outside looking at those puppies."

"Oh, you have to take one," Enid exclaimed. "They're so cute, but I can't handle any more animals. Seth, my husband, would take in any stray he could, and he does. But when his latest refugee had puppies, I drew the line. I just can't. But they are cute, aren't' they?" She smiled.

"They are," I agreed laughing.

"Then take one. Every boy needs a dog," she said then paused. "Assuming you can have one in the city. Do you have a yard? Dogs need room to run. So I suppose if you don't have a yard, you really shouldn't take a puppy, I mean-"

"I was actually thinking about staying out at the lake for a while." I interrupted.

"Really? You mean to live or for a long holiday?" she said, the subject of the puppy forgotten. For now.

I picked up a can of soup and pretended to examine it before putting it in my cart. "Well, maybe to live. Things are a bit mixed up at home right now."

I filled her in on Uncle Ray's heart attack. She'd known him too, and knew what a good man he was. We hugged, but I kept the tears at bay. I didn't tell her the details, but mentioned that I was separated from Andrew and I needed a change. Thankfully she didn't pry.

"Well, I'm glad you're back," Enid said. "I'm just sorry it's under such sad circumstances. But, if there was ever a place to feel better and heal from life's troubles, it's Lake Lillian."

I sure hoped so, but I didn't say it out loud. Instead I asked, "Enid, do you know who I would talk to about enrolling Ben in school? I don't know yet how long I'm going to stay, but he's supposed to start grade one this year, so I should at least look into it."

"I don't know what to tell you. Classes start in a few weeks, but things are a bit of a mess at the elementary school at the moment. I heard the gossip because Seth's a teacher over at the high school."

My mind caught on something. Hadn't Uncle Ray mentioned something about a teaching job?

"There doesn't happen to be a job opening at the school, is there?" It didn't hurt to ask after all.

"How did you know?" Enid asked and her face fell. She'd been looking forward to telling me the gossip.

"Uncle Ray said your dad mentioned it awhile back," I said. "But I don't know why."

"Well, let me tell you," she said and her face lit up again as she launched into the story. "It seems there was a bit of an indiscretion between some of the staff this summer. One of the grade four teachers was caught in a compromising position with Principal Henderson during the dance at the summer festival. They were, um, doing it in the coat room."

I stifled a smiled.

"I guess it wouldn't be such a big deal, but the principal is married and it was the head of the PTA, Patty, that discovered them. Well, Patty went right out to the dance and up on the stage. She grabbed the microphone and announced what she'd seen right in front of everyone. Of course, Mrs. Henderson was there and heard everything. And when the offenders came out of the coatroom with their clothes and hair all out of place, well, I don't think I need to tell you what happened."

"No, tell me," I said trying to hold back laughter. It sounded like a scene out of a bad eighties movie.

"Nothing really very exciting actually," Enid admitted. "Mrs. Henderson agreed to forget it ever happened as long as the woman in question left. She did. So now we're down a teacher and my girlfriend who teaches grade two is not too happy about it because she says everyone else has to cover the space. There isn't really a whole lot of teachers who want to move to a tiny town in the middle of nowhere."

Except me. I thought.

"So who would I talk to about getting the job?"

She looked at me. "Seriously?"

"I am going to need money somehow and you know what they say about timing..."

"Timing is everything," Enid said. "It's like it was meant to be." Her round face broke into a wide grin. "I'll call Seth and get the information right away," she said and disappeared to the back room.

The store was pretty quiet, with just a few customers coming in and out, so I finished up my shopping, checking every few minutes to see that Ben was still playing on the porch with the puppies. It was going to be hard to tell him no, but I didn't think we could deal with one more change right now. Maybe in a few months. I wouldn't say no. Just, not right now. I threw in a bag of Ben's favorite chocolate candies and went to the till.

Enid was ringing up the purchases for a lady I didn't recognize when I got to the till.

"I'm sure it's fine, Mrs. Beaumont," Enid was saying to her.

"Is everything okay?" I said interrupting the conversation.

The woman looked at me; her face was screwed up in disproval. "No, it most certainly is not," she said. "There's another city slicker at the Inn trying to swindle poor old Dex, and I don't like it one bit."

"Mrs. Beaumont," Enid said as she bagged the woman's purchases. "You can't assume that he's there to swindle Dex. Maybe he's a guest at the Inn."

"At the Inn?" I asked.

"Yes, Mrs. Beaumont said she saw a rental car parked out front and a suave, dark haired young man talking to Dex on the back deck."

I froze and the blood drained from my face.

Leo.

I wanted to rush out of the store and find him. Hug him and let him hold me. I looked out to the porch and looked at Ben. No, I couldn't see Leo yet.

"Are you okay, Lexi?" Enid asked. "You don't look good all of a sudden."

"He's there to try and rob Dex out of his Inn and his memory of Jessie, no doubt," Mrs. Beaumont said.

"I'm fine," I told Enid ignoring the other woman. "But I really should go. Ben's waiting for me."

"Sure, no problem," Enid said. "Mrs. Beaumont, please don't worry. Do you need help out with these?"

"No, no, I'm fine. But I just don't know about that poor old Dex," she muttered as she took her bags and headed out of the store.

I tried to listen to Enid's chatter as she rang in my groceries but I couldn't focus. Enid promised to get me the information about the school and after paying her, I carried everything to the trunk of the car and called to Ben.

"But the puppy?" he asked.

"You know what, buddy? Maybe next time," I said. "First we need to talk about something."

I was surprised, but thankful when Ben put the puppy he was holding back in the box and got in the car.

We drove back to the cabin in silence. There was a suave, dark man at the Inn. Leo. I glanced at Ben in the rearview mirror.

I couldn't put it off any longer.

***

I knew I had to talk to Ben. It was time to tell him about Leo. But I was chicken. After a simple dinner of burgers on the grill and oven fries, I sat on my swing and watched Ben try to skip rocks into the flat lake. Uncle Ray had tried without much success to teach him last summer, but he was too little to understand that he had to pick flat rocks and throw them at just the right angle. Ben seemed intent on perfecting the skill now.

After watching his efforts for a few minutes I called out, "Ben." He turned towards me. "Can you come here for a minute?"

He threw his handful of rocks into the water all at once and ran up the lawn at full speed, which is the only speed little boys know. Fortunately he slowed before he jumped onto the swing with me.

"Hey, buddy," I said and pulled him close. "How're you doing?"

"I miss Papa. He should be here."

"I know." I stroked his silky hair and felt him relax against me.

"He's not coming, is he?

Tears burned my eyes. "No, baby. He's not coming back."

I looked out at the lake. It was reflecting the vibrant oranges and pinks from the setting sun and a few stars had already popped out over the mountains in the darkening sky.

"Sara Beth says he's watching us. Is he?" Ben asked.

A tear pushed free and slid down my cheek. "Yes, I'd like to believe that he's watching over us."

"Is he now?"

"I think so."

"Maybe he's a star, Mom." Ben's arm wiggled out from the blanket and pointed to the three stars that had appeared over the mountains, brighter now.

"I think you're right, Ben. See the one on the right? The brightest one?"

He nodded.

"I think that one's Papa, and the two next to it," I spoke through my tears, tasting the saltiness. "Those are my mom and dad, your grandparents."

"Cool," Ben said

"Very cool." I wiped my face and smiled.

Together we watched the sun disappear behind the mountains and soon, the rest of the sky filled with stars in a display never seen in the city.

After a few minutes of silence Ben said, "You know what, Mom?"

"What's that?"

"This is the perfect spot for Papa and Grandma and Grandpa to watch us. I don't think they could see us in the city."

"Even if we can't see the stars, they're still there, Ben."

"But I can't see them," he said his voice took on an edge of panic. He turned so he was facing me. "I want to see them. Can we stay?"

"You want to live here?"

He nodded. "Can we?"

I looked into his dark eyes. Leo's eyes. "I think we

could stay. At least for a bit."

He flung his arms around me and squeezed me tight. When he let go I told him about the elementary school in town and that I might be able to teach there while he went to grade one.

"What about Dad? Will he come?"

And there it was. The moment that could no longer be avoided.

"No," I said. "Dad will stay in the city."

"He has to work, right? Dad likes to work," Ben said with the honest acceptance only a child possessed.

"Ben, what would you say if I told you that you have two dads?" I swallowed hard and waited.

"Does the other dad work lots?"

"Does it matter?"

Ben shrugged. "I guess not."

"So, would it be okay?"

"I guess."

I waited for him to say something else. When he didn't, I said, "Well, you're a lucky boy because you do have two dads, and someday very soon I'm going to introduce him to you, okay? He really wants to meet you."

"Okay."

I shouldn't have been surprised by Ben's nonchalance. He didn't understand it yet. He probably wouldn't for a few more years. I hadn't discussed with Andrew how I would handle this situation and I'm not sure he cared all that much. Despite everything, I knew Andrew must care for Ben, even if it wasn't the way I always wished it was, and no matter what, I knew he would be part of Ben's life in some way.

I rocked us in the chair and when Ben's breathing

changed to slow, rhythmic breaths, I kept the chair swinging, enjoying the weight of him next to me too much to stop. When I saw the flicker of a shadow move next to the tree line I didn't panic. The woods were full of creatures; it was probably a raccoon, a rabbit or even a deer settling in for the night. But when the shadow stepped out onto the lawn and into the square of light coming from the window of the house, my breath caught in my throat, but not because I was scared.

CHAPTER THIRTY-TWO

"Lexi, I-"

"Ssh." I held my finger to my lips and gestured to my lap. "Stay right there." I slid out from Ben's sleeping body and lifted him in my arms. It was harder now, he wasn't a toddler anymore, but I managed to carry him into his bed. I took off his shoes and jeans; he could sleep in his t-shirt. I gave him a kiss on the forehead and pulled the blankets up over him. Closing the door gently behind him, I straightened my blouse and went outside to talk to my son's father.

Leo wasn't where I'd left him. He'd moved to the dock and was standing at the end looking out into the blackness of the lake.

"Leo?" I spoke softly so I didn't spook him.

When he turned around, my first instinct was to run to him and let him hold me. My body had craved his touch since I'd left him. But I held myself back and wrapped my arms around my body.

"I'm sorry if I scared you," he said.

"You didn't. I knew you were here."

His face was mostly covered in shadows, but I could make out a sliver of a smile from the light coming from the house.

"It's a pretty small town," I said by way of explanation. "Word is, you're here to swindle Dex out of the Inn."

"Is that right?" His voice was light and for a moment I forgot everything between us. Everything we still needed to figure out. He moved towards me but stopped only inches from me. "I missed you," he said, his voice deeper now.

"I'm sorry that-"

"Don't be sorry. You had a lot to deal with. I'm sorry. I should've come sooner. I'll never forgive myself for not being here with you."

I couldn't help it. I didn't want to, but I did. I started crying again. Just having Leo near had released the flood of emotions I'd done my best to keep bottled up.

"I asked you not to come," I said between sobs.

"Hey," he said. "Come here." Leo stepped forward and wrapped me in his arms. It felt good to be close to him. He smelt like coffee and wood smoke, like he'd been sitting in front of a campfire. I nestled my face into his sweater and let the tears flow. He rubbed my back but didn't say another word. He let me cry and didn't rush me while I exhausted my emotion. Finally, the tears slowed and I pulled away just enough to look at him.

"Thank you," I said.

"For what?"

"For that. I needed to do that."

"I was going to ask how you're holding up with everything, but I don't think I need to." He wiped a tear from my cheek and the gesture was so gentle and intimate I thought I might start to cry again.

"Come on," I said, "let's sit." I took his hand and led him off the dock, across the lawn to the deck. Once we were in the light I could see his face clearly and the resemblance to Ben struck me again.

He sat in a wooden chair. I grabbed my blanket from the swing and sat across from him, turning my back to the lake.

"I wasn't sure I'd see you again," I said.

"Seriously, Lex?" He sat forward in his chair. "There was no way I was going to let you walk out of my life again. You tried, I know. But I wasn't going to let you push me away. I'm not going anywhere."

I wrapped the blanket tighter. "It's not fair to you," I said. "I mean, you have a career, you have a life. I understand if you don't want...well, this."

"Lexi, stop." Leo grabbed my forearms and held me tight, forcing me to look at him. "There's nothing else in this world that I want more than this. Nowhere else I'd rather be."

I looked up again and saw the emotion on his face. In that moment I knew I was only going to hear what I wanted to. And he was saying exactly what I wanted to hear.

"I'm sorry," I said. "I didn't know what to do. There was so much going on and... I was scared," I admitted. "I didn't want to make you choose because I was, I am, afraid of your choice."

"You don't have to be scared." Leo pulled me towards him and touched his lips to mine. The kiss was brief, the sensation gentle, but there was no doubt of the feelings behind it. He pulled away and released my arms. "And don't you ever worry about me choosing. I choose you. Always."

"What about your job?"

"What about it?"

"You love your career."

"It's a job. I took a leave of absence until I can figure

out how to deal with it. I have no intention of going back."

"What?"

"I told you, Lex." He smiled. "I choose you. You and Ben. I was stupid enough to choose work over you before, I won't make that mistake twice. Once was enough, and I've regretted it ever since."

I stared at him. "You would give up everything for me?"

"Of course." Leo reached for my arms and shook them gently. "When will you get it? All I've done for the last few years is think about you, and when I saw you at the hotel, I knew I'd never let you go again. And then when you told me about Ben...God, Lexi, how could I not be here?"

"I told him about you," I said.

The shock on his face registered and he loosened the grip on my arms. "Ben? You told him I was his father?"

"Well, not exactly like that. I told him he was lucky because he had two dads. In some way, Andrew will always be part of his life too, Leo."

"I know," he said and looked away. "It's just that..."

"What?"

He turned back to me. "Can I see him?"

"Now?"

"Please. I can't stop thinking about him. I need to see him for myself."

"Of course." I nodded and he let go of my arms to take my hand. I rose from the chair, discarding the blanket on the deck. When I turned to head into the house, Leo stopped and turned me into him.

He didn't say a word, but pulled me into his arms for a kiss so passionate that if there had been any doubt of his feelings, or of my own, there was none now. I wrapped my hands around his back and returned the kiss.

It ended too soon.

"Come, "I whispered and led him into the house.

***

Following Lexi into the house I was terrified. It was a struggle to control my breathing let alone take in my surroundings; I kept my eyes on her back and stayed right behind her as she walked through the kitchen and down a short hallway stopping in front of a shut door.

"He's asleep," she said.

I nodded. He'd fallen asleep on the porch swing. My eyes had been riveted on them both as I watched her carry him inside earlier. I remember thinking he looked so little but so big too, like a grown boy.

She put her finger to her lip and opened the door.

The little room was dark with only the glow of a night light illuminating a corner. There he was. I'd seen the picture. Heck, I'd memorized every line and freckle on his face. But it didn't prepare me for seeing him in person. I couldn't move.

"Leo," Lexi said. "It's okay, you can go in."

I tore my gaze away from Ben and looked at her. She was smiling, and when she nodded I walked through the door, being sure to watch my step. I stopped about two feet away from the bed. He was lying on his side, clutching a teddy bear. He had long dark lashes, like mine. I used to complain to my grandma that they made me look like a girl, but now I could see how perfect they looked on this boy.

"He looks just like you," Lexi whispered. She'd joined me in the room and I hadn't noticed. I couldn't focus on anything except my son. She was right. He looked just like me, except there were traces of Lexi too. The freckles scattered on his cheeks. Those were from her. And his nose, with the slight flip at the end, that didn't look anything like mine.

I sank to my knees on the carpet, never taking my eyes off him. Lexi put her hand on my shoulder, squeezed and it was gone. I'm not sure how long I sat there watching him sleep. When I finally turned to look at Lexi she was gone. The door to the hallway stood open.

I turned back to my son. I should go. I didn't want to wake him up.

Didn't I? I did want to wake him. I wanted to talk to him. To see his eyes looking at me. To hear his voice. I needed to hear his voice.

There would be time for that. We would have time.

I reached out and touched his head. His hair was soft. He let out a sigh in his sleep and I withdrew my hand.

I found Lexi in the living room. She was sitting on the couch flipping through a magazine. She looked up when I walked into the room and I took a deep breath and leaned against the wall.

"Are you okay?" she said rising and coming to me.

I couldn't answer at first. I closed my eyes and took a few breaths. "I think so."

"Was he...okay?"

My eyes flew open. "Are you kidding?" I stared at her. Her green eyes that were so different from mine and from Ben's. "He's perfect. Absolutely perfect."

She smiled. "He is," she said.

"Thank you."

"For what?"

"For raising him. He's amazing."

"You don't even know him yet."

"I don't have to," I said, though I wanted to know my son more than anything else. "I know he's amazing. He's yours."

"And yours," she said, and I didn't think I could get any happier than in that moment.

He's mine. I replayed the words over in my head, turning them around and trying them on for size. "He's mine," I said out loud.

Lexi smiled and took my hand. "It's a perfect night for a fire." She led me into the room and this time I took the time to look around. It was like a picture straight out of a magazine. The ceiling in the main room was vaulted and lined with wood panels. A fireplace dominated the large room. The hearth was huge and made up of large, smooth rocks that climbed all the way up the wall. Two overstuffed leather chairs were pulled close with another couch and two large wooden bookshelves in the space behind.

Lexi moved into the kitchen which was just off the main room. It was a bright, open space with a large bay window over the sink facing out to the lake. I watched her open cupboards and drawers until she gathered what she needed and joined me by the fireplace.

"Normally I'd be a little worried that there was a nest or something in the chimney after the whole summer, but Uncle Ray told me he'd used it the last time he was here when the electricity went out during a storm."

"The electricity goes out?" I perched myself on the edge of a chair and watched her stack logs and smaller pieces of wood in preparation.

She laughed. "Of course. We're in the woods here. It's not like a big city where there's a backup plan. When there's a big storm, the power almost always goes out."

I stared at her. I'd never been unable to turn on a light.

"This is pretty foreign for you, isn't it?" she asked.

"Is it that obvious?"

"There's nothing better than being in the mountains. You'll get used to it."

Lexi froze, her back to me. I was afraid to breathe. Did she realize what she had said? Did she want me to get used to it here? Would I even have the chance?

"Lexi?" I asked her and prayed she meant what she said. "Will I?"

She didn't turn around, but shook a match out of the box and struck it against the side. "Leo, we're staying. Ben and I. We've decided to try it, and I think I got lucky with a job. It just seems-"

"I meant what I said earlier, Lexi. I choose you. I won't let you get away again." She turned around and looked at me; her hair seemed to glow as the fire sparked to life behind her. God, she was beautiful. "I don't know how I fit into your plans, but I need to tell you that I will need to be part of your plans because I'm in this."

"You're in this?"

"One hundred percent. Whatever it takes."

She smiled, pushed up from her knees and walked over to where I sat, "Good," she said and sat straddling my lap, "because I want you in this." And before I could say a word, she put her sweet mouth on mine and there was nothing left to say.

CHAPTER THIRTY-THREE

Ben was up early which made me happy that I'd insisted Leo didn't spend the night. It had been taken all the willpower I had to let him leave my bed, but I had to think of Ben. We needed to handle the situation carefully. When I came out of my room, Ben was already outside, still in his pajamas throwing rocks in the water. He was determined to master the art of skipping rocks but wasn't having much success. He threw stone after stone, and each one made a splash before sinking to the bottom. I'd have to show him the tricks Uncle Ray had taught me.

I poured a cup of coffee and started to make my way outside to the deck when a flash caught my eye. The vase. My vase.

I couldn't bear to throw away the broken vase that was my parents. I had so little of theirs. Instead I'd put the pieces in a box and brought them with us, intending to attempt a repair job. But it looked like someone had beaten me to it.

I looked closer. The pieces were held together with what looked like a combination of scotch tape and white glue.

Ben.

Tears filled my eyes and I looked out at my son who

was still doggedly throwing rocks into the lake. He must have fixed it this morning before going outside. And the flowers. A mixture of clover and dandelions. His favorite.

I pushed the screen open and stood on the deck watching. Holding my coffee mug, the heat of the liquid warmed my hand.

"Hey, Mom," Ben called, "watch this." He wound up in a side pitch and hurled a rock into the water where it landed with a loud splash.

He turned back to the house and shrugged.

I waved and he continued his search for the perfect skipping stone.

"Ben," I called. "Come inside and get changed. I need to have a shower."

"Okay, Mom. Just one more." He wound up, just as he had before, and flung the rock out from his side. This time it skimmed the water's surface, once, twice, before submerging.

Ben whirled around. "Did you see that?"

I laughed at his wonderment. "I did, buddy. That was awesome."

He ran up the lawn and into my arms. "I did it!"

"You did. Now come and get changed and after I get dressed you can try again."

Ben was outside again as soon as he changed and wolfed down breakfast. When the phone rang, I stood at the kitchen window and spoke to the Elementary school principal, Mr. Henderson, as I watched Ben skip rock after rock.

"I knew your Uncle Ray," Mr. Henderson said, "We fished together sometimes over the years. He was a good man. I'm sorry to hear about his passing."

"Thank you. He loved it here," I said. "It'll be nice for

Ben and I to be here."

"So, you are staying? Can I convince you to come work at the school then?"

"Well, I'll need a job. But don't you need to see some references? I can get you a list, but I don't know-"

"I'll be honest with you, Lexi," he said. "I'm in a bit of a tough spot here and if you're ready to work...well, knowing your uncle, I think that's all the reference I need right now. Of course you'll have to come in and fill out some paperwork."

"Of course." I tried to maintain a level of professionalism but on the inside, I wanted to scream. Everything was working out.

I finished my call with Mr. Henderson and glanced at my watch as I made my way out to the porch. Leo should have already been here by now. He said he'd come over right after breakfast. It was almost eleven. Before my mind could create a dozen worst case scenarios, I heard the crunching of tires on gravel and a few moments later, Leo appeared around the corner of the house.

My face split into a grin at the sight of him.

"Good morning," he said.

"Almost lunch time actually."

"I'm sorry about that. I had something very important to take care of," he said as he took the steps up to the deck two at a time.

"Is that so?" I teased.

He leaned in to kiss me and as much as my body longed for the touch of him, I pulled away. I gestured with my head towards the lake. And Ben.

Leo turned and watched his son for a few minutes. "May I?"

"Of course, just let me introduce you, okay?"

Leo nodded and I called to Ben who came running up the lawn. He slowed when he saw we had a visitor.

"Ben, I want you to meet someone very important. This is...Leo."

Leo stuck his hand out. "It's very nice to meet you, Ben. Your mom has told me quite a bit about you."

Ben looked at the hand but shied away.

"It's okay, Leo's a friend," I said.

Ben still didn't take Leo's hand but fixed his gaze on him. Leo must have noticed the staring as well because he withdrew his hand and said, "I hope you don't mind, Ben, but I saw something at the store today and I thought you might like it."

The expression on Ben's face shifted. He could never turn down a gift.

Leo looked at me for approval and I nodded.

"I'll be right back," Leo said. "Wait here."

Ben didn't move so Leo ran down the steps and disappeared around the corner.

I took the opportunity. "Are you okay? I told you, Leo's a friend."

"I know," he said, "he looks kinda-"

Ben didn't finish because in the next instant he was running, jumping off the stairs and hurtling towards Leo who had reappeared holding a squirming golden retriever puppy.

"A puppy!"

"I saw this little guy and there was just something about him. I thought he looked like he needed a little boy to take care of him," Leo said. He put the puppy down on the grass and Ben sat down letting the dog climb all over him, licking his face.

"Thank you," Ben said between the puppy's licks. "This is awesome." Then remembering something, Ben looked up towards me and said, "Can I keep him, Mom? Please?"

I did say I'd think about a dog and looking at Leo who was now sitting on the grass across from Ben, the smiles on their faces identical, how could I say no? Of course you can keep him."

Ben squealed and the puppy leapt up at his face, covering it with doggie kisses. He giggled and fell to the ground. Leo winked at me and I knew I'd made the right choice.

***

I spent the rest of the morning watching Ben and Leo playing with the puppy. I struggled to keep my emotions at bay. It was a lot to take in all at once having them together for the first time. The last thing I needed to do was to start crying; that would just upset Ben and confuse him. I tried to focus on the dog instead, and had to admit he was adorable.

Ben couldn't decide on a name for him, so for now we just referred to him as 'dog'. It didn't matter, because he didn't come when he was called anyway. After a few games of fetch, where Ben did most of the fetching, both boy and dog both crashed at the same time.

"How about some lunch?" I suggested. "We can find a warm place for the puppy to sleep and once he's rested he'll be ready to play again."

"Can I show Leo the kayak after lunch?" Ben asked as he followed me inside. Leo trailed, carrying the puppy that had already fallen asleep.

"I've never been kayaking," Leo said.

"What? It's so cool."

"First," I said, "you eat. Go wash your hands. I'll make sandwiches."

Ben disappeared down the hallway and Leo put the sleeping dog on an old towel I'd laid out by the fireplace.

"He likes you," I said to him.

"Do you think so?" He came up behind me and wrapped his arms around me in a quick squeeze. He planted a kiss on my cheek and pulled away before I could react.

I glanced down the hall.

"Don't worry, he didn't see anything," Leo said.

"It's not that...it's just..."

"I get it," he said. "It's okay. I'm not interested in making this situation harder than it has to be. But you really think he likes me?"

I had to laugh at the look on his face. The total need to please.

"Of course he does," I said turning back to the counter where I had bread laid out. "You brought him a puppy. What's not to like?"

CHAPTER THIRTY-FOUR

The water that hit my face was cold, but not icy like I'd expected when we'd first got in the kayak.

"Hey, Ben," I said. "Try to keep the paddle lower, then maybe I won't get so wet."

He giggled and the sound made me relax. How could I possibly be tense when my son was sitting in front of me and was having fun? Life was good.

"Sorry, Leo," he said. "I do that to mom too."

"Okay, let's try this again. Ready?"

"Yup."

"When I say, left, put the left side of the paddle in," I instructed. "And then -"

"Which way's left?"

"This side." I raised the left side of the paddle in the air and Ben turned causing the whole boat to shift.

"Whoa." I dropped the paddle and tried to steady the boat.

"Sorry," Ben said and giggled again.

"Okay, let's try this a different way. Put your paddle in the water."

"Which side," he asked.

"You pick."

Ben put the right paddle in the water.

"Okay, let's say that side is 'boom'. So every time you put that side in the water we'll say, 'boom'."

Ben lifted the oar and dipped it in again, this time he said, "Boom."

"Try again," I prodded. "But every time you say it you have to say it a bit louder and we'll do it together."

Trying to follow his lead I raised my oar and brought it down at the same time as Ben. Together we yelled, "Boom."

Ben laughed and said, "Okay what about the other side?"

"How about when we paddle on the other side we say, 'pow'?"

"Pow"?

"Just try it."

Together we lifted the left side of the oar and this time when we pulled it through the water we said, "Pow."

"That's silly," Ben said.

"No way," I said. "It sounds cool when you do it together, ready. Start with boom." So we did. We paddled right, left, right calling out, "Boom, pow, boom."

"That's awesome!" Ben yelled.

"Keep going," I called.

We scared every bird and fish for miles I'm sure, but I didn't care. I was kayaking with my son. I could do this all day.

I tried to stay in view of the house, but once we got the hang of it, Ben wanted to go a little farther and show me the homes of some of the neighbors. I looked across the lawn and couldn't see Lexi. She must have gone inside.

"Can we go to the point?" Ben asked.

"Okay, but just for a minute, I don't want your mom to get mad at me."

"She won't, I promise."

I followed Ben's lead and soon we were gliding across the water next to the tree line. He showed me a few of the neighbor's houses and the public beach where they'd already pulled in the swim line and the raft for the season.

"I can jump off that dock, ya know?" Ben said.

"I bet you can. You look like a brave boy."

"I am," he agreed. "I have to be."

We stopped paddling and let the boat glide. "What do you mean, you have to be brave?"

"For mom," he said matter of factly. "She's sad a lot."

"You mean since your papa died?"

"No, cause of Dad. Mom said he's not coming."

"How do you feel about that?" I wasn't sure Lexi would like me talking to Ben about this, but he seemed to need someone to talk to.

"I'm glad." He dipped his finger tips in the water, letting them drag. "Cause then we can live here and Mom likes it here."

I didn't know what to say.

"Ben?"

"Yup."

"You don't always have to brave, you know. Sometimes you can just be you."

"I know," he said his voice quiet, then he brightened. "Leo, look!"

I followed to where Ben was pointing and saw a deer standing at the edge of the water only a few feet away. She hadn't noticed us, and since our Boom, Pow, Boom had ceased for a few moments, we hadn't managed to scare her away.

"I don't think I've ever seen a deer this close before."

"For real?"

"Ssh," I whispered, "don't scare her."

"Everyone's seen a deer," Ben said.

"Not true. Where I grew up, there isn't a lot of wildlife. Maybe one day I'll take you to visit."

"Cool," Ben said. Then he paused. "Why?"

"It was just a thought. You never know, right?"

I reminded myself to go slowly, Ben didn't know everything yet and I didn't want to spook him.

After a moment Ben spoke. His voice was so quiet I had to lean forward to hear him. "You're my other dad, right?"

My chest constricted but I asked, "Your other dad?"

"Mom said I had another dad. Are you?"

I thought about lying to him, or dodging the question, but he was a smart kid and more than that, I wanted him to know. "I am."

"Thought so," he said louder this time. "You look like me."

I smiled and the pressure in my chest released. "You think so?"

"Yup."

"Are you okay with me being your other dad?"

"Yup. Mom likes you."

I left it at that and we floated in silence for a few moments.

"You know how to fish, right?" Ben asked quite

seriously.

I laughed. "Yes, I know how to fish."

"Good."

"Hey," I said to his back, "we should get back. Your mom might be getting worried."

Ben nodded and in the way that only little boys can, he summoned energy I didn't know he had, raised his right arm and driving the paddle into the water, yelled, "Boom!"

The deer ran off and we were shooting across the water back to the cabin.

It didn't take long to get back with our new paddling strategy. Lexi still wasn't outside. I pulled the kayak up alongside of the dock with a lot less effort than I thought it would take and Ben jumped out with ease while I held us close.

"Can you hold the rope, Ben?" He took the rope I offered him and using the paddle for balance, I pushed myself into a crouching position.

"Don't fall," Ben said.

"I won't. Just keep the rope..." Before I could finish my thought, the boat flew out from under my feet and I hit the water. The cold took my breath away for a moment. "Tight." I finished as I emerged and Ben broke into a fit of hysterical giggles.

With two long strokes I swam to the ladder. After pulling myself up onto the dock, I stood over Ben and shook like a dog doing my best to get him wet.

We both collapsed in laughter.

Life didn't get any better.

When I looked up I saw Lexi coming down the lawn towards us. She wasn't smiling. Maybe I shouldn't have taken Ben so far in the kayak? I still had a lot to learn.

I jumped to my feet. "Lexi, we were only gone for a minute. Once we figured out how to paddle, we..."

She came closer and I could see she wasn't mad. But there were tears in her eyes.

CHAPTER THIRTY-FIVE

"Hey, Ben," Leo said. "Why don't you go see if the puppy is awake and think about a name for him."

Ben's face lit up as he remembered his new dog, and he sprung to his feet. "Sure," he said and took off running. "I'll think of a really cool name too," he yelled and disappeared up the lawn.

I tried to hold back the tears. Watching Ben with Leo, after all this time was overwhelming. The effect of all the emotions over the last few weeks combined and turned me into a weepy, emotional mess.

"Lexi, what's wrong?" Leo said. He finished tying the kayak to the dock and came to me. "Has something happened?"

"Yes. I mean, no. I..." I was feeling so many things at once I couldn't form a coherent thought. "I'm so sorry, Leo."

Leo grabbed my arms and I jumped a little from the cold of his skin. "Sorry? For what?"

"For not telling you about Ben." I felt a fresh flow of tears threatening. "Seeing you with him, it makes me so happy. But so sad for all the lost time you've had. And I'm-"

"Stop," he said and wrapped his arms around me. He was soaking, but I didn't care. I let him hold me and after a moment I could feel the heat radiating from his skin, through the damp clothes. "We've talked about it," he whispered, "and we can't change the past. The only thing that matters is now. And I'm here now."

"But for how long?" My voice was muffled in his shoulder.

Leo pulled me away from him and met my mouth with his.

The kiss took my breath away, literally. But I didn't need it. Leo's passion fuelled me. He breathed life into me as his lips melded into mine. He had one hand on the back of my neck, the other cupping my cheek and kissed me with an urgency I'd never experienced before. All thoughts flew out of my head and I focused only on the feel of his wet body pushed up against mine, his thumb stroking against my cheek, and the taste of him on my lips.

When we finally drew apart, Leo looked at me, the intensity of his kiss reflected in his eyes. "Does that answer your question? I'm here for forever."

"But, what about your job?"

"I told you, I'm going to quit."

"What will you do for work?"

"Well, as it turns out, I think Dex may need a little help around the Inn."

I reached for his hand and squeezed.

"It's going to be okay, Lexi. I promise."

"I know," I said and for the first time in a long time, I believed it.

"We're going to make this work," he said. "I love you."

I stared at him, tracing his face with my eyes. Everything about him was so familiar. "Maybe Uncle Ray was right," I said after a moment.

"About what?" He reached out to wipe a tear off my cheek.

"He told me not to waste time, that I would have to grab love when it came and never let it go."

A slow smile spread across Leo's face. "Uncle Ray sounds like he was a very wise man. I wish I could have met him."

"So do I," I said and I leaned forward again. This time the kiss was tender and soft.

"Mom!"

We broke apart at the sound of Ben's voice, but Leo held onto my hand and we turned together to see Ben running down the lawn at full speed, the puppy close on his heels.

"Whoa." I caught him with my free hand before he could run right off the dock. "What's up?"

"I thought of the perfect name," Ben said between breaths, "for the dog." He reached down and grabbed the dog around the middle lifting him to his face.

"What's that?"

"Skipper," Ben said.

"Skipper?" Leo and I said at the same time.

"Yeah, for Papa," Ben explained. "He was always trying to teach me to skip rocks and I did it this morning. Right before Leo brought me Skipper."

He looked up at me; the puppy, still squirming in his arms, licked his face.

"I don't think I could imagine a more perfect name," I said.

"Cool," Ben said and put the puppy down. "Come on, Skipper," he called and took off running again.

Leo lifted my hand to his lips and kissed it. Together

we walked off the dock and into our future.

Acknowledgements

When I think about who I want to thank for their support, many people come to mind because, as it turns out, writing a novel is not easy and I couldn't have done it on my own.

First, I have to thank the wonderful and talented Easy Writers. Brad, Susan, Nancy, Trish and Leanne. Thank you for plowing through some of my earlier work, giving me honest feedback and pushing me to 'do better'. Through twice monthly Thursday nights, lots of lattes, a ton of laughs, and a whole lot of work, you've all encouraged and inspired me. Thank you.

A huge thank you goes out to the incredibly talented Crystal Williams for allowing me to use her beautiful photo as my cover art. The moment I saw it, I knew it was my cover. Please check out her photos at http://mscrys.deviantart.com/

Extra special appreciation to my early readers Charissa Weaks, Sierra Godfrey, Lindsay Klug, Leanne Shirtliffe and Trish Loye Elliot. Thank you for giving your time to read and comment on early drafts of NSIV. Your suggestions and feedback were instrumental in creating the final product. And of course, your enthusiasm for Leo was great. :)

A huge thank you to my super supportive friends who've listened to me babble about characters and publishing concerns. I apologize for all the times I hid out in my office, bailed on a girl's weekend, or had to cancel plans in order to make a word count. You're all amazing and I appreciate you all more than you'll know.

Although they've both been named before, they must be singled out. I could not have gotten to this point with NSIV if it weren't for my fellow Wordbitches, Trish Loye Elliot and Leanne Shirtliffe. You two just 'get it' and I feel so fortunate to have found you both so we can support each other through this crazy writing thing!

And another special shout out to Leanne for taking the time to line edit for all the picky grammar, punctuation and inconsistencies that I tend to miss. Especially for taking on this task at the start of your well earned holiday, working under my slightly compressed deadline. You're a superstar!

I can't forget my parents, who may not have always understood my need to write, but have supported it none the less.

Mom, you may be the best P.R. Person a girl could ask for! And to Dad, for reading my book even though it has nothing to do with finance or global warming.

Last, but by no means, least, the biggest thank you goes out to my family. My kids have put up with a whole lot of, "Ssh, Mommy's writing." And burnt dinners when I got lost in the words. They just may be my biggest fans and I'm so proud to be able to show them that they can do anything by working hard and believing!

And of course, to my husband, Rob. There is no bigger cheerleader on earth. Thank you for believing in me so completely and making it possible for me to follow my dream everyday. You are my everything.

Nothing Stays In Vegas is Elena's debut novel, however she has numerous parenting articles to her credit and has been published in multiple Chicken Soup for the Soul anthologies, as well as the Seal Press anthology, How to Put a Car Seat on a Camel- and other misadventures travelling with children.

Residing in the Alberta Foothills with her husband and twins, Elena escapes to the mountains as often as possible and can often be found sitting by the lake plotting her next story.

To learn more about Elena Aitken and her upcoming books, please visit www.elenaaitken.com

12301894R00184

Made in the USA
Charleston, SC
26 April 2012